Motherload

ALISON NANCYE

Published by The Life Kitchen Pty Limited
PO Box 534, Coogee NSW 2034
Sydney Australia.
www.thelifekitchen.com

Copyright © 2017 Alison Nancye

ISBN 978-0-646-97057-8

For information address The Life Kitchen Pty Limited
PO Box 534, Coogee NSW 2034, Sydney Australia.
yes@thelifekitchen.com
www.thelifekitchen.com

Cover Design: Apple Tree Graphic Design

For my beautiful children Bellina & Cicio.
Without you two, there would be no Motherload or
Motherlove.
You help to shape my world.
Thank you.
I love you both beyond words.

ACKNOWLEDGMENTS

To Toni Elford, my Agent, Manager & forever friend. I couldn't achieve half the things I do in my life, work and motherhood without the unwavering, loyal and loving guidance and support you give me. Thank you for everything past, present and future!

To my mumma friends, particularly Rebecca Morgan-Jones, Julie Hale, Jemima Trigg, and Saffrine Nydegger, who support me and my kids through humour, love, sound advice, friendship and babysitting!

To Lyndal Edwards who always wants the best for me and offers support and help in those critical moments of life overload.

To Jacqui Afflick, my childhood friend - although we don't always see each other, we know we've got each other's back. Your wisdom, love and unconditional support means the world.

To Jane Burrows, my Counsellor and Kinesiologist - you helped me through some very dark days and supported me to live in the light.

To Simon Christidis, your unconditional love for me, has helped me create a life sharing my motherhood with a man I love so completely. And to your two beautiful children Ella & Tim, I love you more than words can say.

To my readers, past, present and future. Thank you for reading my books. It means more than you'll ever know.

CHAPTER 1

I can't take it anymore. My morning routine on repeat, day after day, when all I want is one lousy sleep in. Just one. The kids calling out to be fed, someone crying, another needs changing, and then there's the one who wants to be picked up with the third arm my family seems to think I've grown since becoming a mum to three children who haven't quite reached the age of attending school. It's doing my head in! Not to mention my body.

Ed's no help. Ed the absent father, the husband who is missing in action more than involved in the action. I can't take it anymore, I scream inwardly in the hope that someone, anyone, will hear me, and help me get through whatever it is I'm going through...had been going through, for longer than I cared to admit.

Shuffling the kids to the living room, pyjamas still on, tummies yet to be filled, I raised my voice over the crescendo of little people's voices. "It's breakfast in front of the television this morning. I'm putting on Toy Story."

"A movie at breakfast?" Emily, my daughter of four years, said wide-eyed, while looking up at me with mint green eyes that matched my own. "I thought we weren't allowed to watch TV until Play School Mummy."

I absently pulled back Emily's wavy blonde hair as

white as snow - trailing down the middle of her back much like mine did when I was her age - in a band, to keep it from falling over her eyes. "I know the rules darling, but mummy needs to have a breakdown this morning."

Haphazardly, I poured Cheerios from a mega size cereal box into three small bowls decorated in Disney Princess, Shrek and The Wiggles, without a care for the overflow of mess on the rectangle wooden coffee table in front of the television. Milk sloppily added to just skim the peaks of cereal that formed at the top of each bowl. Meal now complete, with banana lazily sliced and moderately divvied out, with Brady my eldest at five years, receiving the biggest serving.

"Can we have popcorn too mumma?" Brady puffed out his chest, excited to be allowed to break the rules for a change.

"No." I replied flatly.

Brady began pouting with an expression that matched his father's when he didn't get his own way. "But mumma," he pleaded, "You always give us popcorn when we watch a movie." Brown wavy hair, bright blue eyes the colour of the deep ocean just like my husband's, hung out in hope.

"No Brady!" my voice shrieked, eyeballs ready to explode from their sockets, suggesting the Green-Eyed Mummy Monster I loathed, but couldn't seem to avoid since becoming a mother, was about to rear her ugly head.

"Zip it!" I shouted, holding up my hand, as Brady

opened his mouth to respond. Since when did kids become such savvy negotiators?

In my day we had to shut up and take it! Now, right now, as the pounding on my brain got louder and the weariness of my body got heavier, what I needed was for three small children to do just that...zip it, lock it and put it in their pocket!

I needed to check out of my life for an hour. Oh hell...I'd needed to check out of my life for a week...a month if I'm really honest. I didn't sign up for this life. I'm sure when I said, "I do," and signed the documents declaring I was officially married, that I didn't sign up for this life.

"It's Toy Story and cereal for the next hour and half," I said firmly, eyeballing six eyeballs staring back. "Brady, you're in charge."

Ensuring the safety gate was locked behind me at the base of the stairs leading up to the second floor, so Harry my two-year-old couldn't break his neck during my breakdown, I escaped to my bedroom at the end of the long hallway.

I fell into an almighty heap on the unmade bed. Tears slowly tumbled in a steady stream. I didn't sign up for this life. I repeated silently over and over, as if saying it in my head would make it real. Rocking back and forth now, I shut my eyes tight and wished I was back in the womb.

How did my life get so screwed up?

Normal childhood, well...semi-normal. Mum and

Dad really should have divorced. They would have been much happier not together than they ever were together. Let's be honest, dad had more fun sleeping around than sleeping with mum. What's the point of staying together if you're not actually enjoying life together?

Maybe that's what I need to do? Maybe Ed and I are meant to call it quits? At least if we split he'd have to take care of the kids more than he currently does. A lot more. I can't even get him to commit to getting home for dinner on time...and let's not get started on Saturdays. He needs a break? He needs to go kayaking. He needs to go hiking. He needs to go cycling. He needs to go catch up with his mates for a drink. Well I need to go jump off a cliff. Can I schedule that in Ed?

Damn this trying to be happy. I want out!

Oh, what is wrong with me? I used to be such a fabulous together package, one that said, "Hot!" I really did. Looked good. Better than good. Dark blonde wavy hair that I tamed each week, well the hairdresser did. Smoothed my wild wavy mane into a bouncy full head of hair that shouted Pantene as I swanked into the office each morning. Designer suits direct from New York and Paris, purchased during one of my many work trips. A curvy size 10 figure with breasts that peaked through expensive and alluring lingerie. Not to mention legs that said Stair Master! And I didn't just look good I did good. I was fantastic at my marketing gig at one of the best beauty labels in Australia. Got to travel the globe, all on the company budget. I was someone! I was going somewhere. Hell...I was somewhere! That husband of mine never had a problem arriving home for dinner on time back then.

I'm over it, I spluttered, wiping my nose and tears with the back of my hand.

Curling up further under the doona and drowning in the knowledge of who I had become...a dowdy housewife and mother of three. A 42-year-old no-body, who couldn't even rustle up breakfast with a sunshine smile for her three small children. I used to manage multi-million dollar accounts and a team of twenty five for God's sake! Now I can't even manage three kids under five. And...to top it off, I've got my five-year-old on babysitting duty for my four and two-year-old. I'm a train wreck.

I knew I shouldn't have gone again after the first two. The third one completely and utterly pushed me over the edge. Everyone told me I was crazy, naturally I didn't listen. No, not the over-achieving Abigail Montgomery. I just had to flaunt my talent for being barefoot and pregnant and popping out babies like they were going out of fashion.

Oh mum...I really wish you were here.

That silly old annoying Shirley that Dad had to go and marry straight after you died is no help. He's obsessed. I can't say a damn word against the woman. She's full of it and the sound of her own voice. Hasn't a child to show for herself mind you, but can't but help but throw advice in my direction. What would an over-bleached blonde with oversized tits, who loves sun and champagne a whole lot more than baking a lamb roast, know about raising three kids? A woman who doesn't lift a finger whenever they stop by for an hour or so, every three or four months in between their latest and greatest world travelling expedition. Expects me to wait on her hand and foot every time they show up on my doorstep unannounced. Well, she can go to hell and so can he...my father that is. Never could rely on him. Still can't. And now I can't even rely on the father of my children.

Screaming into the bed sheets, I pulled the covers over my head in the hope the world would go away. Well, for the rest of the day at least.

"Mummy," Emily whispered from the small crack in the doorway. "Have you had your breakdown yet?" Peaking her head in a little further, green eyes tentatively searching for the knowledge it was safe to enter.

"Oh darling, Mummy's sorry," I said, choking back tears and lifting my heavy head somewhat from the pillow.

"Harry's got a super big poo. It's a real stinker," Emily declared, screwing up her nose and opening the door to reveal the evidence.

Harry, who had just turned two, stood beside his big sister Emily. He was a mini version of Brady, who was a mini version of Ed. My two boys and their father were all gloriously handsome. Brown wavy hair and big blue eyes that reflected the ocean's. Looks that said, "Hey there look at me." Creamy pale skin that loved the summer sun. Both boys already showing signs of the height in Ed's family, as evidenced in the growth charts we regularly marked on the inside frame of their bedroom door.

"Mummy, it's getting super urgent and super smelly," Emily insisted, dragging her little brother by the arm, through to the middle of my bedroom that was covered in oak floorboards the colour of dark chocolate. She pointed her tiny little finger with fierce determination at the evidence running down Harry's legs.

Brown, gooey runny poo slithered downward from the inside of Harry's legs toward my gorgeous chocolate coloured floorboards. Oh no! He didn't seem fussed, mind you.

Well that just tops off my morning! Those new nappies I bought on special at the supermarket are not so damn special after all! You can poo in them, but a word of warning mothers worldwide...these nappies are only suitable for suitably efficient mothers who have their shit together. Mothers that clean up shit the second your children decide to do it!

I stared blankly at two innocent faces, holding onto their breath, patiently waiting for the Green-Eyed Mummy Monster's next move.

Closing my eyes briefly, I sucked in air, before releasing loudly. Re-opening my mint green eyes that were paler than usual, I exhaled, put on my best happy face and dismounted from the bed. Opening my arms wide, I reached out with love for my two babies. Holding them tight in my arms and close to my chest, I squeezed and snuggled and kissed every soft sweet spot of flesh on their tiny endearing faces. They giggled and mirrored kisses back to me.

"You finished your breakdown now Mummy?" Emily said clutching my long leg, not remotely as lean, or toned, as it was pre-babies. She looked up and waited for my answer as if her life depended on it.

"I am sweetheart," I replied, reaching down and kissing her tiny button nose, where a sprinkling of summer freckles already formed. She squeezed even tighter. That's when I noticed her body relax. It's as if whenever I'm stressed out, my kids stress out. But as soon as I tell them, I'm OK, they're OK.

Tears threatened my eyes, guilt choked in my throat. I always thought I'd be a much better mother than I turned out to be. Never realised how often I would fail at this job.

Remembering now the reason my two youngest were snuggled up to me on the wooden floor...it was the stench that gave it away...I took my children's hands into my own. I ushered them toward the change table in the children's room further down the hallway, on the opposite side to my own. "OK Harry, time to check out the damage."

CHAPTER 2

For the next three days, I lived like Ben Stiller's character in The Secret Life of Walter Mitty. Nothing changed. Everything the same. Desensitized to life and the emotions that came with it. It's like I'd switched off from feeling everything, because every time I opened my heart, even just a little, I fell apart.

I am not myself. But just who am I? When did I become this woman that I am not? A woman crawling through motherhood, trying to get back to the woman I once was. But I can't go back. I'm not even that woman anymore. I really need a new identity. A new me. Someone I like. Someone I enjoy waking up to each day. I need a new outlook. A new beginning. If only I could go back to that point when it all fell apart...maybe then I'd have some chance of reclaiming life.

Ed doesn't seem to notice any difference in me. Whether I'm teary or not. Chatty or not. Interested or not. He communicates through text messages. He's got a better relationship with his phone than the little woman at home. And just when did I become that little woman? That woman, a mere shell of her former self. A woman who struggles to be heard without screaming or shouting for someone, anyone, to listen. Since when did a grown woman need to shout louder than a five-year-old, to feel like what she was saying was important, valued, worthwhile?

People talk about how fast kids grow up and how we're supposed to make the most of it. But how the hell am I supposed to enjoy my children when I can't even enjoy myself? I mean look at me. When did I go from being a fit and trim, toned abs and butt size 10 with breasts that more than filled up the palm of a man's hand, to an oversized size 14 who wobbles when she walks. I refuse to buy size 16, even if it does fit better. I am never going to say I made it to that landmark. Ever!

I know I need to exercise. Know I need more sleep. Know I need to put my feet up. But how the hell am I supposed to do all of that when I never get any time for myself?

Ed says his mother, who flits in from time to time, can help. But she's too busy telling me all the things I'm doing wrong to recognise when I'm doing anything right.

"I never did that with Edward," she snoots at me, wearing judgment around her shoulders like she's forever adorned in an oversized faux fur. Well thanks for nothing Meredith. You just stick to your high teas and fabulous fundraisers, helping the families of the world to feel better about themselves, never addressing the real issues within your own family. Meredith, if you had two real, useful, supportive words to say to your precious son it should be, "Go home", "Help out", "Be kind", "Be thoughtful." But the lash of your tongue for my motherhood seems to come out a lot quicker than the critique of your own.

My phone beeped, jolting me from the neurotic trance I was locked into, while sipping tea and tuning out to

Play School, three small children huddled around me on the sofa.

"Be home late. New client just flew in. Remember I'm kayaking at Lake Macquarie tomorrow."

Clenching the phone in my hand, the flame burned within. Rage, and that deep bitter taste in my mouth for this asshole husband of mine, surfaced. "Arghhhh," I shouted jolting my kids from their TV trance. I pounded my phone on the sofa, thrashed it over and over again, imagining it to be Ed's head. Then, remembering my audience of three, I outwardly smiled. "Oh, isn't Play School fun darlings?" inwardly shouting, I don't ever want to receive another text message from that man again!

Later that evening, after putting the kids to bed and pouring merlot to the rim of my wine glass, I sat on the sofa and sipped. No, gulped. Deep, rich, oaky red wine from the Barossa Valley, in the hope that after the third glass everything might finally go numb. What a way to start the weekend!

I wanted to relax. But no amount of alcohol was going to do it tonight. I couldn't get out of my head just how much I hated my husband right now. Wow! I really do not like my husband. Like...at all. This is definitely a self-defining rock bottom moment, when you realise you hate the man you're married to. Hate the father of your children. Hate the man you once loved and was so very sure you could never live without. Hate the man you sleep with sometimes, have sex with occasionally. But it's true, categorically true. I actually hate my husband.

Well Abby, you have definitely reached a milestone!

But if I'm really honest...it's not only Ed I loathe, it's me that I don't like so much.

My life looks something like this, I realise as I gulp more wine...I hate my husband, hate myself, hate my situation, hate my life and have literally no idea how to make anything right, wonderful, delightful, joyful...ever again.

There's only one thing to do. Only one thing that would make the bitterness of my life that little bit sweeter... Sal. She's probably out. My best friend of 21 years. Dangerously sexy, dangerously sassy and dangerously single.

Yep, Sal is probably at some hip bar in Cockle Bay doing who knows what with who knows whom, and I am about to disturb all of that to download my dribble. But I can't take this anymore. I really can't. I simply cannot get through another night in this house, this life, alone, without talking to someone.

I dialled Sal's number, gulped merlot and waited.

"Spill it," a brash voice came loudly through the speaker on the second ring.

Background music blared, people talked, laughter roared in the distance. Yes, it was the sweet sound of people living on a Friday night.

"Sal is that you? Can you hear me?"

"Spill it Ab. No, don't tell me. I've got the picture. You've just poured your third glass of red, and you're waiting for that prick of a husband to come home while wondering when it's ever going to get better?"

"When did you get so good at reading minds?"

Sal and I had been friends since Uni. We met in our first year and it was love at first sight. She was always a mover and a shaker. A total fox with flaming red hair descended from the Scots. Enormous caramel brown eyes the shape of oversized almonds. Breasts a Double D...and then some. An hourglass figure that would have Scarlett Johansson shaking in her boots. Yep, Sal was born, and will be until the day she dies, a total babe! She's got a huge heart with, Don't mess with me balls the size of a soccer ball. Get on her good side and she was loyal to the core, but mess with her and it was safe to say, you were well and truly screwed.

"Alright honey let me have it. Download pronto, because I've got this gorgeous guy from Greece hanging on my every word. And...he's ready to pounce. More to the point, so am I," she roared with laughter.

"Oh look, don't worry Sal. I didn't mean to interrupt. It's just..."

"You're not babe, now spill it."

"I hate Ed!" I blurted out.

"You called me for that?" Sal announced.

I imagined her to be now expertly rubbing her fingers slowly up Greek God's inner thigh, all the way near his crotch. I was certain I could hear her purring.

"Er...sorry to interrupt...and I know I've said it all before but...I can't take it Sal. It's doing my head in. I don't think he's ever going to change."

"Forget about him Ab. When are you going to change?"

"What?" I frowned. "I'm doing everything I can to make this work," I added, deeply depleted of energy, as I reached for the bottle of merlot at my feet to refill my glass to the rim.

"Ab," Sal said more earnestly now, leaning closer to the receiver then calling out to Greek God to fetch another round of drinks. "For as long as I've known you, you've always been the agreeable one. Going along with what everyone wanted. I mean hell...that cake and band you had at your wedding that your mother-in-law organised, were hideous. But you wouldn't say a bad word about it. Had to maintain your super sweet exterior of 'dutiful daughter-in-law'.

"What was I supposed to do?" I shouted in defence, sloshing red wine on the rug at my feet. Excellent. I'm now going to spend the next 20 minutes of my Friday night scrubbing Aussie merlot from the Persian rug. Life gets better every heartbeat.

"Ab, you were supposed to say, "Meredith, I do not like 500 layers of disgusting white icing over a hideously old fashioned fruit cake. And no, I don't care if your best friend Betsy had this band at her daughter's wedding, I do not want that ridiculous Elvis impersonator at mine."

Rubbing my big toe into the wine stained rug in the hope it would help, I retaliated, trying to prove to my best friend that somehow, I really had no choice. "Well what could I do when she had gone and booked and paid for it all without my prior knowledge?"

"Well you tell me Ab...just who's wedding were you putting on? Yours or hers?"

Silence.

Sal knew me too well to lie to my face and loved me too much to sweeten the sting.

"Well?" Sal barked through the phone.

Exhaling I whispered, "Surely I haven't always been like this?" Wanting to defend myself, I added, "Remember when I was once that hot little Miss Something in marketing, running her own show at Avalanche, one of the biggest beauty houses on the planet?"

"But you were always running around Lastminute. com style, jumping when your clients told you to. Cancelling travel plans with the girls and hubby pre-kids to jump when work demanded it."

"I didn't think you minded?"

"Didn't you?"

"But you still took that trip to Fiji, in spite of me ditching you a few days before. And you got to meet that hot guy Foster from Atlanta remember. 10 days and nights with the hunk of all hunks."

"Yeah but I didn't get to gossip and drool over him in front of my bestie. Ab, you were the one I wanted to holiday with, not some random Sex God from Atlanta."

"Oh Sal. I am so sorry. I never realised it worried you."

"It didn't worry me. Buy when a woman's been divorced a couple of times, she kind of looks forward to a trip with her best girlfriend."

"Why didn't you say anything?"

"Because it's you Ab. I get you. But just because I get you doesn't mean it doesn't hurt when you ditch me. Ab, you think you have to please the person that's asking you to jump the highest. Only problem is...you've lost sight of the benchmark you're setting for yourself. You're always working toward someone else's agenda. Now you're doing it with that dirt bag husband of yours."

"Oh, he's not that bad Sal."

"There you go again. Good girl Abigail making excuses for others and their bad behaviour. I swear Abby you do this to yourself. Create this ridiculously unhappy life. All. By. Yourself."

"Oh God, I'm a total mess Sal." Sculling more wine, almost strangling the stem of the glass with my fingers, I let the pain pour out. "I have no idea how to get out of this deep dark hole I've put myself in. How long has this been going on?"

I curled my feet up tighter, tucking them underneath thick thighs that wobbled when I walked, as I anticipated the answer.

"I don't know Ab," Sal eventually said, a softness creeping through her voice. "Maybe your mum dying so young, right when you were finishing high school didn't help a young woman trying to navigate herself through womanhood." After a beat, Sal added, "I'm sure your dad having all those affairs for most of your childhood then re-marrying so soon after your mum passed away... that's gotta have an impact. Maybe you felt you had to behave a certain way to keep the peace. You know...be good...be the responsible one in the family?"

"I'm a lost cause," I said, gulping more wine.

"No you're not. You're just in need of a little time out."

"What do you mean?"

"You give it to your kids all the time when they need to calm down and regroup. You need to do it for yourself too."

I heard a muffled deep male voice whispering in the background; the Greek God had returned with the drinks. I wished I had my own Greek God purring at me right now, massaging my feet on the sofa.

"So," Sal declared, a no-nonsense tone in her voice. "This is what we're going to do. Tomorrow you're telling Ed he's in charge."

"What!" I challenged, stiffening on the sofa. "I can't."

"Oh. Yes. You. Can," Sal pushed firmly.

"But he's got kayaking. Two hours away in Lake Macquarie."

"And," Sal insisted. "You have your breakdown to schedule in darling."

"But..."

"Abigail Steen or Montgomery or whatever you call yourself these days, if I have to phone that rotten husband of yours myself, I will."

Sal was clearly on a roll and you didn't dare stop Sally Douglas when she was on a roll.

"You are going to schedule in your breakdown for

this weekend and I am taking you to the Guru Retreat in Byron Bay for two long, luscious days and nights. Ed can damn well take Monday off and take care of the kids till you get back."

"What!"

"You heard me."

"I can't. I appreciate what you're doing. But I just can't go on such short notice."

"What if this was a real emergency? You know...your health or something vital like that. Something bigger than you that was taking over your life and you just had to grab every damn moment you had and make the most of it?"

Sal had a shakiness in her voice now, a wobble in her delivery. Tears on the verge. It wasn't the Sal I was used to.

"Sal, I know what you're saying, I do," I offered gently. "Why don't we get together on the weekend with our diaries and plan this weekend away a little later in the year. I promise not to ditch you at the last minute this time."

"Abby, you're going away this weekend even if I have to drag you there," Sal snapped, finality in her voice. "Life is short. You never know what's around the corner. You have to damn well do something right this very second to change your life and make yourself happy. You know it and I know it, otherwise what the hell are you doing calling to interrupt my salacious Friday night with Greek God?"

"But ..." I tried to respond.

"I'm not taking no for an answer," Sal said firmly. "Ed can cancel his plans for a change. Give him a taste of what it's really like to take care of his family."

I poured more wine into my glass and gulped. Number four this evening...or maybe it was five. Must remember to take a couple of aspirin and drink a gallon of water before my head hits the pillow.

"Wow Sal," I began to giggle. "This could really shake things up a bit."

"Damn straight," Sal shot back.

The giggle turned into laughter. More red wine spilled on the Persian rug. Oops. Maybe I'll keep the stain to remind me of this moment.

Taking a deep breath and exhaling, I responded with a commitment that came from a deep and foreign place within. "What do I need to bring?"

Sal went into full Event Producer mode now. God knows she's got the talent for it. Managed her fair share of charity bashes for The Children's Hospital over the years, along with her full-on role as Event Producer at one of the biggest investment banking firms in Australia. "Pack an overnight bag. French perfume, stilettos, a couple of party dresses, yoga gear and...don't forget sexy lingerie."

"Sexy lingerie!" I interjected.

"Abigail Steen, oh damn I mean Montgomery, are you still learning that the lingerie is more for you than him? This is your weekend to look and feel fabulous."

"But I'm so frumpy."

"But those tits of yours will look great overflowing in a push up. Go on Ab. We're going to have a little fun in Byron Bay. A little R & R night and day."

Weakening, I added, "I'm not sure."

"No backing out now. You said it yourself. You hate your life. Why waste another minute longer torturing yourself...or me for that matter! You need to check out of the motherload and check in with yourself. I mean it. I love you but I hate to watch you sentencing yourself to a slow dying death of doomed domesticity."

Reaching the wine glass to my lips, Sal added, "Oh and by the way...that overfilled glass of red you've got going on, throw it in the sink honey." How did she know me so well?

"You can talk."

"But you drink to shut it out. It's no fun drinking alone. I'll have a taxi waiting outside your front door at 8:00am tomorrow morning."

"8:00am!" I shrieked, walking to the sink and dutifully tossing the remaining red down the drain.

"Yes 8:00am. I want you ready and raring to walk out that door when I arrive."

CHAPTER 3

I woke at the crack of dawn, to the sun, for the first time in years. Actually, felt like I had a reason to get out of bed for a change. A purpose. A sense of something important to do. To look forward. Something just for myself.

Ed slept like a baby next to me, reeking of alcohol. No idea what time he got in. I'd learned to switch off from wondering or worrying what time he crawled into bed each night. It was as if I was wishing time away, wishing for the day when we become one of those couples in 'the olden days'. Couples who sleep in the same room, separately, in single beds. I'm only 42. Why am I dreaming of being 80 when I've got half my life yet to live?

"Be ready no matter what," I heard Sal's voice snap me out of my dreary daze.

I took one last glance at Ed and shook off the image of us in 40 years, before creeping down the hallway to the kids' room. We had the space for our eldest to have his own room in preparation for starting school next year, but he wasn't ready. My kids loved sharing a room, so we kept Brady's bedroom as a playroom, until he needed some grown up boy space.

He slept like an angel, I noticed as I poked my head in the doorway to reveal three gorgeous children sound asleep. Flat on his back, hands resting underneath his head, legs spreadeagled from one side of his bed to the other. At five, he was a little man in the making. Can't believe he's starting school next year.

Turning my eyes toward Emily, I had to hold back a laugh. She had tossed her blanket and sheet to the floor as usual, but her teddy was tightly tucked under her little arm, long white golden curls dangling messily over the pillow.

Little Harry, who was yet to hit those infamous 'terrible two's', was curled up in the foetal position face down, bottom up. His knees cradled underneath his body, as his head rested to the side in the direction of the rotating castle night-light he'd had since birth.

I caught hold of my breath. My heart ached for these beautiful babies. Every bit of love I had inside me rushed through my heart and poured out like air. Like a blanket of breath, I wanted to wrap them up in. I did love my children. I did love being their mum, but somehow I'd lost sight of loving myself in the process. God I wished my mum were alive. This motherhood thing had become so lonely.

After showering and dressing in silence for a change, I made a mental note to wake early more often. Finishing my slice of vegemite toast and English breakfast tea, I crept back to check on my overnight bag one more time, giggling like a teenage girl when I took in the sight of my sexy black lingerie.

Exhaling, I rocked back on my knees, re-zipped my bag and clutched tightly to the handle. Something about packing this bag, about taking this break was big. I could feel it in my bones. I don't know how. I just knew. I really needed this. Haven't had a night to myself since the kids were born, let alone a whole weekend.

Ed was the first up. I heard his footsteps shuffling down the stairs. Sitting stiffly on the edge of the back steps that framed the back deck and ran off our open plan kitchen dining room, I clasped my hands together in my lap as nerves churned around in my belly. I really wished I were Samantha from Bewitched right now so I could wiggle my nose and magically arrive in Byron Bay. Then I wouldn't have to face the dread at the bottom of my belly about the conversation I was about to endure with Ed.

After finishing up in the bathroom, he entered the kitchen. Frozen in fear, I panicked. What if he says no? What am I saying? A grown woman of 42, mother of three, is seeking permission from her husband to have a life?

From the corner of my eye I watched. He turned on the Nespresso machine, as was his usual routine, then walked to the fridge, drank juice from the carton while inspecting possible remnants of last night's dinner. He stepped over to the window and looked out. Stood at the kitchen sink shovelling cold spaghetti bolognaise into his mouth faster than he could swallow it. Does he even know I'm here? Maybe I'll text him to get his attention!

Knowing I needed to find my voice eventually, I slowly began to stand, body cracking as I rose. I exhaled as if my life depended on it. Bracing myself, I clenched my fists together by my sides for strength, for courage.

"Ed," I called out walking slowly toward him.

"Hey," he grunted, still hoovering spaghetti, without a glance in my direction.

We don't kiss good morning anymore. Did we ever? Can't remember. Lost track of what happened from when we started out till now. Did we love each other when we got married 12 years ago? Can't remember. My mind drifted in and out.

Losing my train of thought, I watched the morning sun beam through the warm kitchen window and rest on Ed's messy mop of dark brown, wavy hair that was now highlighted in grey and tumbled around his ears and down a little over his neck. I do remember, though, how I used to love draping my hands around his strong masculine neck when we kissed. Oh yeah, Ed could definitely kiss. I remember that.

Shaking my head and remembering the crucial task of the morning...why we ended up here in the first place, I wondered some more. Maybe I was only in love with the idea of love? Maybe I liked the idea of a wedding, a house, children? Maybe I did all of those things because that's what you were supposed to do? But the sex, it was good...or used to be. Yes, sex with Ed had been so damn good. I do remember that. And...I remember making every one of those three gorgeous babies of ours...and practising.

OMG. Maybe it was sex that led to marriage? Just sex. But now that we're not having it, well, not enough to rate, our marriage couldn't possibly survive.

Staring hard at Ed, who hadn't uttered a single word

except "hey" since he saw me, I held tightly at my temples with my fingertips and cringed. No, "Hey Ab the spaghetti's great." Or, "Morning gorgeous, how are you?" Instead, I just went on being ignored by the man I had committed the rest of my life to.

I know I don't want to be unhappy in my marriage but I'm damned if I know what a happy marriage is supposed to look like. God knows my parents didn't find their happy. Dad was always away on one of his so called 'work trips', having flings with his latest secretary. Mum did everything for him. She was such a beautiful woman from the inside out. Reminded me of Grace Kelly. In looks and in manner. But all Dad ever did was take her for granted. I was not quite 18 when she died. It was such a crucial age for me to lose my mum. Dad however, never seemed to look back.

It was breast cancer that got her, but maybe she died of a broken heart. I wished I had more time with Mum, but cancer is like the devil once it takes over your body. They say stress is what causes our body to get sick. Maybe that's what happened? She was so stressed from all those affairs my dad indulged in, never really helping at home or acting like he wanted to be there. Maybe her body just couldn't take it anymore? All that pent-up emotion burning, churning inside her heart, turned itself into the cancer in her chest.

As I stared at Ed, who continued about his morning routine as if I weren't there, I absently wondered what he did with all that time he wasn't home. Oh God! Maybe Ed's having an affair? Maybe he's had more than one?

Maybe that's why he never wants to come home? He says it's market expectations, the current economic climate that demands the kind of hours he puts in at work. Says that in advertising you're always wooing the clients and cowering to the big suits that run the joint. The kids have always come second to Ed's work, well third to his kayaking and fourth to who knows what or who else. But me, I am right at the bottom of that list. Possibly don't even rate on the list at all. Oh God...kayaking... completely forgot why I'm up so early with an overnight bag hiding in the corner of the living room.

"Arghhhh Ed," I faltered, grabbing his attention as he made his second cup of coffee from the Nespresso machine we received as a wedding gift that took pride of place on our marble bench top. "Um...about kayaking."

"Yeah," he mumbled tossing the empty spaghetti bolognaise Tupperware container into the sink without an effort to rinse it or stack it in the dishwasher.

"You're going to need to make other arrangements today," I said, adding a touch of huffiness to my voice as if that would help me get through this faster.

"What?" he flashed a look in my direction for the first time in almost 20 minutes.

"Um...well...it's just that I've got plans." Clenching my fists by my side, and rubbing my lips together for strength," I waited for the fight.

"What are you on about?" Ed said with a nonchalance in his voice while tossing back coffee.

"I can't take this anymore!"

"Take what?"

This guy. This idiot husband of mine genuinely looked perplexed.

"Ed...this...us...me...this...family," my voice trembled. "I can't take it. I need a break. And...well...I'm taking it this weekend," a finality began to thread through my voice.

"What are you talking about?" Facing me fully, finally, Ed continued. "I've just gotten up and you're hitting me with this shit at seven o'clock in the morning?"

"Well...when am I supposed to hit you with it?" My voice trembled but I was more than ready to stomp my feet good and solid on the ground if that's what I needed for this man to take notice. "Ed there's never a right time with you. You're hardly ever here. When am I ever supposed to talk to you about what's going on or needing a break?"

"What are you on about? I'm here right now."

"But you're not, don't you see." Tears brewed in my eyes, as I held on tight, trying desperately for them not to fall. "Ed, you got up this morning, walked into the kitchen ... you've been here 20 minutes and didn't even know I was in the same damn room as you."

"Abby. I don't need this shit. I've got to go soon. My mates are waiting. I have kayaking on every Saturday. Why couldn't this have waited till I got back?"

"Because," I said, my voice raising a few octaves, tears on the brink. "I can't schedule my "free" fucking time as "freely" as you do." I spat the words out and held up my quoting fingers for good measure.

We yelled back and forth. I couldn't hear what anyone was saying. No-one gave in. No-one was winning. The yelling, the fighting went on and on and on. Neither of us remotely interested in the other's opinion.

"Ed I'm going to have a breakdown if I don't take this time for myself. I'm serious. I'm not coping. I'm overloaded. Seriously sleep deprived. I need a break."

"Well what about me working every fucking day, every day of the week paying for this lifestyle you asked for," he spat back at me, anger raging in his throat. "When do I get a fucking break?"

He went on and on. I tuned in. I tuned out. He was never going to see it from my point of view. I realised that now.

I just stood there, listening to the noise that was his voice. It went straight through me and all the way out to the other side. I had become a mere shell of my former self. A layer stripped away with each new child I had bared. Each year that passed in this marriage, I'd come to feel less and less for this man. Emptiness washed through my gut, as I watched the father of my children selfishly saying that all I do is take.

"Ed," I whispered. The rage inside me was deep, so deep that I could barely speak. But somewhere within all that rage, there was strength. Just a slithering of strength that I clung onto for dear life.

A voice I'd locked away a long time ago spoke out. "Ed," I whispered a little louder.

He kept raging. I forged on.

"Ed," I said, regardless of whether he listened or not. Knowing I had to get this out as much for me as for him. "Ed, I didn't ask for this life and neither did you. You're not happy," I said quietly. "That's really evident to me now. I'm not happy either. God only knows the impact we're having on the children." I choked back tears. Oh, my darling children what have we done?

"Speak for yourself," Ed spat out the words. "I'm happy with my life and I'll be a lot fucking happier when I jump in my car and drive to fucking Lake Macquarie."

"Ed," I said, eerily calm, as an inner strength rose through me and clung with full force to my throat. "Sal is picking me up in 15 minutes. I'm having the weekend off that I've been meaning to have for years. I'm not trying to hurt or inconvenience you. I'm just trying to help me. I don't know what's left for us but if I don't look after myself, I'm going to get sick...like my mum did."

"Oh, there you go again...on and on about your mother who died before her time."

I just stood and stared, said nothing. The expression said everything. No words needed. He knew he had well and truly stepped over the line now.

"Abby," he faltered, a plea in his voice. He ran his hand absently through his dishevelled hair, taking time to find the words, something, anything, to crawl out of the hole he had just dug for himself. "Look...ah...if you need a break...let's work it out...get someone in ... we can."

"Ed," I cut him off. "I'm going."

"What the hell am I supposed to do with the kids?" he shouted looking to the ceiling where our babies slept, frustration rattling around in his voice.

"Are you kidding?" I yelled back. "Are you seriously fucking kidding?" I had well and truly lost it now. "Your plans. Your Saturday. Your work. Your kayaking. Your friends. Your clients. Well Ed...those three kids up there," I said looking at the ceiling, "Are your fucking kids too. And, if I dropped dead right now then what would you do?"

"Well you're not fucking dead, are you?" He shouted. "But sometimes I wish you were Abby."

My mouth dropped open. Then I heard the tears. But they weren't my own and they certainly weren't Ed's. At the bottom of the stairs, clinging tightly to the safety gate and each other were three small children, unable to hold back the tears. I looked at Ed. His face had gone ghost white.

A horn tooted outside and the doorbell was on overdrive. A deep expression of regret was now plastered all over Ed's face, but his clenched jaw and fists at his sides revealed his unwavering anger.

Emily, who was clutching her one-eyed teddy bear so tightly she might have ripped its head off, choked back tears. "Harry needs changing Mummy."

My heart ripped apart. "Daddy's going to help with the nappy changing today darling." I soothed holding back my own tears.

The doorbell rang again. The horn tooted. Oh give me a break!

"Why do you wish Mummy was dead?" Brady cried out.

"Shit!" was all Ed could say.

"Great response Ed. You really do have the nicest things to say when it counts," I spat back at him, raging green eyes meeting his blue.

"Daddy, do you really want Mummy dead?" Brady sniffed, choking on tears.

With Ed's back still facing the kids, I admired my five-year-old son's courage to stand up to his father.

I ran to Brady now, to all three of my darling children. Opened the lock on the kiddie gate and scooped Brady, Emily and Harry into my arms, wishing I could cut open my heart and tuck them inside to keep them safe.

The knocking on the door pounded ferociously. I glanced at the kitchen clock. Shit. Sal.

Kissing the kids and releasing them from my arms, I ran down the hallway. "Wait a minute," I yelled then wrenched open the mahogany door to reveal one sassy looking Sal.

Hot was most definitely an understatement. Bright pink Kaftan with shades of red and orange running through it. Sunnies rested on top of her coifed siren red curls that fell just below her shoulders. Lips stained in ruby red. Heels to match. "Ready?"

"Oh, God Sal," I moaned. "The shit has really hit the fan."

"We always knew it would Ab," she snapped, tone clipped. "Only difference is, this weekend you're not hanging around to clean it up."

"I really don't think I can go."

"Like hell!" she glared, stomping past me in her oversized heels made for the catwalk instead of a relaxing health retreat in sunny Byron Bay. I didn't have the heart to remind her of our household rule to remove stilettos before stomping all over the floorboards.

"Right," Sal bellowed, storming off to make her grand entrance. With hands on hips, she let rip. "What's going on here?" She glared at Ed, only to soften when she saw Brady, Emily and Harry all huddled together, cowering on the sofa. "All these tears," she soothed, gently stroking the cheeks of three darling children, before returning daggers across the room at Ed.

I stood feebly in the hallway peaking around the corner to see what was going to happen next.

"Daddy says he wants Mummy dead," Brady sniffled.

"I did not say that," Ed defended.

Sal eyeballed Ed, hard.

"Yes, you did," Emily blurted out. "We heard it. That's why Mummy is crying. She wants to have a breakdown and you won't let her." Emily's voice trembled as she held onto her teddy for dear life.

"Look," Ed replied, running his hands through his hair in frustration. No doubt the effects of last night's drinking session with his clients and who knows who else, was messing with his brain right now. "Mummy can have a breakdown if she wants. I just wanted her to plan it with me, book it in so Grandma can come over and help look after us," he smiled sweetly, as if he'd waved a magic wand over the situation and turned everything into a fairyland happily ever after ending.

"Why can't you look after us Daddy?" Brady replied, tension tugging at his throat, the little man in the making speaking up in defence for his mummy.

"I can, but Daddy has to work. He has lots of things he needs to do," Ed said stepping into the living room, getting closer to the kids for the first time since they entered the room.

"But how come Mummy does things and still looks after us?" Emily wondered.

Sal rolled her eyes. Knowing this could go on forever, she hiked up her long flowing kaftan and crouched down in front of the kids. "Mummy's fine. Everything's going to be fine. Mummy just needs a break. A couple of days to get some rest...relax a bit with Aunty Sal."

"Can't we come and help Mummy relax too?" Brady wondered looking over at his mummy hiding in the corner of the living room.

"No darling," Sal replied, giving all three kids one enormous group hug. "Mummy just needs some Aunty Sal time. And time to herself. Anyway, it'll be great with Dad," she said flashing Ed an, 'If looks could kill, you would be my number one target' look. "But if Mummy and Aunty Sal don't leave soon," Sal said tickling each of the kids' tummies, "We'll miss our plane."

"Plane!" Harry spoke for the first time, his eyes lighting up.

"Yes, a plane sweet Harry. We'll take some photos and tell you all about it when we get back," Sal added, kissing the kids and standing up. "Now, come over here Mummy," Sal turned to me retreating in the hall, "And kiss these gorgeous kids of yours goodbye."

Water welled up in my kids' eyes. I held my breath and chocked back my own tears. "Group hug," I smiled.

Launching together, all three kids wrapped their tiny little hands, arms and legs and every little fibre of their body around my own. My heart broke in that moment.

"I love you Mummy. I miss you already," Brady sobbed.

"I do too little man," I trembled. "But it's only two sleeps. Mummy is going to feel so much better when she comes back home."

I gave the kids one last squeeze before turning to Ed who now stood motionless on the stained Persian rug.

"Ed, I'll be back late Monday evening. If you need me, I'll have my phone."

"But she'll have it on silent," Sal interjected.

"So," I looked at Sal then back to Ed, "In case of emergency you can always call."

He said nothing. No goodbye. No good luck. No, I understand. No enjoy yourself. And definitely no...I love you.

The taxi tooted loudly.

"Meter's running babe. We've really gotta run," Sal said scooping up my overnight bag in one hand and yanking me down the long hallway with the other.

The kids ran after us and howled at the closed front door behind me. My heart cracked further and it took every bit of strength not to look back.

"Airport driver. Virgin domestic," Sal said. "And hurry."

CHAPTER 4

Two hours later, Sal and I had landed safely in Ballina, deeply grateful we had only carry-on luggage and able to avoid the wait typical of the airport baggage carousel. Now seated in the hotel's shuttle service, we were on direct route to the infamous Guru Retreat, set high in the hills of the Byron Bay Hinterland.

With half an hour or so drive ahead of us, I rested my head against the minivan's window and allowed my mind to drift back home. "I hope I've done the right thing," I whispered. "Think I may have put an even bigger wedge between Ed and I now."

"Abigail Montgomery!" Sal snapped, grabbing my wrist firmly and turning me to face the rampage. "That wedge honey, I hate to tell you, is the elephant in the room that neither of you want to talk about."

Easing my wrist a fraction, Sal settled in for her sermon. "The only thing you two have been putting your energy and attention into is that wedge. You focus on the wedge day after day and as a result it just grows and grows. You're both too afraid that if you removed that damn wedge, you would be faced with...well...with the...I hate to say it...empty space between two people who have forgotten why they were together in the first place. The intimacy, or lack thereof," she peaked her eyebrow, "That neither of you want to address."

I couldn't help but shift in my seat as nerves crawled around in my belly.

Sal powered on.

"All you're doing is growing that wedge, focussing on all the reasons why the marriage, the life between the two of you, isn't working. It's got to stop Ab. People don't get married to behave the way you do toward each other. It's criminal."

After some silence, I exhaled. "You're not going to slam me all weekend are you? I don't think I could take it," I whispered, lifting my own eyes to meet Sal's.

"No, but I am going to deliver some home truths," she smiled and gave my hand a firm tug before releasing it. "It's time you took some space to absorb it all honey. A little time to reflect on that life you're living...if that's what you want to call it. You're miserable. Abby. but this isn't a new thing. You can't wait for the kids to get older before you start focussing on yourself. You need to do it now. Trust me. It's time to enjoy some good old pampering with Aunty Sal," she winked and held out her arm to announce the almighty view outside that was Guru Retreat.

"This weekend is just what you need Ab. Ed and the kids too, whether they realise it or not."

As I stepped out of the shuttle bus, I was immediately struck by crisp fresh country air. The kind that doesn't come from living in one of the busiest suburbs in Sydney. Guru Retreat was a long way from being anything like one of the most famous and densely populated beaches in the world that was my hometown, Bondi Beach.

But here, deep in the Byron Bay Hinterland there was no traffic to speak of. No loud music blaring out of someone's car window cranked all the way up, while on their way to take in the summer sun. No queues for the supermarket checkout. Here, all you could see, as far as your eyes could take you, was lush green grass, rolling hills and the magnificent Byron Bay coastal landscape in the distance.

My body exhaled as I released a deep, long breath that I had possibly been holding onto since we boarded the plane. Dusty cobwebs that had been clogged in my pores for years, now relieved to escape my body.

As if on autopilot, I reached for the phone in my handbag and stared back at the black screen, wondering what had transpired in the past three hours since my dramatic departure. Sal had insisted I keep my phone switched off after landing. Told me it would be good to hang with the tension of not knowing what was going on. "Good for Ed too," she insisted.

That tension Sal mentioned simmered deep below the surface. Surely everything would be all right? A mild panic began to bubble in my chest, leaving uneasiness on my mind. I began chewing the inside of my gum, my usual habit when I became nervous. But as Sal and I walked into the Oh. My. God sensational, splendid foyer of our retreat, thoughts of home vanished.

My mouth dropped open. I did a slow twirl to take in the view. Shiny marble floors, a long, wide reception area, fitted out with an oversized desk about three-metres-long by one-metre-deep, carved from rich red Tasmanian Oak. All offset with a large centrepiece of native Australian hibiscus flowers. The staff behind the counter, and those floating through the foyer, looked clean, fresh, vibrant and so damn happy in clinical white and chocolate brown uniforms.

Torn between wanting to surrender to this incredible setting that was my escape from my dreary life for the weekend, and wondering what the hell was happening back home with that phone of mine turned off, I clenched my jaw. This was a very foreign experience to not be available for my family at a moment's notice. To just... well...check out...while I check in with myself.

Sal caught a glimpse of my pensive expression. "OK, you can turn it on. Check everything's all right. Then...it's going off for the remainder of the weekend."

"What!" I shrieked.

"We're locking it in the hotel safe," Sal flatly replied, smiling at the woman behind the reception as she signed us in to the Garden Suite for two delicious days and nights.

"That's a bit extreme," I trembled, clutching my phone to my chest. Since when had I become so attached to my phone?

"Extreme measures for extreme situations," Sal snarled.

"But."

"Abby, you don't know how to not be there for your kids."

"But I want to be there for my kids."

"OK, let's try it this way," Sal said blowing flaming red hair out of her smouldering caramel brown eyes, and resting a hand on her hip. "If you really want to start being there for your kids, being present, as everyone talks about these days, enjoying motherhood, you are going to have to ..."

"I enjoy motherhood," I snapped.

"Sure you do Ab." Leaning in closer, Sal whispered in my ear, "Just not all the time."

Huffing now and ready for debate. "What...so I'm supposed to enjoy motherhood all the time?"

"Abby, relax. I'm not judging you. But your judgment, it's clouded. Everyone needs space from their life. As much as I hate to admit this...your unhappiness, is not all on Ed."

"Oh great, so now you're defending him?" I snapped, turning away from Sal and wishing I was as far away from her as possible right now.

"Shit Abby. I've whisked you away, all expenses paid, on me and now you're giving me grief. Give the tirade a rest for a change. 48 hours at least."

"I never should have come," I whispered, my face buried deep in my hands.

Sal stepped closer and placed a soothing hand on my shoulder? "Abby all I'm saying is...sure Ed's a big part of the problem, but he's not the sole reason for your unhappiness. You've lost your mojo girlfriend."

Giving my shoulder a squeeze, one arm fully draped

over me, Sal soothed a little more gently. "I know you're sleep deprived, depleted. But you're going to have to make some changes in you before you even begin to look at what's up with Ed."

"I know," I exhaled. "I do know," I admitted to Sal, as much as to myself. "But he's never home. Well, hardly ever home. I keep wondering why he doesn't want to be with us? With me. It hurts. It really, really hurts." Tears welled in my eyes.

"Oh babe." Sal embraced me in an enormous hug that only a best girlfriend of more than 20 years can. "We don't have to solve it all in one weekend. Let's just take some time to relax, unwind and do a little soul searching. Nothing heart wrenching or exhausting. I want to give you a break from all that," she said leading me to our suite.

"Now," Sal said opening the door in a grand and theatrical gesture, "This is all ours for two whole days and two whole nights."

There was no denying it was gorgeous. We had the Garden Suite, which directly opened to the valley below. Rolling lush green grassy hills ran over the horizon for miles, the Pacific Ocean a distant but beautiful blue blur through the trees.

"Thank you, Sal. This really is truly beautiful," I smiled standing now at the floor to ceiling windows looking out to the private garden.

"Let's get our itinerary sorted," Sal said, tossing her bag onto one of two queen-size beds, decorated in plush white sheets, fluffy pillows and a caramel and charcoal angora wool wrap, loosely draped at the foot of the bed.

Sitting on the edge of my own bed now, phone clutched in my hand, I began biting the inside of my gum as I snuck a look over at Sal. "I've gotta check in Sal. It's driving me batty."

"OK, here's the deal," she instructed. "Switch it on. Check if there are any messages. Deal with them. Then switch it back off and check it in to the hotel's safe."

I raised an eyebrow.

"Extreme measures," she reminded me. "Besides," she added softly and smiled. "I texted Ed the details of where we're staying just before the plane took off."

"You could have told me!"

"Ab, I think you need to learn how to switch off without being given permission."

"Huh?" I stopped, abruptly unpacking my things and neatly folding them into the chest of draws at the end of my bed, phone still clutched tightly in my hand.

"It shouldn't matter what I say," Sal stood at the door, turning her hand on the knob, "It's about finding your own way to let go."

I exhaled as if my life depended on it, and ran my hands through my dark blonde hair, desperately in need of a good wash, cut and blow dry.

When Sal stepped into the hallway, she turned back. "Check your phone, then meet me back at reception."

Five minutes later I strolled up to the concierge and handed over my phone, forced a smile, when Sal greeted me with a, "Well?".

"Didn't text...didn't call," I said, slumping my elbow

on the counter, fist resting under my jaw.

"And you're unhappy about that?"

"Yeah well...I thought he might have at least had one question to ask or at the very least, texted to say they were OK."

"Are you kidding me; you crazy lunatic?"

"What?"

"Abigail Montgomery, if you don't bloody stop pouting and whinging, I'm going to slap you good and hard. Then I'll throw you over the cliff at the edge of that lawn over there," Sal said, pointing her finger out to the incredible vista on the doorstep of Guru Retreat.

My jaw dropped. The lady behind the desk covered her mouth to muffle a giggle.

I flashed Sal my Green-Eyed Mummy Monster look.

"Right," Sal instructed the woman behind the reception, as she went into event producer mode with military precision. Scary. "We'd like to check this phone in to the hotel safe for the weekend." She slapped down the phone on the Tassie oak. "We are not to be disturbed unless it's an emergency or someone is instructing us of our next spa treatment."

Turning to me now, Sal glared. Her caramel brown eyes turned a deep shade of chocolate as she let rip with her dragon lady voice, direct from Scotland. "This is my weekend too Abby. A weekend off from all the shit going on in my life. We all have it. But you seem to have gotten so wrapped up talking about your crap, that you've forgotten how to have a life. Now, stop whinging about everything and just enjoy yourself."

I was too scared to speak. More than two decades of friendship told me that when Sally Douglas was on a mission, those flaming red Scottish hair roots of hers might just light up like a bonfire.

"Are we done here Abigail?" she growled. "Because I would really like to get on with being fucking pampered."

I simply nodded.

Returning to the woman behind the counter, and putting on her best event producer smile, Sal asked. "So, what's on offer?"

The receptionist shared the spa packages, mostly to Sal, occasionally glancing at me in sympathy. She rattled off a long list of delicious, delectable and dazzling experiences one might look forward to in a place named Guru Retreat.

Facials that started at 30 minutes and up to three hours. Three hours? Just how dirty can one person's face get? Mud baths. Now why would they go and scrub your face clean only to get it all dirty again? Nutrition eating sessions. That's a firm no. I am definitely taking a break from meal planning this weekend, thank you very much. Therapy workshops. Oh dear, one session just wouldn't do it. Meditation and Yoga. Mmm...now that I could try, but that Downward Dog thing never ends up being easy for this mere mortal.

"So?" Sal said slapping her hand down onto the counter and turning to me. "What will it be Mrs Montgomery? Massage, facial, pedicure? All of the above?"

"Er...massage?" I replied meekly.

"Make that two," Sal said, flashing her bright, white smile to the receptionist.

CHAPTER 5

We were led down a long corridor covered in more Tasmania oak, wide set floorboards that gleamed. Citrus smells wafted through the air. I was in heaven, well...it smelled like I imagined heaven might. I wanted to lay down naked, here and now, on that comforting wooden floor and inhale sweet citrus. I already felt pampered and I hadn't even stepped into my massage room.

Our guide instructed us that we would now be split up into our own private pamper rooms, for a full two-hour massage, then be taken to the gardens of the Mornington Room for fresh green tea.

I turned to Sal, almost wanting to reach out and hug her goodbye, real tight. It was odd thinking I was about to be alone for two whole hours. I hadn't spent this kind of time on my own since I had the kids, let alone two hours doing nothing.

Stepping into the treatment room now. Oh. My. God. My jaw hit the floor. The view took my breath away. An oversized, five metre by five metre room, decked out in warm wooden floorboards, a plush and inviting massage table decorated in frangipanis at both ends. Fresh white sheets were turned over in a corner, inviting me in. I gazed at the floor to ceiling windowed walls, like those in our Garden Suite. I felt my breath catch. More rolling green hills as far as the eye could see. A garden of fresh roses, frangipanis and lavender stood just a metre from my feet. I was in nature's paradise.

My massage therapist smiled and whispered a welcome, introducing herself as, Kirsty. Had she been standing there the whole time? Her soft sweet voice and mousey brown hair tied neatly in a knot at the base of her neck suggested clean living, healthy from the inside out. She was youthful in complexion, possibly late 20s, and... she was all mine, or more to the point...I was all hers, for the next two hours.

"Take a seat," Kirsty gestured toward the recliner made from cane and complete with two white and green cushions in Asian print design. "A few questions before we begin," she smiled, sitting at the wooden stool in front of my recliner.

Clipboard and pen poised, she began. "Have you had a massage before?"

"Mmmm," I pondered, feeling dreamy from the scents wafting around the room.

"When was your last massage?" she asked.

Mmmm? Last one? My eyes darted from side to side in recollection. Oh yes that's right, "My honeymoon," I reminisced. "My husband and I had a massage by the pool together in Hawaii."

"How lovely," she replied, making notes on her clipboard.

"So, that was your last one?" Kirsty enquired further.

"Yes."

"How long ago was that?"

"Arghhh...mmmmm." I became embarrassed, humiliated really. 12 years since my last massage. "Arghhh...12 years ago," I offered feebly.

"12 years!" she blurted out. Remembering herself, Kirsty clutched her clipboard a little tighter and sat up straight. "Well...you're going to love today then."

"I already do." You could walk me right back out of here now. I would have been happy with the citrus and the view. Not to mention...a little quiet shuteye on that inviting massage bed you have over there.

Smiling, Kirsty continued

"So, what would you like to get from today's massage?" Kirsty probed further.

"What do you mean...get?"

"What would you like the focus to be? You know...do you want to unwind, de-stress, let go, detox?"

"All of the above?"

She giggled. "Of course, but what specifically would you like to let go of?"

"My husband," I blurted out in autopilot, without realising the words had left my mouth before I said them.

She absently chewed on the end of the pen. "So...your last massage was your honeymoon. Now ... 12 years later...you want your next one to be letting go of your husband?"

Cringing, I said, "Well, when you put it like that, it does sound a little harsh. But, yeah...that pretty much sums up the situation."

"Mmmm," she replied, taking notes. Kirsty eventually turned her eyes to look straight into my own. Crystal blue meeting mint green.

"This feels strangely like a therapy session," I mumbled.

"Well, I am a therapist of sorts," Kirsty noted. "You will definitely receive some therapy with your massage."

Sensing my tension, Kirsty rose from her stool and guided me over to the inviting massage table. "Our bodies hold a lot of our emotions," she instructed. "Our tension, our stress, our hurt, our pain...it doesn't just go to our head, it also goes to our heart. And, it travels all the way up and down our bodies. Stored in cells as memories. Painful memories that we accumulate over time. We either hold on to that tension or we let it go. And by the sounds of it, you have some stuff to let go."

I must have looked terrified, because young, but oh so wise, Kirsty assured me that I didn't need to worry about any of that right now. "Just relax, let go. Let me do the rest," she instructed.

Standing directly in front of the massage table now, she asked me to change. "If you could get fully undressed, place your clothes in the basket underneath the table, then lay face down under the covers, with your face in the small hole at the top...I'll be back shortly. I'll add a little chamomile and orange blossom essence into the lavender diffuser while you're getting comfortable. It will help you to relax and unwind."

As Kirsty left the room, my body contracted. Stripping down in the quiet, oversized therapy room, I felt more naked and exposed than ever. I was about to put myself and my emotions in the hands of a stranger. Scary.

Once settled under the clean, fresh, warm sheets and blanket, I heard the slow turn of the doorknob and a voice ask if I was ready.

"Yes," I whispered.

As the lights were dimmed low, a twinge inside my tummy told me that I was saying "Yes" to a lot more than a massage.

"Close your eyes," she insisted, stroking my hair to one side and gently caressing my neck. "Let your body sink deeper, further onto the bed and just relax." She had the voice of an angel. Soothing, willing me, to let go with...each...new...stroke.

Chimes began ringing from speakers in the corners of the room, then triangles gently clinging and echoes of angelic voices, singing in harmony.

"Let go," Kirsty repeated softly, several times, as she began to caress my body with her hands.

Ever so slowly now, she pulled the towels and blankets down my back and neatly folded them lower at my buttocks. Resting one hand firmly on the centre of my spine, as if to announce, "I am here," Kirsty exhaled and continued to rest and hold her hand in the middle of my back.

I noticed an awkwardness...a tightness in my body. What's happening to me? This small, gentle act of placing flesh on flesh, naked palm to naked back, was making me feel uneasy. It's been a while, a long while, since Ed and I had been intimate like this with each other. Slow, unhurried sex that said, 'I have all the time in the world to touch you, and only you'.

Caught unaware, tears sprang to my eyes. I wanted to fidget and wriggle. I didn't want to feel the things I was starting to feel.

Kirsty kept her hand resting firmly on my back, breathing deeply, in and out. "Let go," she urged. "Breathe in, then really let go as you breathe out Abigail. Let go of the tension, let go of the stress. Let go of the worry. Simply let go of everything other than what you are experiencing right now, just for now, and exhale. Listen to the music, take in the sweet smells of chamomile and orange blossom infused with lavender, and just let go."

Tears pricked my eyes sharply. I couldn't stop them. My body became rigid. I tried to let go but this was more difficult than I realised.

Then...finally, she began to move.

Both hands now firmly placed on my back, making slow circular motions, growing bigger with each new breath. She breathed in and exhaled out as her strong, yet soft hands, made their way all over my back, climbing higher toward my neck. Oh, that feels so good.

"Let go," Kirsty encouraged. "Let go of the tension, let go of the inhibitions Abigail," she soothed in her sweet angelic voice as she weaved magic hands all over my neck and shoulders. As the massage grew deeper and longer, she moved both hands all the way up and down my body. Sensations I didn't even know I could have within me, became tiny fireworks that sparkled.

My mind drifted to Ed. Oh Ed I wished you touched me like this.

Random thoughts came fresh into my mind. Arguments re-playing over in my head. Oh Ed, how did we get to this place where we don't even touch each other anymore. I mean really touch each other?

Sensing my thoughts, with my body contracting, Kirsty continued to encourage me to let go.

I must have somehow drifted off to sleep or into some sweet sensual daydream, because all I remembered next was hearing vague and gentle words telling me it was all over and I was to lie quietly for 10 minutes.

A lavender scented eye pillow was placed over my eyes. My eyes! How did I go from lying face down to flat on my back? Kirsty stroked my hair. Lightly, touching the tip of my head with her fingertips. Slowly, ever so slowly, massaging my scalp. I'm in ecstasy and all someone is doing is touching my head. Oh dear, it has been a while.

"Just breathe," she soothed. "Relax. Focus on the natural rise and fall of your breath as you listen to the music. I'll be back in 10 minutes with some fresh spring water."

Ten minutes later, my feet were barely touching the ground. I floated. Carefully, taking one soft step in front of the other. I shuffled like a geisha woman, unhurried.

Kirsty placed me on a comfortable wicker recliner

lounge chair in front of more floor to ceiling windows and helped place my feet up to rest out in front of me. The sun shone brightly on the grass, roses of pink and white framed the garden. Tears stung my eyes in gratitude. I felt very different now to the person I was two hours ago.

Kirsty handed me a cup of something warm and encouraged me to drink. "It's herbal," she whispered, smiling, as she combed my hair with her fingers. Oh, do that again...please!

"It will support your healing process." How did she know? I thought, as piercing blue eyes smiled into my soul. How did she know I was so broken?

"Just relax. Enjoy the view. The tea." And then she left.

Minutes later or maybe it was hours. I had totally lost track of all time. I heard Sal before I saw her.

"Ohhhh miiiiiiii garrrddd. That was insaaaaane," she declared, flopping on the matching wicker lounge chair next to my own. Sal sank her body deeper into the chair as if she might become an extension of it. Her arms flopped loosely on each side arm, as if they were no longer attached to her body. Then she closed her eyes and said nothing. A first for Sal.

I smiled.

As I tilted my head toward her, I reflected that in over two decades of friendship I had never known Sal to be silent. During two miscarriages in her first marriage, then the brutal and heart wrenching divorce, followed by the short-lived second marriage, Sal was never silent.

In all the years and heartbreaks, highs and lows I had witnessed being Sal's best friend, I had never known her to say nothing.

As I turned back into my own silence overlooking the incredible vista, sipping my nourishing herbal tea, I noticed a deep sense of sorrow tremble around the pit of my gut. My eyes twinged with more tears, my belly empty, heart raw. That massage stripped me of stuff I didn't even know I had churning around inside me. The crap I'd been carrying around for who knows how long. Yet now there was a nothingness that left me feeling weirdly unaware of how I might fill it up. The tears rolled down my cheeks, one gentle droplet after another. I'd been so consumed with unhappiness, stress, and pure exhaustion for so long, that I was beyond knowing what to feel anymore.

Sal reached out, touched my hand, kept her closed eyes up toward the warm sun, as my tears continued to drop one by one.

CHAPTER 6

Decked out in runners, leggings and t-shirts- Sal's the crop top, skimpy, low cut version of a t-shirt, and mine the type that said 'Grandpa' -we took off in the direction of the ocean. You couldn't get to the beach by foot from the Hinterland, unless you spent seven hours doing it. But you could, most certainly, stop, exhale and take in that magnificent Pacific in the distance.

Turning to Sal, I broke the silence first. "That massage was intense."

"You needed a good shake up. You've been on a slow and steady roll to burn out. Motherhood is not supposed to be as unenjoyable as yours is."

"Hey."

Holding up her hand, Sal continued. "Before you say another word, just listen. Don't anticipate, don't get defensive, don't butt in. Just listen. You need to make some serious changes girlfriend, and this weekend is just the beginning. I mean seriously, this is the first weekend you've taken for yourself since you've had those three kids of yours."

"But."

Sal held up her hand again, didn't look back this time. Kept leading the trail, further along the cliff face, the main building to Guru Retreat growing further in the distance. "Before you go on and on claiming there is no-one else to look after the kids but you, there is always someone. There is always a way. Geeze Ab, heaven forbid you ever got sick, like really sick...others would have to step in. Ed would have to step in. He'd have to let go of one, probably three of those extracurricular activities he just has to do. And, he'd get home earlier than usual. He'd have to. I'm sure if he managed his time a little better, he would actually be able to fit in more family time. And his mum, I know she's a pain the arse most of the time, but she's still his mum, and did raise two kids herself. She'd manage. Now, I know she won't be as good as the brilliant Abigail," Sal continued without pausing for breath, "But odds are, she wouldn't drop them on their head. Well...not the first night anyway," Sal stifled a chuckle.

"Ab, you're a great mum, you truly are, but you're not really enjoying yourself. We all need a break from the routine, whoever we are, to get some perspective, some time out. Let's face it...corporate workers don't go into the office and never leave the building. We all get to clock off. Switch off. Ab you are always on."

Turning to face me now, looking me dead square in the eyes, Sal's expression grew solemn. "Maybe what's really worrying you is if you switch off, even for an hour, a day, a weekend, you won't be able to switch back on again. I hate to tell you this girlfriend, but if you don't switch off and take some time for yourself a little more regularly, you're going to shut down, completely switch off and not be able to do a damn thing to turn it back on again any time soon. This weekend we're going to unravel you a little. Help you get some perspective." She paused and breathed in fresh country air.

Taking in Sal's words and Mother Nature in all her glory, I had to admit it was nice to take a walk without six small feet struggling to keep up. A little healthy 'me time'. Whenever I stepped outside the house these days, I had three kids in tow, an oversized bag full of kiddie paraphernalia dangling from my shoulder, and a body and brain that was exhausted just trying to keep everyone heading in one direction. Surely, I can manage a quiet walk by myself a couple of times a week?

Later, back at reception, Sal assumed her superwoman event producer mode. She dictated instructions to a healthy looking blonde woman behind the desk, hair neatly bobbed to the nape of her neck, cropped fringe that framed sparkling grey-blue eyes, with a wide smile revealing shining white teeth. She oozed health retreat advertisement. They all look so damn perky at this place.

"Ok that's sorted," Sal declared, turning and looking very pleased with herself.

"What's sorted?"

Leading the way back to our room, Sal continued. "I've booked a cab to pick us up at 4:00pm after we finish lunch out by the pool."

"Cab?"

"We're heading into town for some culture and cocktails."

"Cocktails?" Frowning, then hurrying to keep up with Sal's steady pace. "I thought we were at a health and wellness retreat?"

Turning to pause, hand firmly set on her hip, Sal smirked. "It's taken about six years to whisk you away for a girly weekend, do you think I'm not going to pack in as much as I can? I want to liberate you in all sorts of ways," she winked. "Including," she added with a glint in her eyes, "getting out on the town."

"Now," she declared, leading me to the outside pool surrounded by lush, tall palm trees, "let's go and gorge on sprouts and lentils and all things green before we commit some sins with those sweet massaged bodies of ours."

Later, when we got out of the cab and into the heart of town on a late Autumn, warm, Byron Bay day, I felt like my legs had suddenly grown up to my armpits. Sal had insisted I wear her four-inch silver stilettos and one of her shiny disco ball backless dresses that fell so low it barely skimmed the top of my buttocks. I definitely did not fit the picture of frumpy housewife with three kids, who found herself regularly chained to the kitchen sink, right now.

I stopped, paused and breathed in the scene. One word for it...youth!

Without letting me wallow in self-pity a moment longer, Sal grabbed my hand and led me inside to the nearest bar. "Come on girlfriend, let's get a drink."

As I sashayed with Sal to the outside bar of a hip little place known as Tempted, I became fundamentally aware that my hot little dress was perfect for a venue like this. There was a lot of flesh on display. Taught, tanned and toned flesh mind you. Hot young men with shiny white teeth and a healthy appetite for life. Women swanned. Men sauntered.

"Two Moscow Mules thanks sweetie," Sal purred, leaning on the bar, batting her eyelids and flaunting her oversized breasts over the low plunging neckline of her hot burnt orange kaftan number, complete with one long split that ran right up to the top of her inner thigh.

The bartender, in a tight black t-shit and stone washed jeans, shaggy blonde hair and baby blue eyes, smiled back. "Would you like a little extra mint?" he drooled, leaning closer to Sal. That woman is always on heat.

I had to laugh, thinking back to our uni days. I had way too many late nights partying with Sal. God, I had fun with everyone back then, including myself. Where did that part of me go? That part that Sal exhibited so well...'Flirty at 40'.

Well...if the truth be known, I had never quite had the confidence of Sal and her appetite for men, but I had a little more fire in me than I do these days.

"Keep the change Tom," Sal whispered, leaning in to purr and stroke the bartender's strong arm. He obviously loved lifting weights. How did she already know his name?

We perched ourselves at a table for two looking out at the beach. Byron Bay really was a gorgeous chill-out destination. Apparently that lighthouse is the furthest eastern point in Australia, a real landmark. The kids would love to hike up the hill to see that view from the lighthouse, I daydreamed.

My thoughts drifted back to family life. We never really do go on holidays though. Feels too exhausting thinking about it, let alone packing and driving up all this way along the Australian coast, or catching a plane. We used to have these dreams, Ed and me, when we got married. All these plans to travel with the kids, take them on adventures and live life to the fullest. Now I'm struggling to live each day to the fullest, let alone the rest of my life.

"Cheers," Sal broke me from my sombre silence. "No thinking of Ed or the kids anymore this weekend darling," she winked. "If there's an emergency, they'll just have to deal with it. Anyway, I want to talk about what gorgeous eye candy there is in this place," she said, eyes roaming.

"I was thinking of bar hopping but after seeing the talent here at Tempted," Sal now smiled as she tinkled her fingertips toward a hot young guy that looked like the star of a Levi's commercial. "I think we might just stay put."

Three Moscow Mules later, I let Sal know that my belly was in serious need of food or I would not remember much about the rest of the evening.

"Ok," Sal agreed, "let's take a break, get some dinner, somewhere swanky."

Walking along a sandstone pathway, we followed fairy lights that lit up the tiny lane all the way to Sea Crust, apparently one of the best seafood restaurants in town.

Sal took the lead and sauntered up to an elegant looking maître de with long jet-black hair sleeked all the way down her back, deep blue eyes, an exotic red painted mouth. Assuming her position behind a small wooden lectern, she greeted us. "Evening ladies, do you have a reservation?"

"No, but this mumma," Sal said pointing her thumb in my direction, "has been let out of the house for the first time in five years and she needs to rest that oh so fine butt of hers. Be treated with a little decadence, if you know what I mean?" Sweeping her eyes around the room, Sal added. "Oh, and a fancy glass of bubbles would be a great way to get the appetisers underway."

Flashing perfect white shiny teeth, the maître de gave us a look that said, 'I get your world'. "I have just the table for you. Come this way ladies."

Dressed in a skin tight stretchy three quarter length black skirt and crisp white shirt with the collar standing up to attention, unbuttoned to the point that drew the eye directly to the top of her breast, she swanked and sauntered in the direction of a table for two by the window. Byron Bay's beautiful Main Beach for its backdrop.

"We'll start with a glass of your finest bubbles and a dozen oysters to share," Sal requested. "How do they come?"

"We have natural, Kilpatrick, wasabi and mayo with a hint of tamari and lastly, an infused lime and Spanish lemon relish," our maître de declared.

"Sold!" Sal said. "We'll get half a dozen of the wasabi version and make the rest those infused lime relish ones."

A waitress introduced herself as Mia and informed us that she would attend to our needs for the evening. Our menus were elegantly hand painted in black ink and relayed in great detail, while including the specials of the day. Could I stay a month and have one of everything each day?

Listening to Mia in her animated fashion sharing delectable dishes of lobster and crayfish, prawns and black ink squid, muscles and scampi, I wondered how I ended up with the raw end of the deal. How Ed had continued to get out post children. Wined and dined himself and his clients without a thought for the wife and kids at home, while I cleaned up leftover dinner mush from the floor on a regular basis. I know I signed up for this. Had unprotected sex three times. But I never knew it would be this difficult, this lonely.

I love my kids but I miss me. That independent Abby I used to be. I always thought of myself as a free spirit, but now I feel like I'm locked in. Anchored to this derailed life path I seemed to have set myself on. I want to enjoy my marriage, I continued this rambling of thoughts, while aimlessly gazing at the painting on the wall of a woman floating on her back in a pool of deep green and blue water.

"What will it be Ab?"

Silence.

"Ab?" Sal grabbed my arm to jolt me to attention. "Earth to Ab."

"Huh?" I looked back at Sal, a vague haze glazing over me.

"Oh, you're not doing it again? It's your weekend to stop thinking and just live."

"I can't help it Sal. I don't get any time to myself to think, to breathe. I don't have a handle on things anymore. I don't know why I'm so unhappy all the time, not coping or fighting with Ed. I'm struggling to understand how to get back to me."

"Don't try to solve it all in one weekend," Sal said squeezing my hand. "This is just the beginning. One step at a time. You've spent the last five years in mummyland ... just kind of coping ... snatching pockets of time when you can. Ab, this year you've got to make some changes. If you keep going the way you are, you'll just run yourself into the ground."

Giving my hand one final squeeze, Sal reached for her glass of bubbles to hold it to mine in a toast. "But tonight, we're not talking about it anymore. We're going to eat and drink till we feel so full we can't take anymore. And then we're going to dance our arses off." Sal roared with laughter and hollered to Mia for more champagne.

The evening had now turned to that crazy part of the night where Sal and I had forgotten we were at a health retreat. Forgotten I was married woman of 12 years and a mother of three children for the past five. The sexy little number of Sal's I was wearing was juuuust covering every bit of wobble I had accumulated throughout motherhood. And the alcohol was certainly helping me to feel younger and foxier than my body usually looks and feels on any given motherload day.

As I sat perched on a bar stool, sipping another gin

and tonic, I watched Sal in the middle of the dance floor, swanking and swaying. Making out with her German traveller, Hans, that she met within 30 minutes of walking back into Tempted.

And now his buddy, Karl, was making his moves on me as best he could. It seemed clear, to the late 20 something German, that I was...a given...a sure thing, seeing as I was sexy Sal's sidekick and all. He didn't seem to care that I was married or had three kids. Listened, but didn't really take it in. He was more interested in the only kind of conversation that could happen in a place like Tempted. Up close and real personal.

Karl made me feel sexy, the way he whispered in my ear, and gently stroked the back of my neck. Taking his time to ease my hair to one side, and lean in to whisper what he would like to do with me if he had me alone back in his hotel room. Oh. My. God. Please take me back to your hotel room. Oh. My. God. What am I saying? I'm a married mother with wobble, who is in complete denial she has reached that size 16 destination. But oh...please do that to me again.

Maybe it's just that Ed and I hadn't had sex for six months. Maybe it's been longer. I've lost track. The only thing that seems to be holding us together is the kids, the mortgage, the legal contract we signed 12 years ago. Nothing we say to one another anymore is kind.

Maybe Karl would be a nice distraction for me after all. Oh ... wow ... it really did feel good to have a man's fingers trickling down my back. Oh shit. What am I saying? I have another man touching me and it's not my husband. But ... oh my ... it feels so good.

I was suddenly grateful in this moment that it was jam packed with people at this happening Byron Bay joint, otherwise I might just have to jump this youthful man's bones right here on the floor.

Somehow gaining a brief amount of composure, I searched in the crowd for Sal. True to form, she was giving, 'Baby', in Dirty Dancing a run for her money. Her tongue now firmly planted down Hans' throat, him naturally responding to her mating call. Having the time of their life, touching and matching each other heat for heat, without a care in the world for the fact they were in the middle of the dance floor with over one hundred people surrounding them.

Lost in watching Sal and Hans, I hadn't noticed Karl's hand now hovered a little closer to my breast. My breast! Or...maybe I had.

He slid his fingers slowly, easily, underneath the shiny silver fabric gaping low under my naked arm. His fingers eased their way slower to now fully touching my breast, stroking. Up and down. Oh Karl, you know just how I like it.

My mind wandered in and out of daydream land, as I forgot all about my cold reality back home. Murky territory I know. But all I wanted right here, right now, was to have hot sex with a tall blonde German traveller. Oh, yes Karl, please touch me right there. No strings attached.

I melted closer to him as Karl touched and stroked my naked breast underneath sweaty satin. It felt sooooo good. I'm sure I started purring now, as I absently dipped my head back toward him. I felt the heat of his chest against my bare back. He firmly held my full breast now in the palm of his hand, focussing purely on caressing my nipple. Oh ... wow... He tugged gently, then began squeezing, teasing my nipple, stroking my breast like he'd owned my body for years. I let my head fall back fully to rest into his chest, eyes fluttered closed. I tried to focus my thoughts on the soul band on stage heating up the crowd, in the hope I didn't get lost in Karl, but I was a lost cause.

He drew his hand down my back, caressing bare flesh with a feather's touch. Gently easing his fingertips back up and around to my full breast that yearned for his hand to take me further. Oh...that feels so good. I was about to orgasm, right here, right now.

As he straddled the stool behind me, I let this sweet gorgeous stranger caress and tease every inch of my womanhood. His manhood grew bigger, stronger and harder, pressing into my lower back. As my eyes remained closed, I began to imagine Karl's tongue had replaced his fingers, tasting my bare breast, in the hope that he might move further down my body ... and...Shit!

Panic. What am I doing? I am in the middle of a hot crowded bar named Tempted on the verge of an orgasm with some strange foreigner rubbing my back up against his crotch.

"It's been a while," I flustered, leaping up from the stool, stumbling on my stilettos. Whoa...those cocktails and foreign men are a heady mix.

I stumbled toward Sal, who looked at this point like she and her hot German were in fact Siamese twins, finally reunited, after being separated at birth. Yanking her arm out from where it was happily nestled under Hans's armpit, I pulled her close and all but yelled in her ear. Pleading, I called out. "If I don't leave now, I know my tomorrow is going to look a whole lot different than it has in the past 12 years."

"And that's a bad thing because?" Sal said raising her eyebrow and looking back to purr at Hans.

"Sal, if we don't leave right now," panic creeping into my voice, "I'm going to end up having sex with a stranger."

"Tell me again why that's a bad thing?" Sal said, putting one hand on her hip, while reaching the other hand back to stroke Hans' chest.

"Because I'm married," I said throwing my wedding ring finger in her face. "And, I've got three kids in that package deal."

Hans rested himself up close behind Sal, hands reaching around to caress her lower belly, moving upward toward her breasts." She fluttered her eyelids back.

I yanked her hand to jolt her to attention.

"Oh, come on Ab," Sal cajoled, taking my hands in her own, Hans at her back, still stroking her belly.

Sal tried to tempt me in for a sway and dance. "Maybe a little fling is just what you need," she giggled, looking over at Karl tossing back his beer and looking cocky as hell. "Something to help loosen things up a little."

"Maybe," I said, flashing a look back at Karl. Oh yeah, he was hot! "But I need time to think this through," I said, nervously running my hands through my hair. "I don't know what's going to happen with Ed but I do know that tonight's not the night to turn everything on its arse."

Hans pulled Sal back into his fold a little tighter.

Holding out in hope, I waited for what felt like forever.

"Sorry Hans," Sal said finally, cranking her neck back toward her hot hunky German. "But we're going to need to call it a night."

"Huh?" he said, ignoring her request. Hans continued nibbling on Sal's ear.

I gave her the death stare, my renowned Green-Eyed Mummy Monster look.

Seconds felt like minutes while I waited for Sal to make the call. "Oh Hans darling, it has been so lovely, but Abby here...she's a little, er...rusty in these ahhh... areas ... and well...it seems we need to call it a night."

He drew her in closer. Sal looked about to surrender when she caught my eye. Mouth tight, hands on both hips with a look of, 'Get your shit together and like now!'

Sal reached into her red lacy bra, pulled out her business card and tucked it firmly into the pocket of Hans' jeans, lingering a little longer near his crotch. Call me some time," she cooed, landing one final sweet wet kiss on his mouth.

I looked back at Karl, mouthed an awkward goodbye

and got ready to move quickly. He looked back, confusion in his eyes. Without wanting this to go on any longer, I reached for Sal's hand, held it tight in my own and made a mad dash outside for the nearest cab.

Resting our heads back against the taxi seat, we burst out laughing. "I think I'm going to need another five years to recover from that. I'd forgotten what a crazy cat you are."

"Hah!" she replied. "You met that hubby of yours on a crazy night out where you were behaving just as I was this evening, if I remember rightly."

"Yeah and look where that got me!"

CHAPTER 7

The next morning, I woke with a very sore head. Fumbling around on my bed, I wondered where I was. It took a while to lift from the haze but when I saw Sal on the matching bed across the room, it all came back to me. Needing to get up and slide cold water down my throat to remove the murky, stale, horrid taste in my mouth, I noted that everything pounded like the beat of an African drum, mostly in my head, when I moved.

Great Ab. First opportunity you get to sleep in during the past five years and you go and ruin it with a nice big hangover. Water. I really need water. Oh God, I think I'm going to throw up. Stumbling to the en suite. Please God...don't let me throw up...I promise not to drink again...ever. I promise, I promise. If you can just help me get through the next hour without throwing up, I know I'll be fine. And then I promise to never ever drink again.

Later, with two glasses of ice-cold water rumbling uneasily in my belly, I fumbled my way back out of the bathroom, still willing myself not to throw up. Glancing at Sal, I had to stifle a chuckle. Face down, her flaming red hair tossed in every direction. Legs, arms spreadeagled, as if she hadn't moved an inch since she flopped face down in that position when we arrived back late last night. She was out cold, no doubt about it. The room reeked of alcohol. The stench poured out of our pores.

Ed came home smelling of alcohol most nights. Not like the state Sal and I were in last night mind you, but a few under his belt, on a regular basis all the same. Ed and I never hung out anymore. A quiet night at home, shared over a glass of wine or two. He always drank when he was out. I always drank when I stayed in. Alone.

The sudden pangs of loneliness clung to my croaky throat, my hollow belly. Sure, the kids kept me preoccupied but now I had some space, not headspace mind you, my head felt like it was about to explode, I was able to realise just how lonely it had been in this marriage of mine for so long.

Bile crawled up in my throat, as I scrambled around in search of shoes, anything but those four-inch heels to run away from this stifling, alcohol-invested room. Jogging shoes on, I tiptoed past Sal into the long wooden hallway of the retreat. Unaware of the time, I knew it had to be early, with just a hint of morning sun peeking through the shutters along the corridor leading through to the main foyer.

I shuffled quietly past reception, bowing my head as I walked past the woman behind the counter. She smiled and said, "Good morning." I waved awkwardly, avoiding eye contact altogether. My pounding brain could not take one word of chirpy happy little health retreat conversation this morning.

As I stepped outside and smelled fresh crisp air, morning dew sprinkled all over the lawn, I began to wake up. Well...sort of. The air, the atmosphere in Byron Bay felt so very clean. Healthy somehow. A kind of cleansing sensation took hold of my being. I'd read stories about this infamous Australian destination. Stuff about it being sacred or something like that. A healing kind of place, I had heard. Whatever it was, I could feel it, even with an almighty and horrendous hangover taking hold of me from the top of my head to the tip of my toes.

Finding my stride, as I breathed more fresh morning air, I allowed the fog to leave my brain and Mother Nature to fill my soul. As I looked around at the grassy lay of the land, gardens running beautifully over the grounds, rolling hills on either side, the incredible Pacific straight ahead, I finally felt a sense of space.

Maybe it was just because I didn't have three kids hanging off me. One, two or all three of them squished up in my own bed, laying limbs in every direction at first daylight. They often crept into my bedroom during the middle of the night due to some crazy monster under the bed, or a leg or tummy or toe that was sore. Becoming a mother meant I had no personal space. No breathing space. No headspace. No time to leisurely wake up and exhale and take a few moments for myself to get centred for the day ahead.

As I moved further away from the main building of the retreat, I steadied my stride and set out along the pathway that ran along the finely manicured lawn. To my right in the distance, a group of women were on blue mats, leaning over in a striking upward motion that said one thing...yoga! No, I am not remotely going there this morning.

Diverting in the opposite direction to the yoggies, I continued putting one foot in front of the other in the hope that my head and tummy would remain somewhat sturdy to allow me to make the most of the day. It felt good to move my body. It felt good to have some me-time. If felt good to have some personal space to gather my thoughts. It felt good to not be required to think at all.

No wonder my body had turned to mush, I thought to myself as I continued to walk and take in the glorious view. Since motherhood, I couldn't walk five metres without having to stop and look at that worm or crack in the brick, or some discovery one of my children had stumbled upon in a simple trip out to the supermarket or down the road for a latte. I hadn't exercised my body, well the exercise that didn't involve walking around with a couple of kids on each hip, in years. I needed this. I needed to move my body, walk my body, feel my body.

Later, as I rounded back up near the swimming pool, I heard my name being called. Looking up, I saw Sal leisurely laying on a Hampton's style deck chair painted in white and pale blue, hiding under a big floppy straw hat, skimpy red bikini, peaking out of her purple and pink kaftan. She flashed that gorgeous great smile of hers.

Standing over Sal now, shading her from the sun, she looked up. "I'm totally trashed," she moaned, sipping a concoction that consisted mostly of the colour green.

"Smoothie?" She offered.

Trying not to gag, I declined. "Think I'll start with something a little blacker...and stronger."

"Try it Ab," she urged, "You'll be surprised."

"No thank you. That looks way too healthy for how I'm feeling right now."

"That's the idea."

"I just need coffee Sal," I replied, claiming the deck chair next to Sal's, grateful to be horizontal.

A tanned male waiter all of about 30, wearing a white polo shirt and chocolate brown tailored shorts, arrived holding a tray in one hand. "Morning ladies. What can I get for you?" he said in a way that made me want those gorgeous strong hands to take hold of my body and massage deeply. What's wrong with me? Ever since I unclamped that ball and chain and left it to collect dust back home at my kitchen sink in Bondi, I grew hot and moist for any male in my line of sight.

"What I really want," I smiled, "Is coffee."

"But what she really needs," Sal interjected, is ..."

"You!" I blurted out in a decibel louder than the average. Oh. My. God. Did I really just say that out loud?

He smiled. My jaw dropped. Sal burst out laughing.

"Careful of this one honey," Sal said patting my hand and winking back at our sexy young waiter. "She's escaped from domestic chaos for the first time in five years and any sexy male with a nice clean shave has appeal."

Speechless. I wished she'd lift my jaw from the floor.

"She'll have black coffee cutie," Sal instructed. "And give her one of these green things while you're at it," she said, holding up her drink.

He tilted his head to Sal, smiled at me with a great deal of cheek and bravado, turned and left us with a nice royal view of his arse to longingly gaze at.

Horrified. Mortified. I covered my hands in my face. "Sal I'm a crazy lady," I revealed in muffled tones. "I've been set free for a weekend and suddenly I want to jump the bones of every hot-blooded male who dares to breathe in my direction. But they're all so young."

"Don't be so hard on yourself," Sal said, bending one knee, allowing her kaftan to fall open to reveal her long sexy legs. "You've been locked in confinement for five years so it's only natural that your tits are on high beam." She roared with laughter, drank more green juice and eased herself further down her lounge chair.

I covered my breasts with my hands, looking down at them in horror.

"It's a figure of speech," Sal muffled a laugh. Pulling her sunnies down to the tip of her nose and looking straight across at the glistening swimming pool, framed in large rectangle sandstone tiles, she giggled. "There's that gorgeous little hottie now. Better hold onto your tits Ab, those nipples of yours are peaking through your cami."

"Ladies," he said, creating a shade over me, standing close enough to touch. Finding the courage to look up, my tummy did a flip. Oh, sweet darling, you are gorgeous. I really would like you to put your hands where your eyes are right now., with your mouth soon to follow. Shaking my head in the hope he couldn't read minds, I smiled and sat up briskly to take the drink from his hands.

"Your coffee and smoothie. I also brought a jug of fresh water," he said setting it down on the small white wooden table that sat neatly between Sal and I. "You look like you ladies could use it," he added.

"Thank you. Great. Ok. Lovely. Ok." Oh, shut up Abby.

"We'll come and find you later cutie," Sal winked, rubbing her hand gently up and down her toned, tanned thigh. "See what else we can get you to attend to."

My eyes boggled. The hottie smiled and bowed slightly as he exited.

"How embarrassing."

"I'm sure you made his day Ab. Now get over it and pop your cossie on and get back out here. The day is gorgeous."

I looked out at the crystal blue water in the oversized resort pool framed with mini waterfalls and enough space to float and swim the day away. Yep, I really needed to get some of that ice-cold water all over my body and turn off some of this heat burning from inside me.

Back in our suite, I tossed the contents of my bag in search of my cossie. Why I had listened to Sal when she insisted I only bring a string bikini is beyond me. My breasts were flying all over the place. I looked down at my bulging mummy tummy, then tilted my head over my shoulder in the hope that my oversized rear end I had acquired during motherhood had somehow miraculously dissipated overnight. Damn. Still there. Every inch of cellulite I had gained since having three kids. Awesome!

I reached for one of Sal's kaftans, the emerald green one with weaves of turquoise running through it, and ditched my runners for my flip-flops. I slipped the tortoise shell sunnies that sat on the side table next to my bed on top of my head and drifted back out to the awakening sun. Oh... did someone turn up the brightness? With my sunnies now firmly over my eyes, I exhaled and headed back over to Sal.

"Get some of this green stuff into you honey. Don't know what's in it but it's starting to work magic on my insides."

Later, after a long and refreshing swim and a little sun to thaw me out, Sal declared it was time for us to claim the remainder of the day. She had highlighted the things she wanted us to do. Facial. Followed by a workshop. Workshop? A Life Workshop, whatever that meant.

"Ah Sal...I'm not sure the workshop is for me. I think I just want to go under the radar today."

"You're not getting off that easy. We came to detox. Flush out all things toxic. You need it Ab."

"But ..."

"Look...I know once you get back on home turf, you'll have every excuse under the sun, to not get out again any time soon...especially to a workshop."

"But I'm hung over."

"Exactly the reason why I didn't suggest hiking."

"Ohhhh."

"Facial first," she gave me a comforting smile. "Then I'll meet you back at the pool for lunch. They serve an organic vegan buffet that apparently spreads from one length of the pool to the other. So, I'd say that means they know how to get creative with a vegetable," she chuckled.

Knowing that I wasn't going to win this battle, I shuffled off for my scheduled facial. I'd chosen the Pamper Me option that included a pedicure, manicure, eyebrow shape and eyelash tint. Sal really was incredibly generous, forking out the funds for this decadent weekend. I felt inclined to pay my share and told her so over 100 times last night but she wouldn't budge. Said, "It was good for her soul as much as mine."

I thought of Ed for a minute and wondered how I'd get him to wrap his head around me spending wads of cash on pampering me from head to toe for two days straight. Money had become one of our biggest feuds since he worked full time, and I'd let my sources of income go after Emily came along. I always felt like he had the upper hand. Always felt I needed his permission to buy this, spend money on that. Syphoning away a few dollars here and there to get the re-growth done on my tint, to cover the grey, a little more frequently than he realised.

I never could understand how he could justify his kayaking boys' weekends away and copious nights out without a bat of an eyelid, but should I want a little frivolous beauty treatment or pampering, he could always find a supermarket special that did the job just as well.

Maybe it was time I went back to work. Put the kids in day care and reclaimed my financial independence. But the thought of that depressed me...and exhausted me.

I'd changed since having kids and I was done denying it. I wanted different things now. The conversations I wanted with other women were different to the office banter I had pre kids. But despite wanting independence, I knew I didn't really want my kids in day care, day after day, then nannies taking care of them after dark, just so I could spend long days at work paying for some other woman who wasn't me to look after my kids.

I wanted something more wholesome, grounded, fulfilling and meaningful. But every time I talked to Ed about us making a change as a family, trying something new, an escape to the country, or at least a less expensive address than Bondi to call home, he wasn't interested. Ed still had his perfect little world he lived in and didn't want to make a single change that meant growing up and taking responsibility for raising a family. But I knew I had to make changes, I had to do something, because I really was going to have that breakdown I kept threatening to have, if I didn't do something...and soon.

This weekend had oddly put things into perspective and I'd only been away twenty four hours. Or maybe it started a long time ago, when I wanted different things from life. But having space, time to reflect for just a few hours, gather my thoughts, it's like it hit me all at once. I'd been living in a fog, too afraid to step out of it, or clear out of it, for fear that the dark cloud hanging over me might be more a part of me than I cared to admit. Wow. Not even at that Life Workshop yet and I'm already contemplating life changes I want to make.

"Oh, there you are." A tall woman with strawberry

blonde hair, tied neatly in a low ponytail, grinned at me, her unblemished porcelain skin radiating. I did a double take. She was a dead ringer for Nicole Kidman, only a little more bleached on the blonde.

"Mrs Montgomery, we've been looking for you," she clucked, and ushered me away from the reception desk and toward a room at the end of the corridor. "Your Facial Suite is ready." Facial Suite? She held out her hand for me to make my grand entrance. With eager eyes, I stepped inside.

Facial Suite was an understatement. Stunning. Absolutely spectacular. This Guru Retreat would definitely end up with a 10 out of 10 rating on my evaluation form at the end of our stay.

My senses tingled the further I stepped into the room. Soft, magical ballad style music played on low. The lights were dim and candles paved the way toward my Facial Suite bed. The faint smell of honey filled the room. My heart opened and an outpouring of love and gratitude seeped from me and enveloped the furnishings, floating in the direction of my Nicole Kidman look-a-like, who was about to give me three hours of undeniable bliss.

I was led to a steam room and shower to cleanse my entire body and wash the residue away. Later, I stepped into a plush chocolate brown robe and floated toward my facial bed. I hardly remember lying down. Vaguely heard the words cucumber, oatmeal, milk, and honey, and who knows what other food type that was about to be slapped onto my face, yet missing my mouth entirely.

Layer after layer she enveloped me in another food

item, only to wash it all off over and over again. I wouldn't need to wash my face for a month after all this scrubbing and cleansing and de-cluttering of the pores. And then she just left me "to be", she said. I didn't feel alone though. I felt completely nurtured, look after, and dare I say...loved.

I felt an overwhelming sense of missing my mother all of a sudden. All this nurturing went straight through my heart. I was determined not to cry, especially after all the work this wonderful woman had done with those cucumber shavings around my eyes, I didn't want to walk out of the space all red and puffy.

Stepping back into the room, she whispered for me to "breathe."

I flinched. How did she know?

"Breathe a little deeper each time. Relax and let yourself drift with the music."

The mud mask ritual began. Great, now she was using the soil that the vegetables had grown in, only to pamper my face all over again. Not sure why she just spent all that time cleaning it, only to go and get it dirty all over again.

"Keep breathing Abigail, "she urged, lightly stroking my skin. "Nice and slow, nice and gentle. Take your time to feel the layers peel away with each new breath you choose to take in and let go."

I lost track of time. The music played. The dirt, which had now become cold hard mud, cracked. My body was rock solid and at one with this facial bed. I am a pig in mud and loving every minute of it. Hot towels were placed over my face, one after the other, cracking the mud like it was chiselled from stone. Hot face washers were placed on my skin, only to be replaced with another hot face washer all over again.

And so, the cleansing, toning and moisturising ritual began once more. It's like she was making up for five years of motherhood where I hadn't the time, or inclination, to dedicate myself to a three-step ritual of preparing my face for the day ahead or sleep each night.

Next, I was to just lie there. Lie there...do nothing? Another 20 minutes of breathing and listening to music with a soothing eye mask smelling of fresh apples and mint covering my eyes.

Sometime later, my Nicole Kidman look-a-like woke me from my silent splendour. If I could orgasm while having a facial I would. Maybe I just did, because that felt pretty damn fine compared to anything I'd experienced lately and all she did was clean my face!

Nic and I would become firm friends, I daydreamed. I'd have to come back and visit her again and again. Nic...well let's just call her that for now shall we, led me to a head basin with a full reclining chair. She washed and massaged my head like it was as plain and everyday to touch someone's hair the way she was touching mine right now. She stroked and gently tugged at sections of my hair as she cleansed and massaged the base of my skull, like she had all the time in the world. Well I suppose she did, considering I was paying...well technically Sal was.

Oh Sal, you are going to get a really good birthday

present this year. You have fulfilled your best friend's birthday quota for an entire lifetime. I felt like a brand-new woman, and all Nic did was wash my face and hair. Oh I do love you Sal...you too Nic! How did you know I truly needed this?

Finally, Nic's twin moved me to another reclining lounge, where she dipped my feet in a foot spa. I can see why they call this a suite. So many pockets of pleasure to hang out in and be pampered. She then moved to my arms and fingers, massaging, touching, stroking. I truly didn't think I could take anymore. This woman had honestly mastered the art of touch. And for the final pièce de résistance, she painted my toenails and fingernails in soft shades of pink that I can't even remember choosing. It was so long ago Nic and I stepped into this suite and got...so...well...intimate. Oh Nic, you had me at hello.

I was to recline once more, listening to my melody meditation music. Soft chimes and sounds of sweet angels and something or other playing in the background, like I was the only person the music was singing to in the world.

"Mrs Montgomery. Hello. It's Jade," a distant voice echoed. "You can wake up now. Mrs Montgomery it's Jade.

Huh?

Gently I felt someone touch my arm.

Who's Jade and where's Nic gone? I thought, rubbing my eyes.

I looked up to see Nic. Huh? Did she say her name was Jade? I don't seem to recall her saying that. Oh well...she'll always be Nic to me.

"You're all done. She smiled with a deep knowingness for what she had achieved for me both outside and in.

I looked up, all day dreamy, with an orgasmic smile. You can have my number anytime honey, I thought to myself, as she led me out to the juice bar and a shaded recliner next to the inviting crystal blue resort pool. What am I saying? I'm married with three children and I'm about to run off with my beauty therapist. Abigail Montgomery, you have truly lost the plot.

"Excuse me Mrs Montgomery," I heard a deep male voice call out.

"Huh?" I said looking up in a daze.

"I have a Zest Juice Cleanser. Jade ordered it for you... to have after your facial."

I'll bet she did, I thought to myself. Nic or Jade as she likes to call herself, knows just what this mumma needs. Oh God, what am I saying. Am I really a lesbian being masked in a frumpy wife and mother of three's disguise?

But as I looked up at the taught and tanned, buffed hunk of a waiter staring at me with those gorgeous green eyes, I knew without a doubt that I was not swinging in the direction of the same sex. Nope. Not gay at all. Open perhaps...to being turned on by anyone with a smile and tantalising touch. Yep Abby. You have well and truly lost the plot.

"Shall I set it down here?" he asked.

Oh dear, he actually wants me to speak. Finding words somewhere within, I managed a feeble response. "Ahhh...sure...yeah, thanks." But if you wanted to lay down next me so I could gaze at those gorgeous green eyes and hot buffed muscles peaking from your arms through your tight little t-shirt that would be wonderful,.

He smiled, like he knew exactly what I was thinking. I'm sure he'd heard and seen it all before. What's going on? I'm falling for anyone willing to give me the teeniest scrap of attention. A soft touch, a warm smile.

I felt a sting, a piercing pain directly through my heart. How long had it been since Ed touched me this way...right through to my core? I'm not even sure he had ever touched me the way people were touching me in body, heart and soul here in Byron Bay.

Tears welled fully in my eyes. Wet, sad, incredibly broken tears about to overflow as I sipped juice. Please don't let me ruin my facial.

I had been on an orgasmic roller coaster over the last twenty four hours, and it felt so damn good. Not sure I could take any more of all this pleasuring from the inside out. Ed, you are truly going to need to get your shit together if you ever hope to reach the standard these strangers have set this weekend in turning me on. Or at the very least, start learning to serve me Green Juice Cocktails and braiding my hair!

"Oh, there you are." I heard a familiar voice say. I looked up to find Sal looking like she'd had the orgasmic once over too. She laid down on the sun lounge next to me and purred. "Was that good for you too baby," she said bursting out laughing.

"Oh Sal, you have no idea."

"Oh...but Abby...I do...truly I do."

"How many times have you been to this place? It's mind blowing."

"First time for everything."

"Are you serious?"

"I was saving it for someone special," she said with a sentimental resonance in her voice.

"This weekend means more to me than you'll ever know Sal," I said squeezing her hand.

"And to me," she whispered.

We lay silently for a while like the two old friends we were. Comfortable enough to stay in our silent splendour.

After a while my tummy really started to say hello, like it was beating on the door of an unanswered cry. "Hello, anyone in there? I'm starving...can you hear me?"

"Let's get some lunch," Sal said sitting up. How did she always read my mind?

We walked over to the buffet and wow! Now that is something I had never seen before. A colour coded food bar. The Go Green section had a vast array of food, everything from mint to tabouli, to every type of leafy green vegetable imaginable, to 57 ways to serve kale.

Next was the Purple Pleasure bar consisting of beetroots in every shape, form and size, from raw to baked, to pickled to grated, to peeled in curly slices, to mashed in some kind of dip.

The Ravishing Red bar with tomatoes in every form and other reddish vegan items including quinoa, which I never do seem to pronounce correctly.

Every shade of the rainbow was on display at this delicious food bar. How was a girl to choose? Oh well I guess there's only one way to begin, and that was to pile on a bit of whatever took my fancy and toss it onto the oversized Philippe Starck white salad bowls they handed out. I felt turned on all over again, and all it took was a colourful array of tantalising vegetables.

Sal and I sat quietly munching with sideline chatter from time to time, while we watched some hot, and some not so hot, bodies; frolic about in the pool.

CHAPTER 8

We had our workshop to go to, and something in the pit of my belly said, dread. I didn't want to go, but Sal had insisted. And, as she was paying for this mind altering, body blissful, orgasmic weekend, I felt obliged.

As we re-entered the foyer, showered and changed after spending lunch poolside, we made our way down a long quiet corridor to the Life Workshop. When I stepped into the space, it seemed to have the feel of a church. There were tea light candles trailing all around the room and an arrangement of triangular shaped cushions that sat on the floor forming a large circle.

The sensation of dread went straight to my gut again. We were really going to have to 'go there' weren't we? Purge our feelings. Tell our deepest darkest thoughts and secrets, to a group of strangers.

"I'm not sure about this Sal," I said, reaching for her hand and taking a definitive step backwards from the door.

"Welcome ladies," a woman's voice commanded, from out of nowhere, then from directly in front of us. Her streaks of grey hair spattered through jet black, rested in a short cropped no-nonsense hairstyle that fell just past her ears. She was wearing an unfussy outfit of relaxed beige pants and loosely-fitted cotton shirt in pale green. She was bejewelled with layers of wooden prayer beads around her neck. A beaded bracelet on each wrist and a simple gold band rested on the middle finger of her right hand.

Her pale grey eyes looked into mine, then to Sal's, before returning to hold my gaze. Silent in voice, loud in thoughts, I'm sure. "So, what crap do you two ladies need to purge?" I heard her inner dialogue saying. Yet outwardly she simply smiled and said, "welcome," gesturing her arm and body toward the centre of the space, inviting us to bravely take that first step.

"Take a seat ladies," she smiled, before stepping back to the doorway to welcome more newcomers, an equal amount of terror on their faces. It seemed odd that a retreat would spend a good dose of time, energy and effort to pamper and seduce you with the touch of an orgasmic massage and cathartic facial, only to rip you apart at the seams with an outpouring of your deepest, darkest secrets in a sacrificial Life Workshop.

One by one, women of varying sizes and shades of hair colour, some natural, some not, entered the room.

"Welcome everyone, we now have everyone here," our wise woman with grey highlights declared. "My name is Rachel and today my intention is to lead you on a very personal journey for the remainder of the afternoon. A cathartic liberation from your fears. An opportunity to offload the concerns that are weighing you down or holding you back from truly knowing and feeling that deep happiness and joy that exists within. This will indeed be unravelled over the next few hours.

I will lead you to a deep connection of the highest order and complete the workshop with a cleansing ritual and rebalancing of the chakras."

Shark-what?

"But for now, you need not think or worry about what's coming up next." Oh no, she's already in my head. "We will start with a ritual to let go of the preconceived thoughts we entered the space with," she said." Yep, you've nailed me lady. "By grounding ourselves in the garden. When we return, I will tell you a little about me and the process we will be covering for the remainder of the afternoon."

Motioning everyone toward the sliding doors to the garden outside, she asked us to remove our shoes and place them at the door. "Let's step outside ladies."

My feet squished in the lush soft green grass, caressing my toes as I moved.

Rachel led the way, gracefully floating past a vibrant array of lilies, gardenias, violets and sweet peas. "Walk around ladies. Take your time to connect with nature and feel the earth between your toes. Whatever thoughts you came into the space with, let them go for now. Whatever ideas you may or may not have had about what might go on during this workshop today, it's time to let it go. Just take this moment, this time out of whatever is going on in your lives right now, to be present in this space. To fully hear my voice, hear the wind, smell the flowers surrounding you and feel the glorious grass beneath your feet. You are at one with nature and all its magnificence. This is your time to choose to let everything else go and just be here in body, mind, heart and soul."

I developed a slower and melodic rhythm to my breathing, listening to Rachel speak. My footsteps matched my breath. She had this soothing, yet commanding way, that told me everything was going to be ok and that the time was now to give myself the attention I'd been needing to give myself for so long.

Holding her arms out wide and smiling up toward the sun with a love that crept all over her face, she invited us to join hands in a circle, to stand and face each other and be at one in the space. She encouraged us to look at the person opposite in the circle and simply smile. To feel their warmth radiating from their heart and allow it to connect with our own. She encouraged us to return their smile, with the warmth and love from our own heart.

She invited us now to close our eyes as our hands remaining joined. "Feel the strength," she insisted, "of the earth under your feet from the Mother that commands this earth. Allow this glorious nature-filled land to support you and all the women in this circle. Feel the love," Rachel urged, her voice growing into a more powerful and forceful rhythm. "Feel the strength. Feel the energy. Feel the truth of the space we stand in. Feel the love within."

My hands clutched tighter at the two strangers on either side of me, eyes closed, energetically urging my heart to open a little wider. Rachel reminded us that Mother Nature and her glorious divine spirit was always here to nurture us. She reminded us to stop and allow that connection to touch our heart, body and soul.

Later, when we stepped back inside and took our seats on the floor, fully supported by our triangle cushions, I noticed a twinge in my belly, a rumbling of emotions after what had just passed outside, and what was about to unfold inside.

Except for Sal, I didn't know any of the women in the room, but that ritual outside had somehow connected us all. Equal to one another now, no matter what our personal situations here in this room or back home. Here we could all be recognised as women, the person we were, not the job we had, the marital status we held, the clothes we wore, or the money we made. Not the homes we lived in, or the children we did or did not have. Rachel had somehow brought us together by inviting us to connect to Mother Nature and connect to our own feminine nature within.

Rachel re-welcomed us to the space, informing us we would start by introducing ourselves and stating why we had come and we were there.

My eyes flared wide-open, fear dominating my emotions. Did I really have to reveal my life was a mess... that I was a total failure as both a wife and mother? That I couldn't seem to get a handle on my three kids or entice my husband to love me, even just a little bit, to come home and eat dinner early a few nights a week. To perhaps sit by the fire with a glass of wine in our hands and only have eyes for each other.

"I'm Rachel," our wise leader began. "I am a trained nurse who spent several years living with nuns while training as a nurse and a healer. For the past 25 years, I have been dedicated in service to bring peace, enlightenment and empowerment workshops to women all around the world. I teach the principles of nature's way and health care and maternal nurturing and nursing, along with my training in understanding the human psyche and foundations for our behaviour. I have dedicated my life's work to creating space for women to be empowered and make informed choices about how to live a positive, nurturing, healthy, happy and fulfilling life. I have a strong faith and devotion to the divine, and I bring this belief and philosophy to all my workshops, to give women a profound experience of their own enlightenment deep within."

Please don't make me go first with the introductions. I can't compete with street cred like that.

"This is not a competition by the way ladies, to state one's position over another." Oh great, she's a mind reader as well. Right then, one must not think random sexual thoughts about the hot waiter who served me Green Juice by the pool this morning or the gorgeous German on the dance floor last night.

"Why don't you start dear," Rachel said, calm grey eyes looking directly into my mint green eyes, now a deep shade of fear.

"Me?" I said pointing to myself, eyes boggling out of my head.

"Everyone is having a turn dear. Sometimes it's better to get it out of the way," she said, an encouraging smile forming on her lips.

Oh no...my head was taking me back to that scene at

the bar last night with the hot German tourist...I don't want to reveal my woman-on-heat moments that have been on overdrive ever since I arrived at this retreat. Keep it light Ab. Keep it light.

"Let's begin dear, she said more directly now. "Just your name and why you are here."

Shaking off my nerves and willing myself to get this over and done with asap, I hurried it all out.

"Hi everyone," I said darting my eyes around so quickly I felt I would pass out from the dizziness.

"My name is Abigail. I'm married with three kids and I'm here because my best friend Sal," I motioned in the direction of Sal, seated to my right, "Whisked me away for the weekend on a whim."

"A whim?" Rachel said, her eyebrows peaking in question. "Well done. And why are you here Abigail?"

I stared back, confusion washing over my face. "I just told you. Sal organised it all on a whim."

"Yes, you said that," Rachel replied. "But why this whim?"

"Oh," I said relieved and a little flippant. "She just thought I needed a break."

"A break from what?"

"From life," I replied.

"Your husband, your children? Is that what you mean," Rachel probed.

"Ah sorry," I shifted on the cushioned triangle on the floor, which was now proving to be very uncomfortable.

"I thought we were just introducing ourselves," I said, agitation rising in my throat.

"I'm just trying to get a little context," Rachel soothed, hands resting in her lap, body upright and still. "Abigail, it's safe dear," she urged. "None of us are here to judge. We are simply here to share, to heal. Is something happening at home you need a break from?"

"Just life," I said flatly with a tinge of anger creeping into my voice. "I'm married to a man that doesn't love me and have three children who aren't at school yet and I'm exhausted all the time. Is that enough of a picture?" I said spitting out the words and catching a glimpse of Sal's expression. Was that a look of disappointment?

"Thank you, Abigail, for painting a picture of why you are here. Let's continue clockwise," Rachel encouraged.

The next lady on the hot seat, well the hot triangular cushioned seat, was a rather large woman. Oh, come on...let's be honest...she was a size 20 going on 22 ... at least. The woman was obese!

The cropped red haired woman to my left told us her name was Tina. Told us she was here because... you guessed it...she couldn't get a handle on her food issues. She tries to diet but it just makes her eat more and whenever she tries to exercise she gets an injury and spends weeks recovering. She's single and Tina has now lost all her confidence and hates her job. Rachel, you have certainly got your work cut out for you today.

Next was Kat. She was sexually abused as a child. OMG! Did she just say that out loud? And she's having trouble having an intimate relationship with a man. No shit Sherlock! She insists she prefers men, likes men. But when it comes to getting physical, sexually intimate with someone, she switches off. She has sex but she doesn't enjoy it. Can't enjoy it. Seriously, this could take well over a week to solve all these problems Rachel.

But she didn't flinch. Rachel kept working her way around the room, giving her full and undivided attention to each woman, encouraging them to share their story of why they had come to the workshop.

Later it was Penelope who sat on the other side of Sal. Penelope was overworked. I know what you mean sister! She's caught up in the rat race of working crazy hours for crazy pay and living a crazy life. She took cocaine for a while there to help get her through, but apparently the come down took more effort to get through than sustaining the everyday, stone cold sober.

"Why don't you just leave your job, try something new?" Rachel asked. My thoughts exactly! Hey I'm better at this helping people stuff than I thought.

"I can't," Penelope began to cry.

"Why?" Rachel asked. Yeah, why? I said leaning in and wondering the answer for myself. Thank God, my time to be probed was done.

"I'm in debt," Penelope said bursting into tears.

"Debt?" Rachel questioned.

"I've got a car, an apartment in Kirribilli overlooking Sydney Harbour. Maxed out credit cards. I don't know how to catch up with my bills. I feel like I'm working for the life I'm trying to keep up with. It's all so out of control," she shifted and sobbed. "It's exhausting," she said, finally completing her download.

As Rachel coached Penelope a few minutes more to return to semi-normal, my mind drifted back to Brenda, the woman who spoke right before Penelope.

Brenda thinks her husband is having an affair. Says she still loves him and wants to turn a blind eye to keep him. But it's eating away at her now, and she just can't seem to do anything about it. It's like it's trapped her. Paralysed her. I sat silently in my thoughts. I didn't lean forward when Brenda spoke. Didn't want to know more. It just got me thinking more about my own life and what was really going on below the surface in my own marriage.

When Penelope had finally pulled herself together it was Sal's turn. Knowing that I knew all of Sal's shit, I could finally exhale and sit back a while on these comfortable, yet not so relaxing cushions. It's like I'd been holding my breath while listening to each woman speak. Sharing themselves, sharing their pain and everything that prevented them from being happy. But with Sal, there was nothing we didn't share, so I was grateful for the next five minutes or so, that I could sit back and relax.

"Hi, I'm Sally. But everyone calls me Sal," she beamed. "I don't have kids. Tried to but that didn't work," she shrugged.

My heart panged thinking about Sal and her miscarriages. The first one was at the eight-week mark but the second had reached all the way to seventeen weeks. The baby was almost halfway there. We thought she had the all clear by twelve weeks, even threw her a party at sixteen weeks. Hell...we had already painted and decorated the nursery by then. It cut like a knife through her heart when she lost the baby the following week. Then Jeremy, he left her not long after. Said it was all too much for him to deal with. Too much for him to deal with! Lousy bastard. He didn't carry those two babies in his womb. He didn't get his insides probed, prodded and scraped, investigating without success, why both babies had died inside Sal. "It was just one of those things," the doctor had said, as if it happens to every second woman that walks along the street. Well maybe it does, but it doesn't make it routine when you're the one going through it.

The next marriage to Ben lasted less than a year. Ten months in fact. She never should have gone there in the first place, but I guess she was trying to find a way to move on. I looked around the room as Sal shared tiny pieces of herself, of her heart, past pains and why she was here at this workshop. All these women from different places, all here for one reason...all because we were not happy.

Not satisfied with our lives and certainly not with ourselves, or the people in it. I didn't even know these women, but after hearing their stories I felt like I would walk over hot coals for them if that's all it would take to make them happy again.

As Sal continued her introduction, my mind drifted beyond the room, extending to women all around the world. How many women are unhappy? I wondered.

How many women are living a superficial day-to-day existence on the outside, but inside fighting an eternal battle of pain? Far out, I'm already exhausted and all we've done is say no more than hello and why we are here.

Rachel thanked Sal for sharing and was just about to take us to the next stage of the workshop, when Sal interrupted. "I'm sorry...sorry Rachel...ah...actually there is one last thing. One last thing I wanted to share." Sal glanced at me briefly and returned to focus on Rachel. What was that look in Sal's eyes? "A reason I'm here," she continued.

"Go on dear," Rachel encouraged.

"Um well," Sal grew fidgety in her triangular cushioned seat and took another sweeping glance at me and then back toward the group. And then it came out.

A bombshell that left my knees weak and stomach nauseous. Saliva surfaced in my mouth, slowly, as if it had seeped all the way from my feet through my murky body. I was speechless. There was nothing I wanted to lean forward to hear anymore. Why didn't you tell me? Why didn't I know? I have been bitching and moaning about my life for weeks, months. Oh, let's be real...years! You never said a word. And all this had been going on for the past four and a half months!

"I've got cancer. Breast cancer actually," Sal revealed. Am I really hearing what I'm hearing?

My eyes darted immediately to Sal's oversized breasts. Why do people do that? Why do we look at someone's breasts the second they say they have breast cancer?

"I'm due to have a double mastectomy, but they have to wait and see if it's too far gone." What the hell am I hearing? This isn't happening.

Tears sprung to my eyes. I held my fingertips to my mouth in the hope I didn't explode with the deep gut-wrenching emotion that was stirring in my soul.

Breaking the rule of speaking when someone else was speaking, I turned to Sal and pleaded, tears threatening to outpour. "Why didn't you tell me?"

"Ab," she shrugged, and then smiled. "You've got your own shit to deal with."

"But I could have helped."

"How?" she said sarcastically. "You said it yourself. You're struggling to get through each day with those kids."

"That's not fair," I almost screamed back. "You should have told me," I trembled.

"I'll be fine," she said reaching to squeeze my hand.

Why was she trying to make me feel better when it should be the other way around?

"Sal, I'm so sorry."

"Why? It's not your fault. Just one of those things."

Everything went blurry. My eyes swimming with tears, heart roaring with pain. Everything I had been going through meant nothing, now that I knew my best friend of 21 years could die before the year was out.

I began to cry uncontrollably. Tribal, guttural tears. Sorrow from a very deep place within wrenching out of me. Reaching out to squeeze Sal's hand, I wailed. "I don't want you to die. I can't lose you too."

"Who else did you lose?" Rachel probed.

I looked over to Rachel, and then took a sweeping glance to the other women, delirious through the haze of tears. I can't talk about this.

"Abigail. What happened?"

Silence.

"Abigail. Please tell us what happened?" Rachel urged.

Finally, I let it out. Over 20 years of grief poured out. "My mum," I sobbed.

"What happened to your mum," Rachel gently pushed.

I can't talk about this. Can't cope. This is a lot to take in. My head started spinning. All this talking...purging... it's getting too much.

"I...can't...breathe." Stumbling from the floor to my knees, I cried out, "I...I need some air."

"Stay with the process," Rachel urged firmly.

Are you kidding? "I'm sorry. I can't. This is too hard." I struggled to my feet.

"Abigail, please sit down. Don't leave the group," Rachel pushed on resolutely, yet somehow nurturing, urging me to stay.

I turned back around to Sal who reached out her hand. "Sit down Ab." Oh God, I'm so weak. Such a terrible friend.

"You can do this," Rachel encouraged. "Just a little

longer and then we will all take a break."

Looking back at Sal, then Rachel, then to all the faces in the group, waiting patiently for me to get myself together, I caved. I managed to somehow join the group again and sit back down on the uncomfortable cushion.

"Abigail, I'd like to hear what happened to your mum," Rachel wondered. Looking around at all the women in the group and then slowly back at me. "This is a safe space."

"I really don't think I can."

"Please try."

As Sal squeezed my hand, somewhere deep within, I found the strength to speak. "She died of breast cancer," I eventually blurted out. "She was only 41. A year younger than Sal and I are now. The doctors say they tried everything but they couldn't have...not really... because she died. Didn't last the year after we found out. And Dad didn't skip a beat. He had already moved on to wife number two by then. Well...an affair with his second wife before they were legally hitched at the hip."

The feeling had gone out of my legs. I wasn't sure whether it was the cramping on this damn floor cushion, or the familiar numbness that took over my body whenever I had to share something about my mum dying.

"Do you feel abandoned?" Rachel asked.

The word stung my eyes. "What? Abandoned...by who?"

"By your mother?" she suggested, voice unwavering.

"My mother?" I shrieked. I wanted to reach across

the room and hit Rachel now. Shake her and ask her how the hell could she say such things. "Why would I feel abandoned by my mother? I loved my mum. She was amazing. Incredible. Beautiful. Generous. My mum was the loveliest, kindest woman," I rambled.

"Yes, but she died. And...she left you with a father who abandoned you long before she did...having affairs, as you described earlier. Choosing the love of women outside the family, instead of the love of the two women who waited patiently, lovingly at home to have their love returned."

"What are you getting at?" I questioned in anger. Rage had found itself ferociously swirling around in my belly up toward my throat. I began directing it at Rachel. "My mother loved me. She would never leave me. Never on purpose."

"Of course she wouldn't," Rachel soothed. "That's not what I'm suggesting. Let's leave this for now dear."

Rachel smiled at Sal. "Thank you for sharing Sal." Looking at me now and then at everyone else in the group, a serene smile washed over Rachel's mouth. "Thank you all for sharing so much of yourselves in a space where we are still but strangers."

Rachel addressed the group now as if delivering a sermon. We held her gaze and let the words sink in one syllable at a time. "You can see from listening to everyone today, we are not really strangers. All of us fighting some private battle. Some deep hurt going on inside that many on the outside world have literally no knowledge about."

Motioning to stand now, Rachel announced it was time to take a break. "There's tea and fruit set up in the adjoining room," she said pointing to a pretty little table displaying a fresh platter of berries, banana, apples, oranges, grapes, figs and nuts. A vase of poppies on display in the centre. Hot water in an urn with a range of herbal teas from green, to lemon zest, to quietly chamomile, to fresh ginger.

We were able to have free time in the private garden that joined the workshop room or stay in the space. She reminded us before we took a break, that we still had much to do for the remaining hours of the day.

Oh great. Can't wait for what's coming up next. In under two hours I had discovered that my best friend was dying of cancer, my mother had abandoned me, but not before my father did, and...my life was as crappy as most of the other women at this retreat.

Walking out to Sal in the garden sipping tea by the rose bush, sprayed with deep red and soft pink, I reached for her arm and looked thoughtfully into her eyes, sorrow filling my own. "Why didn't you tell me?"

Exhaling, Sal answered. "Oh, I don't know. I was trying to see if I could just deal with it under the radar and it would all go away. I didn't mean to hide it from you. I really didn't. It's just that once I got over the shock and then summoned the courage to tell you, I didn't have the nerve, knowing how much your mum's death affected you. And well...let's face it, you're not happy. You're not coping. You're miserable. I just didn't want to add to your misery."

I reached out and hugged Sal tight, spilling her tea in the process. "Oh...sorry...but not just for the tea. I am so sorry for so many things. But mostly I'm sorry for not being there for you. Oh Sal...I love you. I'm sorry I've been such a miserable crap friend." I stepped back and held Sal's shoulders firmly before looking her dead square in the eyes. "I promise to get my shit together."

After another couple of hours, and an intense amount of sharing of thoughts, feelings, fears and worries, Rachel had somehow managed to bring us all full circle. The woman was in her element. By the end of the workshop something had shifted in me, and I'm sure in the many women in the room. I had a new perspective on things. A new perspective on life.

I realised I wasn't the only woman in the world with problems. I realised I wasn't the only one who had troubles in her marriage. I realised that for many what was often going on at the surface had nothing to do with what was going on underneath. But what I realised most of all was that my treasured friend was facing imminent death and I should start appreciating life a lot more. A whole lot more.

Rachel had been amazing. That woman truly had a gift for helping people find their way. "Just make small changes," she encouraged as she said her final farewell. Wrapping me up in her arms for a nurturing, motherly, loving hug. An embrace I had craved for so long with my own mum gone all these years.

Although there were just over twenty of us in that space, she had managed to make every woman feel valued and important. She gave us all hope for a better future.

"You can't just survive life anymore Abigail," she spoke to my soul. "You need to go home to that family of yours and claim back what's rightfully yours. Love them with all you have, and open up to the love you deserve to receive from them too."

She had made each of us write a list of priorities, a What Matters Most list, then write action steps we needed to take to make improvements. She was so right about the overwhelm, that sometimes in life, when we have way too much going on, we get beyond overloaded. So clouded by the chaos of our lives, clouded by the dread of all our responsibilities, that we end up not dealing very well or at all.

"But how can something so simple feel so difficult to achieve?" I had asked Rachel, when it came to getting started with the list.

"I think one of our greatest fears is not the changing but the energy it might require to do the changing," she wisely replied. "The effort. The crucial conversations. The standing up for yourself and saying when something is not ok, or how you no longer want to be treated. She assured us that once we found our stride, found our feet, and our confidence, it was like learning to ride a horse.

"When you first learn to ride, it's uncomfortable, it's restrictive," she said. "It hurts, and the next day the pain can be even greater than the actual riding of the horse the day before. But after getting back on that horse, getting more confident in being up in that saddle, you really find your stride," she had smiled. "That exhilaration of moving from a trot to a canter to a full blown out trail blaze. Now that is exhilarating, like you're flying, as if you didn't have a care in the world. That pure feeling of being free. That is what life is meant to be like," she had reminded us. "Go back home and go back into training ladies. Train for the ride of your life. Take small steps to grow your confidence. Then do what you need to do to find your bliss. Find your freedom."

Later back in our suite, I was the first to speak. "I don't think I've got the energy to party in town again tonight Sal."

"Thank God," she replied flopping down on her bed. "They have an open fire by the heated pool and spa where they also serve dinner."

"Sounds perfect," I said, falling face down on my bed and tucking the pillow under my arm for a comforting cuddle.

"When we go back home, let's make a pact," I suggested.

"Mmmmm," Sal murmured, her eyes closed as she lay flat on her back with her arm resting over her eyes.

"Make sure you let me know when you need my help," I urged. "Tell me if you need a friend to hold your hand in one of those gruesome doctor's appointments."

"What about the kids?"

"I'll sort that out. I'm going to make changes when I get back Sal. A lot of changes. Starting with the way I run my life." Lifting my head off the bed to catch Sal's eye I urged. "Just be honest with me. If you need me, let me know. Ok?"

Sal didn't respond.

"Please," I urged.

Lifting her hand from her head, opening her eyes then turning to smile, Sal said "Wow, that workshop sure did the trick."

"It did. More than you know. It seems I just needed a little time out from life, to realise the life I was missing out on."

CHAPTER 9

I could feel the dread in the pit of my gut as the taxi approached my house late Monday evening. Sal had offered to help me check back into reality, but I knew I had to do this alone. Knew I had to face Ed. Face the truth. Face the fact that I wasn't happy. Knew it was time to stop taking that out on Ed and start talking to him about it. It all sounded fine in my head but acting on the stuff that we wrote down on the Life List in Rachel's workshop was daunting to say the least.

When the taxi pulled away, I stood in the dark on the side of the road, staring motionless at my house; my two story, slate grey, rendered renovated home with all the trimmings, including five bedrooms, three bathrooms, and a state-of-the-art kitchen with all the latest SMEG appliances. But for all that flash on the outside, my marriage with Ed had lost all passion on the inside.

The dread swirled around in my tummy like dark clouds ready to explode. Ed hadn't communicated at all while I was away, and something told me it wasn't because he was having the time of his life, or wanting me to do the same. I let out a deep groan as I pushed open the front gate. This was it. This was the moment to have the courage to stay in my heart no matter what Ed dished up. This was the moment to tell Ed I needed help. We needed help. Tell him our relationship needed changes. So why did something as simple as admitting the truth feel so overwhelming, so incredibly scary?

It was eerily dark when I crept inside the front door. The hallway creaked a little as I took one feeble step in front of the other, on what felt like the longest walk of my life, down the hallway. I stood in silent darkness in my empty kitchen. Everything seemed in order but oddly out of kilter. I was hovering in limbo land. Halfway between my Guru Retreat escape and reality. I didn't want to fully step back into my reality for fear that all I had gained and gave myself over the last two days would suddenly disappear with the first sight of Ed or one of the kids. Did Ed even hear me come in? Did he even care?

Suddenly I heard a cry. A scream. My first instinct was to leap. Run to my screaming baby and make everything better. Instead, I stayed motionless in the kitchen. I took a deep full breath of air and filled it into my lungs, holding onto it for dear life.

"Don't jump every time your kids scream Abigail," Rachel had said in the workshop. "You've trained your family to think you will drop everything to be there for them in a heartbeat. Which is of course endearing, but you're not giving them any room to explore their own resilience or resourcefulness," she'd added. "You're not allowing any independence for yourself or for your children. You say Ed never helps but do you even pause for ten seconds to give him the space to react, to reach out and be there for his kids too?"

Her words had struck right through my heart as I stood

listening to my baby scream out my name. "You have been so busy controlling your very existence for fear that if it was out of control, the damage would be too great, too exhausting to deal with," Rachel had suggested.

She softened later when she had said, "I don't think you ever truly gave yourself time to grieve the loss of your mother. The impact her death had on you, a young woman in the making. It forced you to grow up so fast, without the guidance of your beloved mum and the absence of a much-needed connection with your father."

The screams grew louder and my impatient inner controller began taking over my ability to breathe and let go. 15, 20, 30 seconds had passed now. For God's sake Ed, would you just hurry up and deal with it!

"Shit." Ed shouted on the floor above me.

Standing rigid, I waited and listened, my heart in my throat. Ed clambered and banged down the hallway, injuring a body part on what sounded like a tricycle.

The cry grew louder as he opened the kids' bedroom door. Oh God. I can't hold on any longer. Hurry up Ed! He continued to curse as the cries grew to a wail, on a decibel that I'm sure the little old granny at the end of the street could surely hear by now. My palms grew sweaty, frustration increased, but I remained firmly rooted to the black and white large square tiles of our kitchen floor.

Finally! After perhaps a good 10 minutes or so, the silence arrived. I let out a deep exhale as if I had been holding my breath the entire time.

"Didn't think you had it in you," I could almost hear

Rachel mocking. Didn't think he had it in him more to the point, my inner critic began.

I remained rooted to the kitchen floor, cringing when I heard floorboards creak down the stairs and the child safety lock on the gate unclick. Footsteps grew closer as I held my breath. Ed was now standing in the shadows of the moonlight resting up against the kitchen sink. He helped himself to a glass of water, drained the glass and then turned around in my direction.

"Fuck!" he shrieked.

Our eyes stared back at each other like two possums in night fright.

"Fuck Abby, how long have you been there?"

"Not long," I whispered.

"What are you doing?" He said raising his voice yet flustered and banging his hand hard on the sink when he put down the glass. "Shit."

"Just taking a minute for myself."

Eyeballing me now with a look of distaste I had become all too familiar with, Ed spat out his words "What, you didn't get enough time to yourself this weekend?"

"That's not what I meant," I replied, trying not to take the bait.

Rachel had implored me not to take the bait. "No matter what," she had instructed. "Don't dish it up either."

In working through our issues in the Life Workshop late on Sunday afternoon, Rachel had told me that one of the first things I needed to remove in all my unhealthy relationships was the bait. "It's either you or the other party, but someone is always throwing it out there or taking it when it comes to conflict."

"What's wrong with you?" Ed said, his tone angry.

"Huh?" I mumbled, now brought back to the present from my drifting thoughts of all the life learning Rachel shared in the workshop. "What do you mean?"

"Have you gone crazy? Why are you standing here in the dark? Didn't you hear the baby?"

"Yes, but I knew you were here."

"I was asleep. And now I won't be able to get back to sleep for hours."

Oh...that bait...it's dangling under my nose like a great big slab of chocolate that I just have to have. Instead, I breathed and exhaled, taking a few seconds to regroup before responding as Rachel had also shown me.

"Look Abby, I hope you've gone and sorted out your shit because come tomorrow you're back on...back to the way things were. I'm not doing this domestic shit and working my arse off to pay the bills as well."

Oh no...the red flag with an almighty chunk of bait attached to it, was now waving under my nose. "Ed, I hardly think going back to the way things were is the best place for you or me."

"I'm too fucking tired to deal with any of this crap. You've had your weekend, now I need to get some sleep so that one of us in this family can earn a living to pay for the weekends away you're off having whenever you damn well feel like it."

Oh no...red rag to a bull...I can feel it coming and there is no stopping it. Well...I inhaled that bait like it was the last line of cocaine on the planet. "Damn you Ed," I spat back. "First, you didn't pay for my weekend singular not plural, Sal did. I did not spend a single cent of your money, which I always thought was our money. That was the first weekend singular, I have given myself off in five years since having our kids."

"Fuck this shit. I'm going to bed," Ed said, storming toward the stairs with literally no regard for a single word I had said.

Racing toward him, anger leading the charge, I grabbed his arm hard. "You always do this. You start it but you never finish it."

"Sounds like our sex life," Ed snarled, opening the child safety gate and firmly slamming it behind him.

Sorry Rachel, I found myself mouthing to the ceiling. The bitter bait had been well and truly injected into my veins and there wasn't a thing I could do to stop the flow. No counting to ten and breathing was going to stop me now.

I stormed up the stairs, following Ed into our bedroom, and refrained from slamming the door. I needed the kids asleep so I could get this out. Five years of pent up anger, possibly more. Somewhere in between the time of saying, "I do" to twelve years down the track, I had become my mother, only dressed up in a different guise. But now I had to let all that fear go of shutting up and putting up and let him have it.

The rage roared out of me, somewhere deep in the pit of my belly. Deep, dark rage. Anger at Ed. Anger at my father. Anger at myself for living this life I loathed for so long. It eventually ended with tears, the only way I knew how. Venomous words exhausting me to the core. I finally broke down and wept on the floor. Legs hugged tight to my chest with my back resting against the wall for some sort of meagre comfort.

Ed roared in response to my rage. "If you don't like this life, then get a new one. Stop fucking complaining all the time and work your shit out."

I sniffed hard, snot seeping from my nostrils. Tears unrestrained, streamed down my cheeks. Everything ached inside. My heart had completely broken in two.

Without another word, Ed stormed past me and closed the bedroom door with a heavy hand behind him. I huddled up tighter on the floor, too tired, too exhausted to crawl up into bed. I reached out to the corner of the pale blue and cream doona dangling from the bed, pulling it over me, eventually falling asleep on the floor in the foetal position.

CHAPTER 10

I woke dazed and disoriented to the sound of crying. Looking up from the bedroom floor toward the white wooden deck outside, sun crept through the closed shutters that were also painted in Antique White.

The pounding of my brain gained momentum. I wanted to move my toes, stretch out my legs, but pins and needles took hold of my limbs. Why did I ever think it was a good idea to sleep crouched up on the floor all night?

My head thudded. My mouth craved saliva. The cries grew louder. Scrambling to my feet, I managed to somehow put one tingly foot in front of the other. But my head...oh how it ached. I flung open the door to the crying, only to have it cranked up to what felt like a maxed-out volume of 10.

Wincing, I picked up little Harry as he clung to me with every fibre of his being. He wailed while my heart ached for this beautiful little boy in my arms.

Brady and Emily, who had been in a trance playing with Lego and Barbie dolls, tossed them aside to race over and grab hold off my legs. "Mummy," they shouted in unison. "Mummy. Mummy. Mummy."

I held all three of my children close to my breast now and felt the love pour all the way through me.

When we finally made our way downstairs to begin our morning routine, Ed had already left for work. No note. No text. No good morning. No goodbye.

As I'd slept in, the kids were now in high demand for food. Harry's nappy was in grave need of being changed and Brady and Emily were both in desperate demand for my attention. I need paracetamol and now!

Later, with breakfast devoured, dirty dishes neatly stacked in the dishwasher and all three kids and myself washed clean and ready for the day, I noticed we had just a couple of hours before returning to the next food and cleaning ritual, lunchtime. My head, thanks to paracetamol, had finally lost the fuzz.

I wanted to claim the time left. Grab a couple of hours in the fresh air while the window of time remained and before daytime sleeps dictated the day. First stop was the park that sat with Bondi Beach for its backdrop. Then it was back home for lunch, followed by an afternoon sleep, then Playschool, then afternoon tea, then the afternoon walk, then back home for dinner, then bath, then play, then story time, then bedtime, then cuddle time. And so, the repeat routine continued.

It was survival of the fittest for a mother to maintain routine. Without it...all roads did not lead to Rome. It led to tears, tantrums and the torturous cries and wails, the pleas for attention and pleas to fulfil every whim and needy request that only a child could demand from its mother.

Stop complaining Abby. Just find a way to enjoy your day. Enjoy your motherhood. This was a vow I had made myself. To Rachel. To Sal. And to all the women at the workshop.

"One chapter at a time," Rachel had insisted. "Take small steps to recovery. That road to fully enjoying your life and finding that balance between letting go and immersing yourself in your roles as wife, mother, friend and woman in her 40s."

When 9:00pm ticked over on the black and white provincial clock that took pride of place on the kitchen wall, my temper began to rise. Still no word from Ed. No text. No call. Nothing. Is he trying to punish me?

Later, when I sat on the sofa in the quiet of the night knowing my children slept soundly, yet unaware of my husband's whereabouts, I reflected on my feelings for Ed. I realised I was beyond anger. Beyond hurt. Beyond hope. I was literally in a place of nothingness. I had reached this place of feeling totally and utterly nothing for Ed. Nothing for our marriage. Nothing for myself.

I don't make 'me plans' anymore. It's as if I am in some sort of holding pattern. Hovering in limbo land. Waiting for the kids to arrive at some magical golden age when everything was going to be OK. Maybe it really was finally time to go back to work? But I couldn't go back to what I was doing. There was no way I could sustain that life of late nights and endless travel with three kids and a husband that doesn't even call at 9:42pm, I noted, picking up my phone.

Moving to the en suite, I brushed my teeth on autopilot to complete my evening ritual before getting into bed. I sat rigid, upright under the doona, attempting to read the local newspaper, while watching time tick over slowly on the alarm clock beside my bed.

Damn this. I picked up my phone and dialled my husband's number.

After several rings, Ed responded. "What?"

Don't bait, don't bait. I kept willing myself.

"It's late," I exhaled. "Where are you?"

"Why?" he spat back.

Don't bait, don't bait, I urged myself further. "Ed. When are you coming home?"

"Why?" he yelled back.

"Because you're my husband and I'd like to know," I said in a very even tone that even I did not recognise.

"I'm in a cab," he replied, tone clipped.

"On your way home?" I wondered, trying to remain calm while desperately trying not to take the bait.

"Yep," he replied.

"Ok. I'll see you when you get here," I said hanging up before my temper took hold of my voice box.

I didn't want to push it further and ask where the cab was. Where he was coming from. Wondering at that moment why I gave him the courtesy of every little detail of my life. Maybe I needed to be more like a man?

Looking back at the time again, it was now 10:37pm. I crawled further under the covers and let my head ease deep onto the pillow. My eyes fluttered closed, the newspaper dropped from my fingertips.

I never heard Ed come home. Never saw him leave the

next morning. The evidence on the kitchen bench told me he had stumbled in, eventually. Fantastic. Another day gone and no mention of the oversized elephant in the room. Surely Ed didn't want things to keep going like this?

But the days ticked by, those mind-numbing days where one blends into the next. The sleep-deprived mother, depleted of energy and lacking in intimacy from anyone above the age of five. Nothing changed. Everything stayed the same.

I'd been back from my retreat for a whole ten days and Ed had always managed to find himself in the company of others when I approached him to talk. He was doing everything to avoid it. Why wouldn't he talk?

I was done waiting. Done waiting for any opportunities to suddenly present themselves for us to work through the changes we so desperately needed to address in this marriage. I took out the Life List from my purse and stared hard at the first item. Have Truth Talk with Ed. Looking over at my kids still heavily immersed with their craft activity, I gripped my phone and psyched myself up and dialled Ed's number. It went straight to voicemail. Come on! Stay with it, I self-talked as I texted him. "Call me urgent." No salutation. No kiss. No smiley face.

Two minutes later, the phone rang and I jumped from the kitchen stool. So, he was able to talk when it counted?

I picked up the phone, fear kicked in. "Hi," I said softly.

"What's so urgent? I'm in a meeting."

Oh shit. "Ah...Ed...Will you be home for dinner?"

"Not sure. Is that what's so urgent?"

"Ah...no...it's not," I stammered.

"Well what is?" he snapped. "I'm working."

"Ed. You...me...we...we have to talk."

Fuming, he replied. "Can't this wait?"

"No it can't wait," I replied flatly. "I've been waiting for the past ten days and you've been doing everything to avoid talking about what's really going on."

"And what's really going on?" He flared up.

"Come home sober," I said with finality in my voice, before ending the call.

Every minute felt like an hour as the slow grind of the day dragged on. Ed finally made it home as I was putting the kids to bed. Once they were down for the night he just glared at me.

"Abby, don't ever text me at work again and tell me to call if it's not urgent."

"But it was urgent," I said my voice even. "It is urgent."

"What's so urgent...us talking?" he laughed without any humour in his voice.

"Yes. It's us Ed. And this marriage. This ridiculous facade of a marriage that is on a downhill spiral to nowhere."

"Oh, here we go again," he flared up.

"Ed, you may be able to avoid this conversation for the next ten years but I can't. Taking that time for myself recently showed me that this us, this you and me, we are not ok. Far from it."

"No shit Sherlock," he spat back.

"Well how come you don't want to talk about it?" I questioned, deeply confused.

"What's there to talk about? You became a mother then you changed. You bitch and moan about everything. You're not grateful for the hard work I put in. You're always too tired for sex. By the time I get home of a night, I get the remnants of all the drama that went down in your day. All the dialogue of what's so miserable about your life. You never want to hear about my day. My kayaking trips, my success with my clients, because you're too busy bitching and moaning about your lack of independence."

I was speechless. I sat there on the stool at the kitchen bench, mouth agape, wide eyed with wonder at how his point of view was so very directly opposite from my own.

I listened to him rant. I tuned in. I tuned out. It all became a blur after a while. None of it was good, from what I could decipher. Listening to him now, it all seemed beyond repair. A marriage so deeply unravelled at the seams, barely hanging on to the fraying edges of fragility. He ranted and raged some more. He was on a roll. Nothing I could say or do would change his point of view. I could see that now. Finally!

"Ed, we need help," I blurted out, when I found a small window in his rant. I grabbed hold of my courage and kept going. "Ed, we need to see someone. Couples counselling," I confirmed.

"Couples counselling?" he laughed, yet my instincts told me there was nothing he found remotely funny about this reality.

"Yes. Couples counselling. Whether we stay together or not, we need help. Because standing here, listening to everything you've said, I've realised, really realised," a lump forming in my throat, "that you and I agree on very little. You have your view and I have mine. I can't see how any of this is going to get better if we don't go and see someone."

"What's the point?" he said, with what sounded like sadness now threatening his throat.

It tugged at my heart. Emotion made its way to my eyes. Please don't cry.

Devoid of emotion, he spoke. "It's done. "We're done."

I pressed my fingertips to my lips to stop the tears from flowing, willing myself to stay with what I had set out to achieve.

"That may be the case, but those three kids of ours upstairs," I said tears threatening to break free, "God knows the damage we have already done. To Brady, to Emily, and our baby Harry," I choked back tears. "Whether we do or don't stay together Ed, we need help. We need to find some common ground. A place you and I can meet half way...for the sake of the kids."

Anger flared from his eyes and roared from his throat. "What the fuck is a therapist going to achieve?"

"It's not an option. If we end this now, you and I still

have no idea, no civilized way we can meet each other half way to raise our children, even if we're apart. We've got to stop focusing on ourselves, start focusing on our kids."

Drained, but knowing I needed to get it all out, my eyes fell empty onto Ed's. "I'm beyond caring whether we do or don't end up together, but I'm not beyond caring about our kids' happiness. It's not an option anymore. I'm booking someone this week. I'll get Sal to watch the kids." Oh God, I can't ask Sal. Not now I know about the cancer. "Or a sitter or someone," I added, flustered. "We're going to do something about it."

He opened his mouth to speak. I cut him off. "Save it for the counsellor."

CHAPTER 11

After making a few enquiries throughout the next week, I finally managed to find someone. I tried to find a man, someone Ed might feel more on the same level with but a woman would have to do.

Aunty Sal was all set up with the kids on the sofa. Brady tucked tightly under her right arm, Emily under her left and Harry snuggled up in a little ball on her lap. A picture book entitled, Cooper's Day Off, in her hands ready for reading.

I hadn't wanted to ask her, now I knew about the cancer, but she had insisted. Said she needed to keep doing things that made her feel normal...made her happy. Said hanging out for an evening with three of her godchildren was, she was sure, just what the doctor ordered.

I ensured everything was set before Sal arrived. Kids fed, washed and changed into their pyjamas. Toys put away. I'd even vacuumed and mopped the kitchen floor! Didn't want to give Sal a single thing to do, other than to be with the kids.

I looked over my shoulder from the hallway to glance at the door. Still no sign of Ed. He'd sent a vague text this afternoon saying that if he wasn't home in time, to meet him at the session.

About ten scenarios entered my head of all the reasons why Ed wouldn't show. I had zero confidence in his ability to make it home in time. Excellent, our first couples counselling night and I'm going stag.

Sal gave me a sympathetic look before insisting I get going before I didn't arrived late to the session.

Dr Greta Bower stood to greet me when I walked into her consult rooms. Oh dear. I didn't expect her to be so good looking. Not remotely my vision of a shrink. She looked more like Monica Bellucci than Nancy Drew. Someone who would give my husband every reason to leave his marriage than investigate why he didn't want to be in it in the first place.

Her thick mahogany hair fell effortlessly past her shoulders in large, soft curls. Her musty pink blouse barely covered her full breasts. Her slim black tailored pants only did more to accentuate her perfectly rounded buttocks, neat waist and trim thighs. Holy shit! This shrink is hot!

Well...I considered as I drooled back at the steamy Dr Greta Bower, this was one way to get Ed to turn up to couples counselling.

"Welcome Abigail," the good lady doctor smiled, offering me a chair opposite her own. Did she just purr? This is going to be harder than I thought.

I caught a glimpse of my appearance in Dr Bower's mirror behind her desk and inwardly shrieked. I'd opted to stay in my navy blue leisure suit for comfort, warmth and to relax. But now, looking at the foxy Doc, I realised I should have made more of an effort. Oh my hair! I tried to re-adjust my ponytail to be less...well...messy. Didn't my hair once upon a time look like the good lady doctor's, only in soft shades of the most glorious sand that one lavished about on a deserted island?

Those wonderful days of sitting in the hairdressing salon, having my weekly wash and blow dry were a distant thing of the past. My hair had mostly looked like it was permanently plugged into a power socket of late, hence the ponytail. Oh, how I longed for my hair to be steamed straight with the endless drying only a professional could manage.

After making ten minutes of small talk, my husband finally arrived. Huffing and puffing, he came armed with drivel and defensive ammunition. But suddenly, he fell silent. A stillness washed over Ed's body as colour heated his cheeks.

I refrained from reaching into my bag to fetch my husband a kiddie wet wipe to scoop up the drool. Catching a glimpse of the look in his eyes, he had certainly caught hold of her breasts and somehow managed to find comfort in holding his gaze there.

"Mr Montgomery? How do you do?" she said, reaching her long slender hand out to hold my husband's. "I'm Dr Bower but you can call me Greta." Is he rubbing his index finger on the inside of her palm? Oh why didn't I search harder for a male shrink!

Greta, finally, released her hand from Ed then offered him the chair next to my own before closing the door gently behind her. She sat legs crossed; clipboard poised, and gazed back at the two of us.

Eventually Greta broke the silence. "These things are never easy," she said evenly. "Why don't we start with you telling me a little about yourselves? I know you're married, but what about kids? Those sorts of things?" she smiled.

Silence.

"Who would like to go first?" She probed.

"You can," I said turning to Ed then back to Greta.

Shifting in his seat Ed was all charm, flashing a gigantic toothy grin at the sexy psych. "That's OK Ab. Why don't you start?" The little shit was going to play happy hubby. Right, I fumed, if that's the way you want to play this, you're on!

Smiling sweetly, I rattled off a picture-perfect life that told a fairy tale story of our twelve-year marriage, dating for fifteen. Three healthy children, living in a house, in a lovely street in one of the loveliest eastern suburbs of Sydney, Bondi.

Next it was Ed's turn. He went on and on about all the family outings we had. Didn't mention the fact that the two vacations he noted were the only holidays the family had ever taken together.

We smiled back at Greta, radiating from the afterglow of having painted a sickening sweet picture of the perfect house and family life that we did not have.

Greta rested her pen in her mouth and paused. Pondered. Then, she slowly, ever so slowly, arched back to reach to the desk behind her and placed the clipboard and pen on it. She leaned forward now in our direction, mostly Ed's, exposing her breasts a little more. Who is this woman? I took a sideways glance at my husband who was now sitting upright to attention, ready to hang on her every word.

But she just stared. Didn't say a thing. Just held her gaze so intently that it left an uncomfortable feeling in my belly. Dread. It felt like twenty minutes had ticked by but I'm sure it was only twenty seconds.

Finally, she spoke. "Thanks," she smiled with what looked like sarcasm dripping from her lips. "So, that was the pretty little bullshit story about how fabulous your lives are. How wonderful," she oozed. Deepening her gaze now, she let rip. "How about the real version. The, no holding back edition, of why a couple can't even show up as a "couple," she held up her hands to quote, "To couples counselling. And," she declared leaning even just that little bit closer to Ed, tantalising him with those breasts! "I'd love to hear why a husband is more interested in making eye candy with his therapist's breasts, than the woman who gave birth to his three children."

Ed motioned to interject, but Greta was clearly on a roll.

"And...why a wife who's acting like she has very little to say on the subject of her marriage, when I'm sure she spends all her spare time bitching and moaning to anyone that will listen." Smiling sweetly to me now, Greta added, "I'm sure it's all you ever talk about with your best girlfriend."

Reaching back to her clipboard and resting it firmly

on her lap, she finished her rant. "Need I say anymore? "Well?" she questioned. "Which one of you is going to give me the real story?" I thought this therapy thing was supposed to help?

Silence.

Greta looked at her watch and motioned to stand up. "Look Mr and Mrs Montgomery, this is a total waste of my time and yours. Not to mention your money, if you sit here a minute longer without offering the real deal."

"Wait," I urged. Holding my hand up. "You're right." Looking over at Ed and back at Greta I fessed up. "We need to give you the truth."

Greta sat back down, smoothing her black pants over her toned thighs, motioning me with a brief nod to continue.

I let her in. Let her in to a small piece of my insanity. The daily grind of motherhood. The overload of being responsible for three small children 24/7. The sadness, the deep, bottomless pit of sadness that stirred in my gut on any given day that my husband didn't look at me the same way he'd been eyeing off our therapist for the past twenty minutes. The fact that I'd lost sight of who I was. And that being out of the workforce meant I had no real opportunity to be praised, acknowledged, or recognised for any milestones. I'd lost my way, I moaned, as I continued with the download. And, I didn't have a single clue how to find my way through it. Exhausted, I slumped back in my chair and let out a massive release of air.

"Thank you for your honesty," Greta said. "It's given me a really solid picture. Something for us to work with."

She turned to Ed now. His body had grown tense at some point during the outpouring of my soul. The unburdening of my reality. His shoulders stiff, jaw clenched, fists tight in his lap. He was ready to explode.

Looking at her slim black watch on her wrist, Greta softened. "Ed we've got about ten minutes or so till we wrap up. Do you have anything to add to that?"

Ed could barely move his body. Saying nothing told me everything.

"What's left to say?" he remarked, flippantly. "Looks like Abigail just said it all. Painted the picture of how things really sit."

"That's her picture. What about yours?"

He waited. Pondered. Then let it out. "You know what Doc, this marriage has been really shit for a long time but the way Ab paints it; we may as well end it now. What's the point?"

"There's always a point. But it's important to get a clear picture of what's going on before you can even begin to create a new picture for the future."

Turning her attention fully to us both, Greta continued. "Whether this is going to end between the two of you or continue to improve, the fact is, you have three children to consider. They're young. They have so many years ahead of them where they will rely on your guidance, direction and love. Whether that comes from the two of you as a tight unit or the two of you as separated individuals, the love needs to be there for your kids and for yourself."

Placing her clipboard back on her desk, Greta wrapped up the session. "You've got some work ahead of you, there's no denying that, but staying where you are currently, is no solution. The bitterness will grow. The unhappiness will become more apparent. You have to make changes. But you both already know that, otherwise you wouldn't be here. Our time is up for today but I suggest we book your next session in a week's time, two at the latest. Please get in touch with my receptionist tomorrow to make an appointment that's convenient for you."

She began walking us to her door and sighed. "Try not to dissect the night with each other. Just accept the place you're both at right now isn't great. Just agree to be honest about that. Don't try to work it out or solve it before our next session. Perhaps just observe. Take some time to observe the situation and your part in it. Maybe start to identify why you're not happy with your partner and not happy with the marriage. Just observe for now and next session we can work through it."

Later as I drove home alone, the deep pit in my belly left me feeling empty. A profound sadness overcame me. I think I had let part of me inside die...and I only realised that tonight. That part that gave hope to a happy marriage and to a loving partnership. But I let it die because the pain, the void, of not having it, was too much to bear. But in the aftermath of that counselling session, all I felt was sorrow, longing, and deep regret. How did I get to this place that left me feeling so much pain, every single day?

I pulled over to the side of the road and let out a guttural moan. The tears came, flooding out of me, heaving into my chest as I bent over the steering wheel. I screamed. I yelled. I moaned and allowed an explosion of tears and frustration to cascade over my cheeks.

A sudden rap on my window sent me flying high and hitting my head against the car ceiling. Ouch!

I turned to see a man in his mid 50's, spectacles low on his nose, dark beady eyes, glaring back at me through the closed window. I reached for the central locking and pressed down firmly on the button, panic ripping through my fingers. He mouthed something I couldn't make out.

Great, this is all I needed to add to this downward spiral of my life. Marriage is in ruins. I feel like the most incapable mother in the world. I had no idea that my best friend of twenty years could die before her next birthday and the highlight of my day, is walking with my three loud and hell blazing kids to pick up my morning latte at the local café that is usually cold by the time I get home. My life's a mess and now it's about to get messier. Assaulted or murdered by a beagle eyed stranger on the side of the road.

Instincts took over. I placed my foot on the accelerator and revved the engine. I snarled my face at him to show that I meant business. He stepped back, softening a little and placed both hands in the air as if he were in a bank hold up. Now who's accosting whom? This is just plain weird. I decided to ease my window down a little after releasing my foot from the floor, letting in just an inch of air.

"I didn't mean to disturb you," he whispered through the very small gap of air I had created. "You looked upset. Wondered if you needed any help?"

I watched his lips move to try and make out what he was saying. I urged my eyes down further to his collar and then lower to the remainder of his outfit. Black coat and pants with a stiff white collar firmly around his throat. Oh God! He's the local chaplain at the church I never go to. Remember now seeing him outside smiling and greeting and welcoming the parishioners on Sunday mornings. He always gives the kids a smile and a wave but I never go in.

"I didn't mean to startle you," he whispered through the window. "I just wanted to see if you were all right. I just finishing packing up from this evening's mass and you looked...well...unhappy," his dark brown eyes, now full of concern.

"I'm ok," I replied meekly, tilting my mouth up toward the one-inch window of air I had allowed sound waves to travel through.

"I'm Father Michael, do you want to come in and talk about it?" He suggested, pointing his thumb back in the direction of the church.

"I can't Father," I smiled. "I've got to get home to my kids." Oh, shit the kids. Sal...she'll be wondering where I am.

I reached into my phone and saw three missed calls and several text messages. I'd forgotten to switch my phone back on.

"Thanks Father, I'll be ok. I've just come from a couples counselling session and it hit me a bit hard actually. Just trying to get myself together before I go home."

"Trouble at home?" he called, pursing his lips through the tiny gap of air.

"That's an understatement Father."

"Sure you wouldn't like to come inside and talk a little?"

"I really do have to get home Father."

"Well you know where I am if you need to talk," he smiled.

The very last thing I felt like doing right now was talking. I was all out of purging myself...but there was something in his voice that comforted me and I wanted to hold on to that.

"I'll keep it in mind Father. Thank you."

CHAPTER 12

By the time I reached home, Sal had left. Ed yelled random words at me in no apparent order, saying something to the effect of, "Where the hell were you? The kids...Sal...you could have called ..." and then I lost track.

I just stood staring at my husband, numb, devoid of emotion, depleted from all the crying and severely drained from his never-ending dialogue, a dialogue that haunted me daily.

"I'm going to bed," I said flatly. Ed reached out and grabbed my arm firmly, stopping me from walking past him. I glared back at him and through clenched teeth I said in an even clipped tone, "Glad our counselling session improved our situation."

I tugged my arm away but Ed clung tighter.

"Let go of me. I'm going to bed."

He opened his mouth but I freed my arm, slamming the child safety gate behind me before heading straight to our bedroom upstairs. Closing the door, I stripped out of my clothes and dressed for sleep in autopilot. When my head hit the pillow, it fell heavily, as if I were wearing a motorcycle helmet. My body collapsed in a heap along with my head.

The remainder of the week came and went. Ed and I managed to avoid each other more than usual. Maybe we were making progress? We weren't yelling at each other, but then again, we weren't talking either.

I maintained my usual routine with the kids. Latte run after breakfast. Park when it wasn't raining. Crayons and Play-Doh indoors when it was. All the while, holding out for that afternoon television time of Playschool, so very grateful it started promptly each weekday at 3:15pm.

I was not really living, not enjoying life like the other mothers seemed to be at the park. The other mums that maintained that inner and outer glow I struggled to attain internally and in my physical appearance. I always felt a little more dishevelled than most. Coffee never failed to stain my clothes.

I spoke to the other mums from time to time, chatted politely but careful not to delve deep. Who had the time to chat with three kids to control? My kids always ran in entirely different directions, which meant I never had time to sit and relax. Why did I feel like the only mother who did not have her shit together?

On Saturday, like every other Saturday, Ed had his kayaking. In fact, he was due to be away all weekend with his mates. They'd had this booked for months he told me, couldn't cancel just because of one little couples counselling session.

I was looking forward to Saturday night for a change. Sal was coming over and we hadn't seen each other much since the retreat. Now that I knew about her cancer, I didn't want to trouble her with all the regurgitating details of my boring, mundane and deeply dissatisfying life. I just wanted to be with my friend.

"I brought grape juice with bubbles," Sal announced upon entering with her big breasts and scary three-inch stilettos.

I couldn't help but notice her breasts and wondered whether the cancer growing inside them was slowly killing her. As tears stung my eyes, I sucked in air and held on tight to the breath I really didn't want to let go of. Tonight...well...more than tonight, I wanted to be strong. It was my turn to be there for Sal for a change. God knows she'd been there for me on more than 50,000 occasions.

"It's organic," she announced, unscrewing the bubbly non-alcoholic drink, pouring it into two long stemmed crystal champagne glasses she claimed from the kitchen cupboard. "I'm on a health kick," she announced. "Only organic. Only vegan. No alcohol. Boring clean living from now on."

"Sounds great Sal," I said, enveloping her in a great big hug. "Are you scared?" I asked, encouraging her to sit down in the living room by the fire. I enjoyed lighting it at night now winter had just settled in.

"Sure," she said. "Who wouldn't be?"

Sal kicked off her heels and tucked her feet underneath her legs on the sofa. "But fear isn't going to help me Ab? I've got to stay positive, well so the doctors keep telling me. Feed myself with healthy thoughts, healthy food and maintain a healthy lifestyle and all that. I've even started meditating. Can you believe it?" She laughed out loud. "Doctors say I need to calm down, centre myself. Some sort of crap like that." Smiling, Sal sipped her non-alcoholic grape juice and continued. "It's actually helping to put things into perspective though. Realised I'd held on to the anger of my prick of an ex Jeremy far too long. God knows how long all those toxic thoughts had been eating away at my insides with the shame of not being able to see those babies through to long term. That crap takes its toll on your body."

Turning to me now, those gorgeous caramel brown eyes stared at me with sincerity. "Honestly Ab, you're going to have to sort your shit out. Not just for your sanity but for your body as well. Those kids of yours need you honey."

My chest tightened. Throat choked. I couldn't hold onto it any longer. Couldn't pretend to be strong for Sal anymore. Soft tears gently dropped down onto my cheek. "I'm scared Sal," I trembled. "I don't want to lose you."

Sal squeezed my hand.

I wiped the tears away on my cheek. "How are the treatments going?" I wondered out loud.

"They're awful," Sal replied bluntly. "Pumping me full of drugs, nuking me like my body is a war zone. They're doing everything they can to try not to cut them off." Sarcasm dripped from Sal's lips while an exaggerated roar of laughter exhaled from her lungs. "Got to be honest, didn't dream when I was a kid running around in fairy wings that I'd grow up and have chemo!"

Reaching out, I squeezed Sal's hand. "I wish you'd let me come with you, help out a little more with all this."

"To be honest, I don't want you there."

Her words cut straight through my heart, leaving their mark on my face.

"Sorry, but it's the truth. You've been a mess for so long. I don't need a mess to help me get through this. I need someone who can be strong, positive and together."

"I can be all that," I choked.

Sal's eyebrow rose, yet she smiled.

"I can," I declared like a child who wanted to show her parents she was growing up.

"Just sort yourself out honey," she squeezed my hand and held it there a little longer than usual, staring me deeply in my eyes as if she were trying to reach my soul. "Get happy again. Then you'll be doing me some favours."

"Anyway...enough about me. How'd the counselling session go?"

"Nothing's changed," I declared flatly. "It might even be worse," I said, biting my lip for strength.

"Ed and I have barely spoken since. It's like we're trying to avoid being honest about how bad our situation really is." Running my fingers through my hair now, I let it out. "It's just so bad."

"Give it time," Sal soothed. "It's only been one session. You and Ed have been doing it the same way for so long, you've stopped knowing how to be nice to each other." Offering me a cheery smile, Sal added, "Look, we all know it can't go on like it is. The good thing with a counsellor is, neither of you can avoid the obvious anymore."

I wanted to change the subject. Steer it away from my misery. "How long do we wait till we know if the cancer treatment's worked?"

"Weeks, probably months to really know the results," Sal revealed.

As the weeks rolled on, Ed and I kept up counselling. Sessions two, three and four, came and went in a blur. Greta maintained her stunning appearance. It unnerved me the way she always looked so impeccable...not to mention hot. We'd managed to maintain fortnightly visits. Same pattern repeated. Travelled separately. Ed turned up late, offering a new feeble excuse each time. We talked. We listened. Greta led the way. I left each session exhausted, drained, and desperately unhopeful.

At home, we talked less and less, to the point where our responses became automated, as if the television remained on mute.

Meanwhile, Sal had regular bouts of chemo to kill the cancer that raged inside her body. We waited, wondering if she would live or die.

My life was a living time bomb. Tick. Tick. Ticking away. No hope for a brighter future. Very little had changed between Ed and I with the counselling. Although, I did think I was making more of an effort with my motherhood now. I focussed on enjoying my time with the kids more and I was getting better, slowly, each day. But the emotional strain of a loveless marriage and a never-ending identity crisis, was gravely taking its toll.

"You're wasting our time, not to mention your money," Greta barked at Ed and I during session number five.

"We're ten weeks in and I've seen no progress. Neither of you seems interested in doing anything to make changes in this marriage. We talk about suggestions, new improvements you can both make but another two weeks roll on by and not a single thing is done." Smoothing her slender hands down her sleek marine blue skirt, she looked at us in wonder. "Why are you here? I mean... why are you even bothering?" Frustration growing, she leaned forward in anticipation of the answer, offering more than a glimpse of her full cupped breasts that pushed their way through her crisp white collared shirt and lacy white bra.

Catching Ed's eyes through the corner of my own, I noted that his were boggling out of his head. Did he even hear a word she was saying or was he was too busy gawking at her cleavage?

"Ed let's start with you." Greta suggested.

"Why me?" he snapped like a kid being told he had to have the first bath.

"Why not?" she glared, sitting with her back up straight, pen poised at her clipboard.

"Fine," he groaned.

Greta leaned in closer. I mean did she really have to squeeze her arms so close to her breasts as if it were the most comfortable position to take notes? One thing was clear...Ed didn't look at me like that...not any more... maybe not ever.

"Why are you here Ed?" Greta wondered.

Shrugging his shoulders. "It was Abby's idea."

"So, you are capable of trying something your wife suggests, something for the wellbeing of your marriage?"

"Huh?" Ed replied, fidgeting in his chair.

"Well...every fortnight you go away with a whole list of things you could do to change and improve your marriage, suggestions Abigail has made, yet you do nothing, absolutely nothing about it."

"Oh right, so this is all on me?" Ed glared.

"No," Greta said flatly, "Just making a point." Leaning in and smiling a little more closely at Ed, she added, "Don't worry, Abigail's next."

Turning to me, Greta asked, "And Abigail, what changes are you making? You keep saying you want Ed to help with the kids, notice you a little more, act like a devoted husband and loving father. But what are you doing to make an effort to get him to notice you? What are you communicating to him about what you would truly like him to do?"

I began chewing the inside of my gum.

"Take it from me," Greta remarked, looking to Ed and then back at me, "The man hasn't got a clue!"

Eyeballing Greta, Ed spoke up. "Hey!"

Holding her hand out in defence Greta replied. "He hasn't got a clue because his wife hasn't enlightened him. Hasn't told him what's in her heart."

Ed and I sat in silence. Like two kids who had been taken into the headmaster's office and given a good smack over the knuckles for not playing nice in the playground.

Taking a deep breath, Greta announced that we were going to do some sort of role-play. Oh seriously? Please, anything but that. Never was any good at those corporate development workshop things back in my Avalanche days where we had to pretend we were someone we were not.

Sensing our unease, Greta grinned. "Don't worry, you're not trying to win an Oscar. You're just trying to get a little perspective."

Standing up and encouraging us to do the same, Ed and I grumbled as Greta turned us this way and that, until finally we were facing each other, in character and in position.

This felt weird. Ed and I standing face to face, looking directly at each other. I hadn't really looked at him lately. Looked at the man underneath the unhappy husband I had been staring back at for so long.

She led us through this silent exercise where we had to notice what appealed to us about the other. "Was it their eyes?" she asked. "Their smile? Colour of their hair? Shirt? Height?" she probed further. Then she made us go deeper, beyond the physical. "Can you think of something you like about the person standing in front of you? Something a little deeper than what you can see at first glance?"

And so, the layers began unravelling, getting us to dive deeper and deeper until she had us claiming something that genuinely appealed about the other person standing before us.

Oh, that was hard. And I mean really hard. Staring

at my husband for a good fifteen minutes, trying to see something decent both inside and out.

Greta now gave us explicit instructions to take this exercise further once we left the confines of her clinic. "It's like you're on a field trip for the next two weeks," she chuckled, tucking her long luscious dark brown hair behind her ears.

"Throughout the next two weeks I want you to make a conscious effort to notice the good in each other. Take the time to recognise something the other person has done that appeals. Write it down in the notebooks I gave you in the first session. It's time to put those books to good use."

It had been a good two and a half months working with Greta now, and finally she was giving us something concrete to do that would see how we measured up.

"You have to find something good, every single day, for the next two weeks. Fourteen things that appeal to you about your spouse, ensuring to write it all down in your book. Bring the list back to the next session."

Standing up to indicate our session was now at a close, Greta added one final stipulation, her voice becoming serious. "You are not to share your notebooks with each other, or anyone else for that matter. Just yourself." Ah Greta, can we go back to the role-play thing? I'm certain I'd prefer that to this excruciating daily exercise you have planned for the next two weeks where I have to find something I like on a daily basis about the man that I loathe.

CHAPTER 13

The next morning while at the park with the kids I reached into my handbag for Greta's notebook. It was a rare moment when all three of my children were pre-occupied. They were happily playing in the sandpit, bellies full, bladders empty, tinkering with trucks and tea sets brought from home. I looked down at the page blankly; empty of thought, almost willing the words to magically appear on the page. Wished this would come easily. Wished I could think of something about Ed over the past twenty four hours that I enjoyed. Just one little thing Abby, I self-talked. Greta insisted we not let a day go by without writing an entry into our notebooks. "State it and date it," she had declared. Said that if we couldn't find something, we weren't looking hard enough.

She had asked us back in session three if we were attracted to each other when we got married. Explained that attraction is a way to ignite passion, interest and desire, regardless of whether a couple were or weren't having sex. She had asked us for now, not to focus on whether we did or didn't love each other but instead to find ways to re-connect the attraction. "We can look at love later," she had said. "For now, we need to create spark."

She had reminded us in session four to stop questioning

our marriage. Reminded us we had three kids to consider and that whatever came of these sessions, at the very least, her intention was for us to come away from them focussed on being the best parents we could be.

Looking up at the kids in the sandpit and then back at the blank page, I willed myself to dig deep. Nothing came. No matter how hard I tried, the words, the feelings, they didn't arrive.

Ed surprised us by coming home earlier than usual that evening. He was home in time to help feed the kids. It ended very messy, with more food on the floor than in the kids' mouths, but they were all laughing when I came out from claiming some time out to shower.

As I stopped and looked at this scene from a distance, I realised I enjoyed Ed in this moment. I liked that he was smiling with the kids and they were smiling back. I have my first one Greta! I shouted silently. With my towel tightly wrapped around my body and another around my head, I leaped up the flight of steps to my bedroom to grab Greta's notebook from my handbag.

"State it. Date it," Greta's voice echoed in my head.

I faithfully scribed. "This evening I really enjoyed watching Ed and the kids have a great time during a feeding frenzy over dinner. As messy as it was, I liked watching how happy they all were together."

Hope rumbled in my belly.

With each new day that followed, I continued to search and struggle to dig deep, to discover something that appealed to me about Ed. I was damned if I would rock up to our next session not having completed the task. I felt like a failure in so many areas of my life, I did not want to fail at couples counselling as well.

Session six had finally arrived. Time to present our notes and observations of all the good we could find in each other. Honestly, it had been a struggle. I wasn't proud admitting to myself that I found it easier to like a Facebook post some random stranger or long lost friend I hadn't seen in twenty years had shared. But, somehow, I had managed to write an entry every single day. Fourteen in total. Satisfaction rumbled around in my belly now.

Greta started with me. The exercise was for one person to share while the other person listened. The recipient wasn't allowed to comment or interrupt. Greta would then let the other person share after her debrief.

After sharing my list, Greta asked more questions. "How was that exercise for you Abigail?"

"Which part?"

"All of it actually."

"It was difficult," I blurted out without thinking, covering my mouth to stop the overflow.

"Go on," she encouraged, smiling at Ed and giving me the nod. "Why was it difficult?" Sensing my hesitation, Greta urged me to continue. "Abigail, you have come so far, been so open and honest. It was a wonderful list. But I do appreciate this hasn't come easily. Please let us know why. It's important for Ed to understand what you're going through."

Moving my hand from my mouth, I let go. "Ed and

I don't spend a lot of time together," I shrugged. "He's rarely home to eat with me, which makes it really hard for us to communicate...to talk...to share ourselves with each other. It's hard to find things that you like about someone when you're not thinking about them very much or interacting with them." I wondered who I was admitting this to more, Greta, Ed or myself.

"And if you could choose one thing on that list," Greta probed, "One thing, something you liked about Ed, enjoyed, wanted to see more of, what would it be?"

"The kids," I replied without hesitation. Turning to Ed without thinking, I spoke. "I really enjoyed seeing you with the kids."

"Wonderful sharing Abigail thank you," Greta remarked.

It was Ed's turn now. He shifted uncomfortably in his chair.

Looking at Ed curiously, Greta began the probing. "Got your notebook Ed?"

"No," he replied flatly.

"No?"

Where's he going with this? I thought fidgeting uncomfortably in my seat now.

"Ed, did you complete the exercise?"

"Sort of."

"Perhaps you could explain a little further," Greta delved deeper. The woman had patience. I'll give her that.

"Well, " he began lazily. "The first day I forgot all about it actually. The next day, time got away from me. The third, I realised I'd left the notebook in my car, ended up typing it into my phone. The next day I missed, then I picked up a couple of days in a row...wrote bullet points on my computer at work. My work schedule has been crazy lately."

And so, the dribble continued.

I was fuming inside. One simple exercise. All he had to do was think of fourteen things over the course of fourteen days that he liked about his wife, the mother of his three children, but he couldn't do it. Or didn't want to. But I couldn't say a thing. Greta's rule not mine. The other person had to zip it while the other person got gruelled.

"Ed, do you want to be in this marriage?" Greta asked, an acute directness in her voice.

"What do you mean?"

She repeated the question, devoid of expression.

"I'm here aren't I?"

"Ok thank you, I'm glad we cleared that up," Greta's voice remained even. "Let's continue with the exercise. Are you able to remember your notes, from your er... computer...iPad...phone...wherever you decided to store all of that vital information?"

He shrugged. "I'll try."

"Great, any time you're ready," Greta encouraged.

Five, ten, twenty seconds past. It felt like hours waiting for this damn husband of mine to say something bloody nice about me. I fiddled ferociously with the corners of my own notebook in anticipation.

Stalling, he eventually began. "She's pretty good with the kids."

"That's lovely Ed. Could you be more specific?" Greta probed deeper.

"Ah...not really."

"Understood. And anything else you recall noticing over these past two weeks?"

My eyes closed in disgust. Didn't want to hear anymore. Didn't want to see anymore. Had gone well beyond the point of not feeling anymore. It was clear to me now how little respect my husband had for me. Yet Greta continued to engage with the man. He faffed and fluffed, vaguely attempting to deliver something meaningful, yet not remotely being specific.

"Ed," Greta stared blankly at him. "You do realise that if you want this marriage to work, you're going to have to make an effort?"

Turning to me now and back to Ed, she added, "You both are."

Greta paused to gather her thoughts. She looked down at her notes on her clipboard before finally returning her gaze back at us, a look of sympathy washed over her.

"How things are right now...I'm not going to lie to either of you...they're not great. If you want to stay in this situation the way it is, fine," she said shrugging her shoulders and holding her palms open, as if she was channelling her inner Italian mumma. Shaking her head at us now. Oh no. Not the headmistress tone.

"But that kind of unhappiness...you need to know... need to understand... it will only lead to a lot of bitterness and blame. But what you need to keep top of mind...in your hearts...is that all of this impacts your children."

With a deep pause and another moment to catch her breath and reconnect with her notes, Greta looked back at us and let out a big breath. "Ed, I'd like you to complete this exercise in full by the next session. I'd really like you to put in the effort this time. I know this may feel a little out of your comfort zone and I know you are busy, but a couple of minutes a day to think something nice about your wife is a good thing, trust me on that."

"And Abigail," Greta said a hint of empathy in her voice. "I'd like you to use the next two weeks to write an entry each day about yourself. Something you like about you."

"Myself?" I exclaimed.

"Yes, yourself," Greta smiled. "You did so well on delivering an entry every day on Ed, now I'd like you to turn that attention to yourself. Please don't go to bed," she urged, "without thinking of yourself."

After Greta noted the time on her slim black watch, she leaned in closer, forcing us to do the same, her breath a mere whisper. "I've got a degree in human psychology, honours actually, and another in relationship counselling. I've been successful in my career for the past twenty years...I do actually know what I'm talking about!" Almost as an afterthought she added, before standing up to cue us to do the same, "It's really simple...you take time now to make the changes, or time will get away from you. If you don't, you'll wind up wondering what you've been doing with your time all along. You'll have nothing to show for it. No growth. No evolvement. No emotional development. No self-awareness. And I guarantee...a lot less joy in your lives."

Walking to her office door now and shrugging her shoulders, she turned back and held us firmly in her gaze. "But, it is your choice after all."

Ed and I stared blankly at each other on the street. Greta's truth serum had cut through to the core. Eventually, we stammered something to the effect of, "See you at home."

CHAPTER 14

Sitting now in the quiet of my car, I turned my phone back on in autopilot. A dozen missed calls. A bunch of text messages. What! Something to the effect of Sal had collapsed and my darling little Brady had run next door to the neighbours to get help. Oh. My. God. The ambulance had taken Sal to the hospital and the kids were fine, but being taken care of by a neighbour. Panic ran through my veins.

I dialled Ed and put him on loudspeaker as I slammed my foot flat on the accelerator, intent on running every red light and incurring a speeding fine on the way home.

"There's be an accident," I cried, on the verge of tears, when Ed answered the call.

"What? What happened?" Ed cried into his own phone on loudspeaker.

"I...I...don't know," I shuddered. "All I know is...an ambulance came to the house...our neighbour is with the kids.

"What?" Ed shouted. "Where's Sal?"

"At the hospital," I shouted in response, my voice reaching hysteria.

"Who with?"

"What? The ambulance," I shouted back, pressing my

foot down harder to run the next orange light.

"Who did she take to the hospital?" he screamed as if yelling was going to help me understand him better.

"What are you talking about? Herself?" I screamed out loud. "She took herself to the hospital."

"What? Why?"

Are you kidding me! We can't even communicate accurately in a crisis.

Intensely exasperated now and clutching the steering wheel tightly for strength. "Something happened to Sal. She collapsed. The neighbour called the ambulance. The neighbour is with the kids. Sal is in hospital."

Looking up and squinting at the next set of traffic lights, holding my breath in the hope it remained orange as I pressed harder on the accelerator, I continued yelling at Ed through my loudspeaker. "I'm driving straight to the hospital."

"What about the kids?"

"Ed!" I shouted. "The kids are fine. They're at home with our neighbour. "Go home and deal with that. My best friend has just collapsed. I need to see how she is. Call me as soon as you get home to let me know how the kids are."

Nearing the hospital car park, I ended the call.

I ran frantically into the emergency room, gasping for air, beads of sweat trailing down my face from the marathon I had just run from the car park. "Um... hi... Sally Douglas please." Pausing to catch my breath, I added, "An ambulance brought her in."

"Are you a relative?" The nurse behind the clinical white counter asked.

Frustration took over my body and mind. Why do you always need a marriage certificate or blood lineage to see a loved one in hospital? "No," I said through clenched teeth, "But I've spent the past twenty one years of my life every bloody day utterly devoted to her." Tears threatened to break free.

"I'm sorry," the nurse said. Smile bland. Tone flat. "We only give out that information to relatives."

I wanted to rip my hair out in frustration or dive across the counter and rip the nurse's damn hair out. "But she was looking after my kids," I shouted. "I was out having marriage counselling." The ramble continued. "My husband and I...we don't get along anymore you see...I'm not sure when it all fell apart."

The woman's eyes glazed over.

"Um...what I meant to say...is...Sal...she would want me there. Please I need to know if she's all right?" I begged.

"As I said, only relatives and next of kin."

My head jolted. "Next of kin? Did you say next of kin? I'm next of kin." I patted my hand proudly on my chest. "She's godmother to all three of my children and the sister I never had. She has breast cancer. She's been undergoing treatment and...please...I really need to know if she's all right."

Silence.

I held my fingertips close to my mouth as I struggled

to hold back the tears. "Please." I urged. "I'm next of kin."

Mouth taut, the nurse replied in a cool tone. "Wait here."

My phone rang, vibrated in my handbag.

"The kids are fine," Ed said, when I answered the call. "A bit shaken up. What was Sal doing collapsing?" Ed asked, confusion, fear and frustration threaded through his voice.

"She's got cancer Ed," I said flatly.

"What!" Ed softened a little. "Ab."

Emotionless, drained, I asked about the kids.

"They'll be fine. What about you? What are you going to do?"

"I need to stay." Choking back tears, I added, "I'll be home by the morning in time for you to go to work. Call me if you need anything. I've gotta go."

The nurse returned, telling me Sal was sleeping and couldn't be disturbed.

"Please," I pleaded. "I have to see her. I won't make a sound. I just want to see her."

The nurse considered my plea and eventually gave in. "Ok, just for a minute."

Relieved, I wanted to reach out and hug the nurse, but instead muffled a, "thank you."

When I walked in and saw Sal, the blood drained from my face. She was attached to a bunch of monitors and a drip was taped firmly to her hand. Her heart pounded steady and slow as her eyes rested closed. That gorgeous luscious red mane of hers was swept to one side from her incredibly pale face.

"Oh Sal," I whispered, taking quiet steps toward her. "I'm sorry I wasn't there for you."

After gaining permission from the nurse to sit with my darling dear friend, I stared blankly at the flaming red head. She'd lost the spark in her flame. Seconds turned into minutes. Minutes turned into hours. I lost track of how long I had been there. The nurse came in from time to time, to check more on the visitor I think, rather than the patient. They'd given Sal something to sedate and stabilise her I was told and that she would be out of it till at least the morning. The nurse suggested I go home on more than one occasion and come back fresh in the morning. I'd have the kids with me then so if there was a small glimmer of hope that she would wake tonight, I wanted to be with her when she did.

I couldn't remember falling asleep but I woke to the sound of the nurse patting me on the shoulder. "It's morning. Go home, get some rest."

Dazed and confused, I looked around to get my bearings. The cold reality settled in. My best friend was lying in a hospital bed with tubes and electronic devices keeping her alive.

"What time is it?" I mumbled.

"Almost 6:30am," a nurse I didn't recognise replied.

"Really? I better get going. You have all my details. Please," I pleaded, "Call me if there's any change...

anything...I really want to be kept up to date."

"Is there anyone else we can call?" The nurse asked.

"No." Both of her parents are dead. She isn't married. Doesn't have kids. Her brother and sister both live overseas. I'll get in touch with them," I sniffed, trying not to choke on tears. "I'll phone her work to let them know she won't be in." The tears trembled in my throat and caught up with me by the time I reached the elevator.

I arrived home haggard, dishevelled and just plain worn out. Ed was scrambling in the kitchen. Flustered. The kids ran toward me, screaming out my name in joy, and possibly relief. They virtually crash tackled me in the hallway, covering me with kisses all over my hair, face, hands and arms; hugging me like I'd been gone a whole month.

"Oh, my little darlings. Mummy loves you so much," I said squeezing each of them tight as if they might disappear.

"Thought you'd never get here," Ed said.

"Is that all you have to say?" I glared at him. "Don't you even want to know how she is?"

"Is Aunty Sal ok," little Emily asked?

"She's sleeping darling," I said, stroking my daughter's white blonde mane.

Pouring orange juice into three small cups decorated in Disney, Ed fumbled with his words. "How...how is she?"

"I don't know," was all I could say.

Brady reached over and stroked my hair gently.

"Mummy looks tired," he said then snuggled under my arm for another cuddle.

"Mummy is tired darling. But I'll be ok."

Turning to Ed, I asked when he needed to leave for work, knowing I could do with an undisturbed shower. I needed to wash away all the hurt, pain and worry that seemed tangled inside me.

A couple of hours later, with the kids happily playing on the rug in the playroom, with a bunch of blocks, dolls, soft toys and old cardboard boxes scattered in front of them, I stole a few minutes to regain my composure and call the hospital. I looked over at the kids before I dialled and was relieved they were all playing so nicely together without needing my assistance. Kids are so clever, I thought. I didn't have to say a thing. They just knew I was hurting.

When I phoned the hospital, they told me there was not a lot of change. Sal was stabilised and comfortable. "Come and see her this afternoon," the nurse had instructed.

I had asked Meredith, my mother-in-law to watch the kids in the afternoon before Ed arrived home. She had responded with formality in her tone, telling me it was a little inconvenient, being that it was her Tennis & Ladies Lunch Day. Somehow...eventually...she had managed to oblige.

That afternoon when I walked into Sal's hospital room all self-talk of trying to keep it together and stay strong was forgotten. Rushing to her bedside and reaching tight for her hand, the tears tumbled hard. Vulnerability overtook me and shook me to the core. I hadn't felt like this since my mum died.

The doctor later informed Sal and I that the cancer had now spread, beyond her breasts to her lungs. They weren't sure how much longer she had. A few weeks, months maybe, a year at best. I couldn't believe what I was hearing. It all seemed so surreal. They just wanted to do whatever they could to make her feel as comfortable as possible. Apparently, Sal had experienced these falls more than once. She had been struggling with the treatment of late.

An ache clung to my heart. I was gutted for my friend, the sister I never had, who had been going through all of this, so much of it on her own. My best friend was dying and there wasn't a damn thing I could do but make an oath to be there for her no matter what.

Later in the quiet of my car, sitting outside my house, I replayed Sal's words before I left the hospital. She urged me to step up in my life. To sort out my crap with Ed. "Be with him, don't be with him," she roared. "Just do something about it before it's too late." She urged me to find myself again. To re-create a new identity. Implored me to discover what makes me happy, whether it involved Ed or not.

Stepping inside my house now, nothing could have prepared me for what happened next.

Ed picked a fight the second I walked into the kitchen. I'm not sure why, something about troubling his mum to look after the kids when she had plans. He'd forgotten to mention my friend, to feign interest in her wellbeing.

He'd failed to look up when I moved toward him, and notice my despair.

"I want a divorce," I muttered. "I don't want to do this anymore."

He lashed back out at me in response. I ignored his rebuke. My jaw clenched as I raged inside for this man that stared back at me. I knew now I had reached the other side. Had crossed the line that meant I'd had enough. To that destination that said, "I can't do this anymore."

I stepped away from him and began to make my way upstairs, instructing Ed to sleep on the sofa and make arrangements for somewhere else to live. I had told him when I ended it - emotion clinching to my chest, tears framing my soft mint green eyes - that my best friend was dying and I needed to find a new way to live.

CHAPTER 15

I woke up feeling different. A real awareness of what I had to do. I'd hardly slept a wink. Tossing and turning as I fretted for Sal, worried about how I would raise three kids on my own. Technically, I was already doing most of that myself, but I wondered how I could afford to raise my children. How I might contribute financially having been out of the workforce for several years.

I had originally opted for maternity leave when I had Brady, but once I got into motherhood, I wanted to stay home more and go to work less. My marketing job, enticing people to buy what they did not need or could not afford, seemed violently opposed to what became important to me when I gave birth to not one, but three children. As a mother, I had changed. Or perhaps this part of me always existed and I had just failed to acknowledge it pre-kids. But now, with the news of Sal dying, and under no illusion that my marriage was dying too, I had no choice but to find a way out of this and choose to come to life. I'd be a coward to throw away any chance of happiness and vitality while staring into the eyes of my dying best friend. I knew I had to stop focussing on how I got to this place and just accept I was here. Had been for quite some time. I'd been hanging out in this unhappy place, growing comfortable with the bitter taste I had in my mouth. It stopped being Ed's fault a long time ago. I could acknowledge that now. I'd spent so much energy focussing outwards, blaming everyone around me for my unhappiness, my failure at succeeding in life. But I was now painfully aware just how much this constant blame was the undoing of me, and prevented me from making a better life.

I looked out my bedroom window, taking a little extra 'me-time' in bed as the rain pelted down. The ferocious stream of water thrashing on my flowered pot plants, leaving pools of water on my white-washed weatherboard deck. That rain would settle in for the week and I knew I'd go crazy cooped up indoors with the kids. I needed to get out, in more ways than one.

Shaking off my gloom and thinking of Sal's bitter reality, I reminded myself of my new oath to make the most of life. Summoning all the energy I could muster, I leapt from the bed and ran into the kids' room.

"Good morning my little darlings," I beamed, then squeezed each child tight and gave them soft, wet kisses all over their cheeks. "We're going to Kiddie Land today," I announced.

"Yay!" Emily cried, jumping up and down on her bed.

"Really Mummy?" Brady asked, his big blue eyes full of love.

"You bet," I said swinging him in a twirl from his bed to the floor. "It's going to rain all day and mummy thinks it's time we got out and had some fun."

"Yay." Emily screamed and leapt from her bed to rummage through her chest of draws. She claimed pink tights and her red tunic dress with bright pink polka dots all over it for the occasion.

"Yay," little Harry cried, mimicking his sister and jumping up and down on his bed.

Later, with the kids settled into their favourite spots at Kiddie Land, which involved squealing down slides, jumping on blow-up castles and building block towers as high as the Empire State Building, I had some time to breathe.

I took out Greta's notebook and a pen and absently flicked through the pages. Sipping my latte, I read pages of notes I'd made about Ed, about me and even about the kids. I had begun to use this notebook for more than just completing Greta's fortnightly homework tasks. It had become a sort of companion. A confidante to declare my thoughts. I'd had so much stuff bottled up inside me for so long. It felt cathartic somehow, to pour it all onto the page. Thoughts and feelings that had been trapped inside and steadily feasting on negativity.

"Negativity breeds negativity," Greta had said in the session before last. I heard her at the time but wasn't really listening. It had begun to sink in a little now. You see with Sal in hospital, dying each day, the cancer eating away inside her; I'd understood exactly what Greta had meant. Exactly what days after days of negativity could bring to my life.

I looked up to search for my kids and smiled when I found Brady steering the rocket ship up so high. His toothy wide grin spread over his little face, muttering something to the cute little blonde haired boy beside him.

I beamed when I saw little Emily lost in the dress up box, fairy wings on her back, a tiara on her head. Suzanne, the woman who ran the place, had a real talent for entertaining the kids.

Harry was sitting to my right on the floor, fully engrossed in the train track that ran all the way around the eastern side of the centre. I held back from reaching out to touch his soft tuffs of brown wavy hair, for fear I might interfere with his focus.

I rested my head back on the chair, sipped more of my latte and took in the scene. Children, as well as my own, delighted and engaged in brightly coloured activity, wonder and noise. I mused inwardly at myself, wondering why I didn't come to Kiddie Land more often.

Thinking of Ed now and driven by the need to share my thoughts with him in writing, I reached for my pen and began to offload in my notebook.

I knew I'd never get out what I wanted to say to him in person without his interruptions or switching off at some point. Writing a letter meant I could get clear, claim it and state it in the process.

My hand trembled as I wrote the first few words. Ending my twelve-year marriage and the three years we had dated before was big. Each time I faltered, I heard Sal's voice inside my head, encouraging me to make a change for good. "Do something, anything," she had urged. "Just start finding a way to be happy."

I wasn't even sure if ending my marriage was going to make me happy, but I knew how things were right now, was not a good place to stay.

So, I wrote.

Dear Ed. I'm sorry. I'm sorry things have gotten so out of hand. Sorry that we have somehow both ended up so unhappy. Sorry that we have become so disrespectful to each other, so unhelpful to one another and in turn grown unsatisfied in this marriage. I don't know at what point we made the decision to go our separate ways, to be enemies instead of allies. But I do know that it's not ok for us to pretend anymore or put up with how things have turned out. I know I'm not making you happy and I'm certain you are not making me happy. But the serious implications of this, are without a doubt, not good for our children.

We are not the role models to our kids that I know we can be. Somewhere in all this motherhood I started putting myself last, and in the process, I have become a person I don't like. I have put my needs, my desires, my wants, last on the list for so long. But I can't do it like this anymore. It's never going to turn out well if I do.

The only way I can see my life improving, your life improving, Brady, Emily and Harry's lives improving, is for you and I to go our separate ways. It pains me desperately. Please know that it does. It hurts me so deeply to be here at this place with you. This place where we have run out of road and no idea where to turn next. It's time we created something new to look forward to, something different from how we are living right now.

Who knows whether those individual paths will lead back to each other, but for now I know those paths need to be separate. Of course, we will always stay in touch for the kids. It will be a different kind of family unit than we first imagined. But for now, I need to let us go, because I can't find a way to build you into my future when I've lost sight of who I want to be in that picture myself. I have no idea where this separation will take me but I know I must try to find out.

I would like to talk about some sort of formal arrangement for how this all comes about. What our new life might look like for the kids. Home life, how our new living arrangements might be. I think it would be wise to do it formally and with the support and guidance of our counsellor. I think we're at a place where we need to focus on the facts. Let go of emotions for a minute. Practically work out how this new arrangement might look right now and a little while down the road.

I hope you'll understand why I had to write it all down in a letter and share it with you in this way. Quite simply, I just needed to be heard Ed. I needed for you to listen. I look forward to finding a way to be better, even though we will be apart. Abigail x

Harry waddled over to me now and snuggled up onto my lap for a cuddle. Clinging to me tight, he oozed love. Oh yes kids have an insight into these things. I squeezed him as tight as I could without breaking a bone. Told him over and over how much I loved him.

Later, after bundling up my exhausted yet deliriously happy children and completing the routine of our day, it was almost time to face Ed. I'd checked in with Sal to see if I could visit her and texted Ed of my plans to leave for the hospital when he got home.

I sat poised on the sofa, as the kids quietly played on the rug at my feet, my hands

gripping tight to Ed's letter. Nervous to openly share my thoughts. Nervous to have those thoughts potentially thrown back in my face.

I heard the kids before I heard Ed. They often had an intuitive sense before he walked in the front door.

"Daddy, they yelled and giggled, pushing and shoving against each other along the hallway to claim the first cuddle. I heard a scream and then a succession of tears. I drew on all the inner strength I had to not sort it out. Ed can deal with it, I self-talked. Somewhere along the way to the front door, it appeared Emily had been trampled on by her older brother.

"I didn't do it," Brady pleaded.

"It's all right mate," Ed said, patting Brady's head while scooping Emily into his arms to wipe the tears from her cheeks. Harry now clung to Ed's leg, willing him not to move. My heart panged. When did I stop noticing this glorious scene of daddy returning home and the kids getting swept up in this wonderful ritual of competing for the first cuddle?

Ed stumbled down the hallway clumsily, all three kids hanging off him in some fashion as he made his way to the living room.

I couldn't stand to be in the space a moment longer, with the knowledge that I held between my fingers. Almost throwing my letter at Ed in defence, an act I would surely regret later, I adopted a sort of huffy tone to hide the emotion that clung to my throat. I could barely make eye contact with him. This was harder than I thought. I rattled off something about, "It all being in the letter" and that I was, "off to see Sal in hospital and I'd be home late."

I leaned over to kiss Emily goodbye.

"Don't go Mummy," she said, reaching out to pull me close to her cheek while still resting high in Ed's arms.

I eyeballed Ed. He eyeballed back. We hadn't been this physically close, this intimate, in so long.

Emily drew the three of us tightly together, clinging to both Ed and I equally now.

"Family cuddle," Brady squealed jumping up high.

Harry mimicked his brother. "Family cuddle," his little voice squeaked.

All three kids screamed and squealed, using all their limbs, will and heart to bring the five of us together.

Did they sense something? Did they sense we would soon be apart and that's why they were drawing us closer?

"Hug Mummy, Daddy," Brady ordered.

Brady moved Ed's awkward arm around my waist. I sucked in air and held my breath. The five of us became one. A smothering took hold of me. An awkward suffocating feeling in this space. I was the first to pull away. I had to. I hurriedly waved goodbye and rushed down the hall, quickly closing the door behind me.

CHAPTER 16

I sat in the hospital's car park, ignition turned off. In the eerie darkness of my thoughts, I closed my eyes and let myself get swept away in dreaming my mother was here with me now. I imagined her floating in a haze of fluffy white clouds as light as fairy floss and as soft as sheep's wool, drifting in the air above. I imagined her to be just sort of floating, hovering above the hood of my car, arms open wide, with a smile that came from her heart, calling out.

"Welcome, sweet child," she whispered. "Let's sit a while, so you can tell me all about it. Tell me your woes, release them to me and do tell me how that sweet child of mine is doing. I can see my darling daughter has lost her way. Come here now lovely Sally and stay with me a while."

My eyes leapt open. "Sal!" I screamed leaping from my car, slamming the door behind me and racing to the hospital lift.

I jumped three feet off the ground when the lift bell rang, announcing its arrival to the seventh floor. As the doors opened wide, I flung myself out, tripping and nearly landing face first on the blue carpeted floor on the other side.

I heaved myself up off the scratchy carpet and ran and

rushed and panted on a mission to get to the sign that said Oncology. I bolted past the nurses' station, down the corridor, turned left, and then ran some more. Turned right and panted again, until, finally, I reached room AE9. I ran inside shouting out her name without a care for the three other patients that shared her room.

"Shhhh." I heard a familiar voice whisper when I peeked behind the drab grey curtain. "Have you gone crazy?" Sal lifted her head slightly, trying to ease herself up onto her elbows.

"I thought you were dead."

Sal's eyes sprung wide open.

"Sorry. That didn't come out right."

Rambling, I sat at the edge of Sal's bed, and clung tight to her hand. "I drifted off in the car park somehow and began imagining I could see my mum. She was calling your name. Sort of welcoming you...to the other side...I thought you were gone."

Trembling with tears I reached out to hug my dear friend, then let her know my darkest fears. "I was worried I'd never see you again." I sniffed back tears. "I'm not ready to let you go. Not nearly ready to send my best friend off to be with my mum." Almost as an afterthought, I whispered into Sal's neck as I held her tight in my arms, "I'm not ready to be alone."

Pushing me back a little so she could look directly into my eyes, Sal declared with a hint of humour in her voice, "You're going to have to get a grip Ab. After all, I am the one who's dying here."

"Don't joke about this," I cried.

"Why not? Who said we have to be so serious all the time when we're dying? Who said one can't have a little fun, find the humour in life, even when life is coming to an end?"

"I'm not sure I can find the funny in this."

"That's ok," she winked. "I've got enough funny for the two of us."

"But how can you be like this? How can you not feel so...so ... ripped off?"

Sal let me cry a little and catch my breath, and spoke again when she felt I was ready to listen. "I've had a little time these past few days to think about a lot of things. To think about life and all that we make it up to be. There's really no guidelines for happiness, except that we must do what makes us happy. Who said we can't laugh when someone is dying?"

My eyes launched open, astonished.

"I don't mean laugh at the fact that someone is dying," Sal defended herself. "But why can't we see the funny side of life even when life is coming to an end?" Struggling to sit up to gain more of my attention, Sal pushed on. "I'm here. I've got cancer. That's where this road has taken me. I'm dying and there's not a thing I can do about it. It's too late for me. But Ab, anyone could walk out of their house and get hit by a bus, be in a car accident, have a heart attack." Sal leaned closer now as if instructing me to really take note and listen. "But it's the crap we dish up for ourselves, that's so crazy messed up."

I wiped the back of my hand over my tear-stained cheeks and looked up at Sal and frowned.

"Your passion in your marriage Ab, it's been dead so long, yet you've sat resigned in that knowledge. Your identity has been locked away without the key for more than a few years. The willingness to find the beauty in the everyday has been buried possibly for as long as your mother has been buried. You've grown that little bit bitter every single day since she died."

The truth stung, but I couldn't speak.

"For God's sake Abigail Steen...oh I mean... Montgomery...get some fire back into your lungs girl... some strength back into your bones. Find the will, the drive, the deepest need in your gut, to claw yourself up from that cave you've been hiding and just get out there, embrace life and have some fun."

I listened. Took it all in. Waited for more wisdom.

"Abby," Sal breathed softly, energy slowly leaving her body. "I now have the luxury of knowing exactly what you're missing out on."

Tears welled in my eyes. "I wish we had more time."

"We still do. So let's make damn sure it counts," she declared with a fire that would do her Scottish ancestors proud.

Resting her head all the way back on to the stiff hospital pillow, Sal let her eyes flutter closed. "But I've got to get out of this dreary ward. I mean seriously," she said, opening her eyes again. "Why they make hospitals so luck lustre is beyond me? People are dying in here.

The least these interior designers and architects could do," she said waving her hand in the direction of grey curtains, bleak white walls, and colourless shelves, "is... bestow a little colour on a dying girl. A quilted bedspread made of rich reds," she dreamed, allowing her eyes to fully close. "Dusty pinks and seaside blues wouldn't go astray in a place full of sick people."

After a moment catching her breath, Sal spoke again with a little more determination in her voice, "Prop me up...I've been thinking."

"Mmmm," I murmured in response.

"Look," she said in her no-nonsense tone. "There is no way I'm going to spend my dying days holed up in this dreary hospital. I'm morphed up to my eyeballs, can't feel a thing. Fine, give me a pill or two to ease the pain, but don't stop me feeling altogether," she roared. "I know I'm dying. Know the cancer's killing me. So just let me feel it."

"Ahhhh Sal...you've lost me?"

"I'm taking a vacation," Sal declared, resting back against the pillow and smiling in a way that reached her pretty blue eyes.

"What?"

"Not a cruise around the Riviera," she laughed. "Just a nice relaxing seaside escape." She reached unsteadily for her phone that sat on the plain white table beside her bed, passing it to me after she pulled up an image on Google.

I held her phone now and frowned. Neat little

cottages made of weatherboard, painted in all the shades of a pastel coloured rainbow, all lined in a row along a white sandy beach, came to life on the screen. Some with blue trims, others yellow, several green and a few in soft burnt orange. Pretty little picket fences ran along the rim of each house's garden where the soft white sandy beach merged with the front of each house.

"Picturesque isn't it?" Sal chimed.

"Gorgeous," I said, taking one final look at the images before handing the phone back to Sal.

"I'm spending my last dying days, weeks, months... who knows how long I've got...in one of those sweet little houses," she declared.

"What?" Concern washed over my face. "Who's going to take care of you?"

"Well...as much as I'd love it to be you old friend, you have three kids to look after...but more importantly...you have you to look after." Leaning in closer, Sal revealed what had clearly been bubbling in her mind for some time. "I want you to find your happy honey. That's more important than taking care of a dying friend."

"Oh Sal," I sniffed back more tears. "How can anything be more important than that?"

"Because," she said wincing as she tried to gather the strength to sit up a little straighter. "None of us know... not really...just how long we've got."

"But how will you take care of yourself? You can barely sit up straight on your own at the moment," I said fussing with Sal's pillows.

"I'm no fool," she laughed. "Why I'll have someone doting on my every need of course! What a way for a girl to go huh!" She gaggled.

"You're crazy," I declared, smiling for the first time in an hour.

"Not crazy. Just doing the most sensible thing I've done in ages. I've got enough savings for this. I'll put my home on the market and use the Super, health insurance and savings and anything else I have stashed away. I've got plenty of cash really. It's just time that I don't have a lot of," she choked on her last words.

"Oh Sal," I soothed, leaning closer, unable to hold back the pain in my heart. "I'm sad."

"I'm sad too," she declared. "But if I sit here feeling ripped off about it all, I'll waste the time I have left. I've lived Ab, I truly have. Married twice. Some people go through their entire life never having got a divorce, but look at me...I've had two of them!" she chuckled.

"Overachiever," I threw back at her and laughed.

"Damn straight," she cackled.

"Ab, I've had the beauty of being godmother to your three gorgeous children. Aunty Sal to all your kids, as well as my brother and sister's kids too. Sure they live overseas, but I've still had joy in all of that. Joy during the Christmas holiday visits I've had with them, flying into Toronto and London. I may not have had kids of my own, but I've had kids in gorgeous destinations throughout the world to travel to, be with, and love."

"This is all so big. What are you going to tell them?"

I choked on my words.

"The truth honey. But give me a week or two to find my way, settle in a little to my new digs. Then, I'll release the press release to the masses."

"Aren't you going to tell them now?"

"I need to do it this way...for me. Need to be a little bit with my own thoughts before I can be with everyone else's. I mean look at you...you're a blubbering mess. It's exhausting watching you."

"Oh God, I'm so selfish."

"No you're not," she said, squeezing my fingers. "You're just being you. Expressing exactly how you feel, and you should. It's just that it kinda hurts too. Seeing you in pain. But then I can see when you're trying to be stoic too. All of it is perfectly ok. I want you to be all of that," she said, squeezing my fingers again. I just need a little time for me," she revealed, curling to get a little more comfortable on the bed.

"How far away are these cottages?" I asked, picking up her phone to take another look."

"Two hours south of Sydney."

"What! When am I going to see you?"

"It's not that far," Sal mumbled.

"Do you really need to be that far away?"

"Yes."

"Surely there's somewhere close by?"

"I want to be there," Sal said, her eyes fluttering closed and open. "You'll come and visit...and take a weekend or two, without the kids. You need it and Ed needs it too. You'll bring the kids with you sometimes as well."

Urgency reached my voice. "We'll talk on the phone still?"

"Of course but Ab, I'm getting on with my life and I want you to do the same. I'm getting on with the business of dying and I want to find joy in that. I want to fill myself up with all the memories of being alive. I want to find happiness in the everyday. Find joy in the birds that chirp for God's sake. I want to find joy in watching the waves roll in, then roll out, all over again. I want to watch and wander in it all." Sal let out a big sigh as she sunk deeper into the pillow. Her eyelids fully closed now as she breathed deeply. "I've begun the arrangements already. Come back and see me tomorrow old friend."

I sat and watched Sal's chest rise and fall as she drifted off to sleep.

After sitting in the quiet of my car outside my house for what seemed like hours, I mustered up the energy to step back into the motherload of my life.

I noticed the light from the fire flickering brightly when I reached the living room. Ed was sitting in the dark on the sofa, a glass of red wine in his hand. I stood on the fringe of the living room, slowly inching further into the space. The embers of the fire sparkled, throwing a surge of light through the room now.

My eyes turned to Ed's. I whispered his name.

"I know," he said, letting his eyes softly close.

I stood rigid in the spot, unsure of what to do.

"Is this where we truly are?" he whispered, eyes still closed, with what sounded like a choke in his throat.

I looked down at his hands. The letter was resting on his lap.

"You read it?" I said, easing into the room a little.

"So, this, is it?" he said, sipping his wine, his deep blue eyes lost in the fire.

"I don't know what to say Ed." Tears stung my eyes. The pain shot right though my heart.

"I think you've said exactly what you wanted to say," he said clenching the crumbled letter tightly in his closed fist. Exhaling a deep, dark sigh, he tilted his head to look up at me, and stared silently for what felt like minutes. I stood rooted to the spot, fear crippling me from saying or doing anything I might regret.

"Sit down with me a minute Ab," he said, patting the sofa cushion beside him.

An unwelcome fear travelled through body. I opened my mouth to speak but couldn't release the words.

"Ab. Sit down," he said more forcefully. "We need to talk. There's never time for you and me to do this. The kids are asleep. It's got to be now."

Reaching for the half empty bottle of red wine that sat upright on the Persian rug, he held it up to me with a half-smile. "May as well grab yourself a glass."

When I returned with an unfilled glass in my hand, I trembled as I sat to Ed's left on the sofa. He slowly turned toward me, holding his quiet gaze while steadily filling me with wine. "How's Sal?" he finally asked.

Careful not to touch his hand, I noted the rhythm of my breath had increased and become unsteady. "She's dying," I said, choking back on my words.

He reached out to squeeze the free hand in my lap and began softly stroking my hand with his thumb. Instincts it would seem, told my husband, the man who had been my lover, my companion, for so many years, to comfort and protect me. He continued resting his hand on mine and silently held my gaze. The light of the fire framed his face in the glow.

"This er...cancer," he began, "It's big?"

"Bigger than big," I said, releasing my hand from his to reach out for my glass and sip the warm, welcoming wine, two hands holding tight. Resting my glass in my lap eventually and balancing it with my fingertips, I let my head fall back against the sofa. My turn now to gaze silently at the flickering flames.

We sat for some time in the stillness of the night; unspoken words filled the tension in the air. But for tonight, we were content to listen to our breath, the rise and fall of our bellies rhythmically tuning in with one another.

Ed broke the silence first, shifting in his seat to turn his body toward me, one leg bent slightly and resting on the sofa. He placed an outstretched arm behind my head and began gently stroking my hair. I sucked in my breath and held onto it tight. It's been a while since Ed touched me like this. The hairs on my neck stood to attention with the anticipation of what might happen next.

He allowed his fingers to rest lightly against the back

of my neck now and began slow, soft strokes in feather light touches that lifted up and then all the way down my tingling skin. My blood rushed up to my cheeks and a burning fire stirred deep inside my belly. He shifted his body once more, turning further around to face me fully. Ed's fingertips curled through my hair as the breath of his exhale reached my neck. I tensed my knees tightly together and stared uneasily at the fire. I didn't want to move, too afraid to turn to meet his gaze for fear the desire he was suggesting he had for me right now might also be somewhere deep inside me too. He breathed out once more, the rush whooshing toward my lips. My body melted a little. Control slowly slipped from my mind.

What's happening? Why is my husband turned on suddenly? And...why is he trying to turn me on?

Shaking it off, I wanted to find my composure. I began gulping more wine, only to find my senses heighten as the tantalising tannins slowly made their way down my throat. Senses further sharpened as my husband's hand fed hungrily on my neck. I needed to regain self-control, so I fixated on the sensation in my throat from the wine rather than the sensations in every other part of my body.

His words spoke with the same longing that was running through me. "It's been a while Ab."

Ohhh … wow! I let a rush of air leave my lips as more wine touched my mouth.

"It's been a while since we did this," his words lingered. "Sat together, relaxing by the fire...the kids out of the picture."

He shifted again and began kneading my neck in a

way that said I want you...and now! Oh...please don't touch me like that. It feels too good.

I pressed my lips firmly together after taking another deep mouthful of wine. In fear of the anticipation of what he might do next, I stayed firmly fixed on the fire, body rigid yet so deeply aroused, as Ed stroked the fabric on the sofa that rested behind my head, lightly, ever so lightly surprising me, delighting me, each time he touched my skin.

Oh, how I had longed for this for so long Ed. Longed for my husband to want me. Longed for you to want to sit in this intimate space that exists between man and woman. Breathing together, talking together, touching together, loving together.

He shifted a little more and moved even closer. I contracted every muscle I had and held my breath. I felt like a teenager all over again. He turned to move closer to my mouth. Oh dear God. I remained fixed on the fire, Ed's familiar scent wafting through me, desire in his eyes matching my own. I stayed rooted to the spot in fear that if I looked into his eyes, I would cave and let him take me here and now, on the sofa. I knew if I turned, his mouth would be on mine and from there; there would be no return.

"I don't know how we got here Ab?" he whispered. "But I do know what I remember." Oh God. My breasts tingled, and I grew wet at the hope of what was to come. I sipped...no gulped, more wine.

"I remember this girl, this bubbly young woman with thick luscious sand coloured hair." He brushed his fingers ever so gently over my hair now. Oh, that feels so good. "She tamed it with her straightening iron but I loved it most when it was all messed up. Her messy morning maze of hair that shimmered in the morning light from our love making till all hours the night before. Those large, wide wavy curls," he soothed, taking bigger clumps of my hair now in his hand, slowly easing my head back further as if he might soon take my mouth.

"She tried to tame that gorgeous golden hair," he chuckled deeply. "I loved it though," he stroked my neck softly, "When she let herself get ruffled up. Touching my ear lobes, he began stroking them ever so softly. Oh dear God. "Forgetting to put her earrings on for work that day," he mused, "after a session of hot sex before breakfast."

Stroking my shoulder, he let his fingers run down my arm, with the soft touch of one finger that felt like the power of ten. Please take me now.

"I loved her sexy text messages," he soothed, a smile tickling his throat. "At any time night or day. I'd be in a meeting with a client and she'd pop up on my phone. "Not wearing panties today," she'd say. "Want to grab a bite at lunch?"

His finger moved around to my throat, teasing my skin with his touch. He was careful as he moved lower down my body to stop his feather light touch to rest just above the crease of my breast. "I really did love it when you remembered not to wear underwear." Oh, dear God Ed, this is driving me crazy. My eyelids fluttered closed as his finger ran along the line above my breast. Where has this man been hiding for the past five years?

Reaching back up to caress and knead my neck, his hand fully taking hold. "I miss that girl, that woman I once touched like this," his voice wistful as if drifting into the open space.

I shifted in my seat now, the tension, the aching need for this man's touch had overcome me. Caught between wanting so desperately to be taken on the sofa by the man that sat beside me, yet knowing that one night of hot sex would not bring back the love lost in our relationship.

Taking a breath to sip my wine, I let go a little as Ed's sensual kneading of my neck began to relax me even further. I allowed my eyes to fix on the fire as my thoughts drifted back. I'd poured my love into the kids. He did too, I do know that. Yet when he felt left out...or unwanted perhaps...his instincts were to turn outwards. I could see that now. Understand what our pattern had become. His clients. His friends. His kayaking. His activities. All his energy and time had twisted outward.

"Did I do this?" I whispered the words to myself...yet somehow let them slip out loud.

"Do what?" he replied, curling my hair between his fingers and tugging me gently a little closer to him.

"Did I get us here? Did I get so caught up in the overload of motherhood, that I forgot to love you back... forgot to touch you?"

His hand stopped the caress to rest on the sofa behind my neck as if to gather his thoughts. He didn't speak. Just sat quietly while I waited for the response. "I'm not sure which one of us rejected the other first," he eventually said with a sigh, reaching for his wine. "We both got ourselves here Ab. The wrongdoing is not so much who started it but the fact that we never stopped." Shifting in his seat to turn his attention more fully to the fire, his hands did not touch me now as he prepared to speak. "Circumstances didn't separate us, we did. Our kids didn't take our time away from the two of us spending time together, we did.

I clung to his words to let their meaning rest fully on my heart and stay with my mind. Unclear of what to do next, Ed challenged us to go further. "Abby look at me," he urged.

Afraid my desires would lead my actions, I stiffened uncomfortably in my seat.

"Look at me Ab," he willed me, grabbing my arm to turn me toward him.

I turned in hesitation, not fully shifting my body. Preparing myself for an escape.

He held my gaze and said nothing with his mouth, yet so much more with his eyes.

"I wish I could read your mind right now," I whispered.

"You don't spend fifteen years with someone and not know what they're thinking," he replied, deepening his dark blue gaze at me. "More importantly," he added, "what they're feeling."

He was challenging me like he used to when we first became lovers. I would often plead for him to reveal his thoughts to me, yet his response remained fixed. "If you need me to tell you what I'm thinking, then you're not looking close enough. Look deeper," he would urge when we first began falling in love and I was insecure of his feelings...and of my own.

Was he challenging me now? I really didn't know if I had the energy to pursue all this depth. It's been a long five years this motherhood thing, with a challenging marriage and a heaviness that sat deep in the pit of my heart daily. I'm not sure I could go there anymore, to that place so deep that was only the space that two lovers shared.

"Do you love me?" he wondered out loud.

My eyes flashed open suddenly and shifted over to his.

"Your letter," he said, looking down at it briefly and back to gaze intently into my eyes. "You said you were sorry but you didn't mention you love me." Oh Ed. "Are you separating from this marriage because you don't love me anymore or because you have separated yourself from what it means to be married?"

I frowned. Ed had always challenged me. Knew how to get me to go deeper than surface deep. I'm suddenly remembering that quality in him now.

Holding the letter up to me he spoke gently, a love that touched his lips. "Ab, you haven't revealed yourself so intimately to me for quite some time as you have in this letter. You say you want to end it, that you can't see any other way. But is it the marriage you want to end or the feeling of being lost in the marriage?"

Oh no, he was doing it again. Challenging me to go deeper. To a place locked away in my heart.

He leaned forward to rest his wine glass on the rug at his feet then shifted a little closer. Oh no...what's he doing now?

"Easy Ab," he said reading my thoughts. "I'm just topping up your wine." I held the glass firmly with both hands, enjoying the red stained taste that lingered on my lips.

"If we end it, we end it," he said with a practicality in his tone. "I'm just wondering though, if that's the direction you want to take?"

I stared silently gazing at the fire, too afraid to speak.

Resting his arm easily on the sofa behind my neck and sipping wine from the other hand, he fell into a comfortable rhythm revealing his thoughts. "I love the way you cook poached eggs."

I flashed my eyes at him, confusion written all over my face.

Deadpan, he continued. "I love the way you throw your hair about like an untamed wild woman, ferociously trying to dry it and tame it with the hair dryer in several short minutes that only a woman with three small children would have the time to allow."

I turned to hear his thoughts, staring open mouthed in silence.

"I love how you tie a knot in your summer dresses in the hope they won't get wet when you pick shells on the beach with the kids, only to wind up fully drenched anyway." The lips of his mouth began to curve. "I love how you try to salvage a burnt-to-the-crisp base of chocolate cake the kids have tried to make without your assistance and only their dad to guide them.

I love that you haven't mastered the technology in this house and simply cannot get the Wi-Fi working when it goes down."

My nostrils began to flare. His smile widened further. "But I love that you try all the same."

"I love that when the kids are sick, you devote yourself to welling them better by setting up camp on their bedroom floor. Being available at a moment's notice to attend to their every need should they wake in pain, fear or delusional from a fever."

My breathing grew rapid. I'm not sure when it began. What is he doing? Did it start with the poached eggs or when I first sat down on the sofa and he began caressing my neck?

I suddenly realised the woman sitting beside this man for the past hour or so was the woman behind the veil of motherhood. The woman who longed to be touched by her lover, the woman who longed to hear what brought that lover to his knees. The woman who made his lips curl up into a smile. The woman who made him feel things so deeply that no other woman could possibly touch in this lifetime.

Tears threatened my eyes. Please don't let me cry, I self-talked with all the strength I could fathom.

"I love it when you leave my dinner warming in the

slow cooker, even though I've been a total prick and stayed out too late, ashamed of my own failure as a man."

My mouth agape, no words came out. Why was he saying all of this to me?

"Ab, I think there's an unchartered path yet for you and I to explore. That's the path of two people. Man who loves woman."

I couldn't help the tears anymore. They slowly began to stream down my face.

"Man who wants to learn what it means to be married."

The tears were well on their way to winning an award. He spoke fully to me, without flinching. "Ab. I'm not going to deny that path...that new road to explore...is not going to be unchartered territory for both of us. I'm not going to deny that I won't fumble or stuff up along the way."

I trembled as I stared frigid at the fire.

"Come on Abby, give me a break," he pleaded. "Will you please look at me!" He grabbed at my wrist and yanked it to command my attention. Seeing my swollen eyes now, compassion filled his own. "Oh babe, I'm sorry too. I'm sorry we got here," he said tucking a stray hair behind my ear. "I'm sorry I don't even know how it happened. But I don't even care."

My nostrils flared. I opened my mouth to speak.

"I didn't put that right. "Let me try again," he whispered gently.

"It's not that I don't care about you, about us. It's just that I'm beyond caring what went wrong. Who did what, who brought what shitty piece of baggage, or a whole collection of luggage into this relationship. All I know is, that I care about moving forward. I care about your happiness. Care about mine, and care about those three incredible kids of ours. Care that we somehow forgot to have fun. We have been so overloaded and trapped in the task of parenthood, we forgot to lose time with our family and find ourselves in the process."

I roughly scuffed the back of hand against my nose, now dripping snot as tears streamed down my face.

"I had fun with them today," I exhaled, finally relaxing for the first time since sitting in this space with Ed.

"You did?" his lips turned into a soft curl.

"I did," I smiled. "I took them to Kiddie Land. You know that place where all the fun happens indoors?"

A quiet confidence began to grow as I sat by the fire... sharing my day...sharing myself with my husband. It had been so long since I'd done this. "They loved every minute of it. I did too."

He smiled, shifted to relax and ease off a little and take another long sip of his wine.

Cautiously raising my eyes to meet his now I shared myself some more. "I wrote your letter there today. You know Ed, I hadn't even realised that I don't give myself any space. Space to breathe, space to think, space to process whatever it is I am feeling on any given day. I feel like I've been running from one thing to the next for five years. Afraid if I don't stay with the 'always got to be in control, firing on all cylinders' momentum I've set for myself, that I might just fall apart. Isn't that stupid? Without pausing for a response, I stayed on my roll. "But in trying not to fall apart, staying vigilant with the task of motherhood, not addressing my marriage problems, our marriage problems, I was quietly falling apart. I was slowly becoming unravelled. Yet in the fight to do exactly what I did not want to do, create that separated and strained marriage of my parents, of my father not appreciating my mother, I went ahead and blindly did it anyway."

Allowing my mint green eyes to find trust in Ed's, I purged. "The reason I wrote about letting go and moving on is that I don't know how to be any different. I don't know how not to be the person I don't want to be. I don't know how to be the woman, the mother, the lover, the wife, the friend, and still somewhere in all of that, know what it is that I want to give to me. I don't know who that woman is. But I know that trying to find that out while my life is falling apart around me is going to finish me. Ed it's drowning me," I wept now.

His eyes ached when I spoke, but he didn't speak. His deep blue eyes held my own. I took in his beautiful face, rugged and manly, framed in deep brown waves like that of my two darling boys.

"I'm drowning Ed," I pleaded, tears overflowing.

He reached out and held my hand. "Ab, I'm dying here too." He stroked his thumb over the soft pad of my hand as he revealed his own heart to mine. "Dying to love the woman in front of me that blessed me with three amazing children. Dying to love the woman that took my hand in marriage and made me her own. Dying to love the lover who once reached for me in her sleep without knowing she was reaching. Dying to fight my way back through these murky unchartered waters we have travelled for so long. Ab, I am dying to find my way back to you."

I wiped the tears from my cheeks, as I hung on Ed's every word. I let my head fall back against his arm on the sofa, cradled in the fold of his chest. I rested my eyes on the fire and let my eyes flutter closed more than once. I was tired. Drained. Devoid of any knowledge to figure this whole thing out.

We sat a while longer, I lost track of time. Ed's fingers clutching my own, listening to the hum of the fire that had slowly turned to embers.

I broke the silence first, a whisper leaving my lips. "I need sleep Ed."

He squeezed my fingers tightly, then released them to lay limp on their own, resting on the quiet comfort of the sofa. "Go to bed Ab," he urged. "I'm going to throw some more wood on the fire and sit here a while."

"Sure?" I whispered.

"Yeah," he smiled.

"Ok good night," I whispered to stand and turned my eyes in soulful search of his.

"Good night," he whispered back.

CHAPTER 17

The next morning, I woke to a whole lot of noise in the kitchen. Alarmed, I jumped from the bed, threw on my slippers and dressing gown, fastening it tightly at the waist as I raced out of my bedroom. I ran downstairs, only to find three kids perched in their respective high chairs and stools, giggling at their father who was shouting loudly to be heard.

"What's this?" I asked, a little confused, rubbing the sleep from my eyes. Ed glanced sideways at me then returned to the task at hand, turning out soggy poached eggs onto burnt toast on the plates of three eager and hungry mouths.

Brady was the first to dip his toast in for the tasting. "Not as good as Mummy's," he declared with his brutally honest food critic hat on.

"I'm sure," Ed smiled, taking another sideways glance at me. Was that vulnerability I detected in his eyes?

"Not as good as Mummy's eggs Daddy," Emily revealed then shrugged, "But thanks for trying."

I had to laugh at the fierce honesty of a child.

"I'll keep trying to do better," Ed said to the kids, but looked directly at me. Was he talking about the eggs or us?

"Ok, now Mummy's up, Daddy better get a move on." He smiled and handed me the slotted spoon.

"Sorry," I said, reaching out to take freshly squeezed orange juice from the jug in his hand. "I didn't mean to oversleep."

"You needed it."

"Er...sure...thanks." I faltered. Was this Ed's way of making a fresh start?

Ed tickled each of our three children's tummies before planting soft wet goodbye kisses on their cheeks while they giggled. He walked toward me now, and stepped into the space that held my breath. As if catching himself on autopilot, he sidestepped me to reach to the bench beside the sink for a cold piece of vegemite toast.

"Don't fix dinner," he called out from the hallway, passing to turn and speak before he left. "I'll take the kids out for sushi when I get home from work, so you can go and see Sal."

"I love sushi," Emily yelled out.

"I hate sushi," Brady moaned. "Can't we have pizza?"

Ed laughed. I had to laugh too. Glancing back at me, he added before he left, "I'll be home by 6:00pm."

I stood in the kitchen, rooted to the spot, drifting my thoughts to the man who just left my home. Where has this man been hiding? Is this what it had to take to get him to reappear? The threat of me leaving? Or was it the fact that I let my guard down? Let him know my inner most thoughts through that letter?

I found myself hours later that day in exactly the same

spot when Ed returned home. "I'm home," he called out as the front door opened. I looked at my beloved French provincial clock...5:55pm. Five minutes early spoke volumes.

The kids were all rugged up in their hats, coats and gloves to venture out in the cool night air that clung to the end of winter, for a feast of sushi, pizza or who knows what.

"They're all ready," I said with a small smile, a hint of caution forming on my lips.

"Great," he replied casually, stepping toward me, then turning to get down on his knees so all three kids could crash tackle him on the black and white tiled kitchen floor.

Dumping his laptop bag on the kitchen bench, he directed the kids to the door.

"Bye Mummy," Emily reached out. "Have fun with Aunty Sal."

"I will darling," I replied, leaning into her soft warm cheeks for a cuddle as I rested up against the front door.

I kissed Brady and Harry goodbye and held a little distance between Ed and I, unsure where this was all going. He was definitely making some changes since 'the letter', but could I really be sure he wouldn't change back? How could I know that he wouldn't run off in his carefree, no commitment manner, at any given moment?

Trust...that's what was truly lacking here I realised. I didn't trust Ed anymore. I was still trying to work out if I loved him. But without trust there is no love. I'm not sure I could go back to trusting him again. But then there is that new path he mentioned that we should try creating together...maybe a big part of that is trust.

Later, as I reached into my handbag and fumbled for my car keys, I found myself taking out my notebook instead. I opened to a new blank page and marked it with five big bold letters. T R U S T. Somehow, I knew I had to find it. Find a way to live with that again if I was to ever love Ed, and want to stay in this marriage.

Later, I peeked my head in to Sal's hospital room, wanting to make less fuss and noise than I did last time. I clutched a posy of sweet peas tightly in my hand I'd picked up on the way in at the hospital florist. I didn't go in at first, just stood in the doorway and watched. Looked at my friend and wondered how much time she had left.

It seemed ironic that I was finally finding my voice, letting the woman inside me roar out. The unclaimed woman who had been locked up for so long, who was yet to share herself with her best friend. Ironic, that I shared so much of myself but left out the best part.

I breathed her in a little longer. She looked frail, vulnerable. That life and fire inside her that came out to play at any given time of the day, was not in her eyes or her body that lay so very limp.

She would have made a fantastic mum. It seemed criminal she was denied that honour.

"Can I help you?" a voice spoke from behind jolting me from my trance.

I banged my elbow on the doorway. "Ouch."

"Are you going in?" the nurse enquired stiffly.

"Ah...I just wanted to check first...see if my friend is up to having visitors."

The stern nurse with a pouting mouth, framed with very fine lines, allowed her eyes to drift into the room before glaring back at my own. "Which one is your friend?"

"Sally Douglas," I whispered.

The nurse poked her head in the room with the efficiency and speed of experience then returned to glare into my eyes. "She looks perfectly fine to receive visitors." Glancing at her watch, she huffed, "But you better get on with it. Visiting hours will be over in fifty two minutes."

"Ok. Thank you," I said, walking toward Sal and muttering quietly to myself about the, "biddy old cow."

"Taken to talking to yourself now have you?" Sal chuckled.

"Oh, that stupid old witch of a nurse out there," I fumed in autopilot. But then I stopped mid-sentence, realising all this hot air was pointless. Here I was with my best girlfriend, cancer crawling up and down and around her body, and I wanted to use my fifty two minutes sharing useless crap about some nurse having a bad day.

"Forget it," I said, handing Sal her flowers. "How are you feeling?" I asked, finding the courage to smile, even though the image before me told me Sal was not looking good.

"Well, the meds help," she said flatly. "But these bleak grey walls, drab furnishings and curtains are killing me. I'm dying here for fuck's sake."

My eyes flashed open wide. "Don't joke."

"Ab, there is no way I'm going to sit here feeling sorry for myself. I just won't. And if I can't make bad jokes about dying, then who can?" she said.

Patting the bed to motion me to sit down, she reminded me that none of us knew how much time we had. "All we know is we gotta make the most of it," she added then ordered me to put her flowers in a plastic yellow water pitcher that looked as dull as the drapes. "Sit down and tell me the latest," she smiled.

Propping up Sal's pillows and noting that we now had a total forty six minutes left together before Nurse No Friends would come back to haul me out of here, I exhaled.

I revealed every single intimate and intricate detail of the letter, Ed's reaction to it, the first stirrings of starting something by the fire, and how things were at home right now. I shared my own realisation too, that I was in grave need of changes. Needed to create my own fresh path for me, just me.

Sal listened intently, expressing her wonder, surprise and happiness through a combination of raised eyebrows, popped out eyes and cheeky smiles.

I realised how exhausted I was from the download and laying it all out in the open, and taking the time to observe it for myself. To really see my situation from a distance, I realised how cathartic and draining it was to purge.

I looked down at my watch. Damn. Eleven minutes till Nurse No Friends would hunt me down.

"Ab," Sal whispered, leaning forward as if she had a share a secret. "I think our little girl is growing up."

"Huh?" I replied, screwing up my nose the way I always did when I couldn't make sense of something.

"Ab, I think your mum dying when you were just at the beginning stages of womanhood stunted you. You were so afraid to grow up into the woman that you were meant to be because you were afraid that you might die young just like your mum." Waving a hand over her body she added, "And ironically, it seems, like me.

"But did you realise there was a part of you, a huge part inside that you forgot to nurture and love like that of your own children. Don't be so afraid of death Abby that the living you are doing sucks the life out of you anyway."

Moments ticked by. "I've been such a fool. Why have I wasted so much time missing out on all the things I truly wanted?"

"There's still time. There's always time," Sal soothed.

"But I'm already 42!"

"It doesn't have to take a long time to work out how you truly want to live life. Work out what really makes you happy. It's just about making the time to let yourself shine...finding things every day that brings a smile to your lips, warms your heart and gives you the courage to try."

"One-minute till lights out," snapped Nurse No Friends, from the doorway.

"Damn woman," I groaned. Can't she see I'm having the most enlightening conversation of my life! I wanted to shout and scream out loud.

Sal squeezed my hand and smiled. "I leave tomorrow for the coast. Come visit me in a couple of weeks once I'm all set up."

"Oh Sal."

"Visiting hours are over," Nurse No Friends glared, standing with her hands on her hips, hovering over me like a hurricane about to let loose on all the strays on the ward.

I growled. Sal laughed. "See you in a couple of weeks. Now give us a hug and be off with you before Nurse No Friends here (the nurse let her mouth drop open) drags you out by your ponytail."

I burst out laughing and squeezed my best friend tight like it might be our last time we were together. Holding back the tears, I kissed her cheek and turned my head away trying to stay strong, despite my crushing heart.

I sat in the quiet of the car, key unturned in the ignition. I wasn't ready to go home. The kids would already be in bed but Ed...he would still be up, seeing as our new arrangement had him sleeping on the sofa.

I didn't want to talk tonight. Not about us anyway. To be honest, this whole breakdown of our relationship was exhausting. Every spare second I had in the day had been consumed with going over and over in my head all the things I loathed about Ed. Loathed about our relationship.

It seemed Ed finally wanted to work on us. Improve us. Focus on us. Fix Us. But all I wanted to do was work on me. Improve me. Focus on me. Fix me.

"It's broken Ed," I found myself saying out loud in the quiet of my car. "But first, I need to mend me."

I texted him, telling him not to wait up. Told him I would be late and just wanted to fall into bed when I got home. Said I was drained from seeing Sal and just needed a good night's rest. In part that was true, but not the whole truth. I couldn't face him. Too much of a coward right now to say I needed a break just for me. That I knew no amount of hand holding, wine sipping by the fire, stroking of my skin or my soul, was going to change any of that right now.

CHAPTER 18

The next day, Ed greeted the kids and I with a great big smile at breakfast, fresh from showering and dressing for the workday. I was too afraid to look up into his eyes in fear of him reading my thoughts. Sensing my distance, he focussed on the kids while making light conversation with me.

He glanced at me later, willed me to look at him before he spoke. "I've ah...I've got to go away for a few days," he winced.

I breathed a sigh of relief. Grateful for some distance... some space. "Sure ok," I replied casually, smothering Harry's toast with avocado on top of vegemite.

"Sorry," he stumbled, "I mean...I know we are trying to er," hesitating, he looked at the kids and caught Brady listening in, and although he was only five, that young mind would surely know more than he needed to if we kept talking openly the way we were about to.

"It's all good Ed," I said simply. Looking at the kids now, I added, "We understand." Pouring orange juice into Harry's Wiggles cup that had a handle on both sides, I added. "I'll call Greta and reschedule."

Ed winced before adding, "And...er...I've got another kayaking weekend coming up...it's the evening of the same day I get back."

Looking at Ed's face, I could see the guy was torn.

Knowing that he needed to make some real changes right now if he wanted to salvage his marriage but trapped by his own situation. A career that took him away on a regular basis and forced him to late nights, entertaining clients. And the one downtime he truly enjoyed, took him away for hours at a time, to hang out with his mates, a long way from his family. Time away from all the responsibilities of his own load, he too was carrying. A time-consuming hobby mind you! Took the best part of the day...half a day at the very least. Then there were the monthly retreats of course, where all the men would get together and challenge themselves to the bitter end. Signing over their lives to death waivers, stating that if they died in the hands of nature or misfortune, that the event organisers would not be liable for the limbs that became dismembered or the lives lost that were no longer able to return to their families.

As I watched Ed hold his breath, anticipating my reaction, I wondered why I had chosen a man, a partner for my life, not unlike that of my own father? A man who found a million other reasons, not to be with his wife, not to be with his kids. But for now...just now...it seemed that my man was truly trying.

"Don't worry about it Ed," I shrugged. "It'll all still be here when you get back."

I watched him hug the children goodbye, laptop bag and overnighter in his hand. He seemed to squeeze them tighter than usual, much like I did with Sal last night. He kissed me neatly on the cheek, more for the kids benefit I'm sure than anything. But then he lingered longer to rub his cheek gently against my own. His breath whispered in my ear before wrenching himself away. I briefly looked into his eyes that revealed so much, and wondered if I might be looking into a mirror for my own.

It was Emily that broke the space we held. She had knocked juice all over the table. "Sorry Mummy, I didn't mean it."

"Don't worry darling," I soothed, dashing to grab anything on the table that remotely resembled a cloth.

Ed reached for a dishcloth in the sink and dived at the juice that was about to drip to the floor. I covered his hand with my own, rested it there before letting him know I had it covered.

The next couple of days went down pretty well in motherload land. I had found a way to get a little more organised with my time and with the kids' time as well.

While Harry and Emily had their daytime sleep, I set Brady up with his own personal headphone system and portable DVD, all tucked up tightly under the doona on my bed. "A special treat," I told him, and was glad to rid the guilt I had put on myself of no television before Play School.

I decided to claim this middle of the day rest time for me, to not clean the house, not put on another load of washing and most certainly not catch up on Facebook, glimpsing into other people's lives, rather than spend time glimpsing into my own.

I used the time to download my thoughts in Greta's notebook that had firmly become my own. Legs tucked underneath me on the daybed that sat out in our backyard garden random thoughts and feelings poured out. I let the words stir and release onto the page, unedited and unjustified. Completely pouring out every fibre of my body, heart and mind, and revealing my deepest soul.

I hadn't kept a journal since I was a teenager. It really did help me back then. Confused thoughts of boys, hormones racing around, wondering what part of myself to give or not give. Misunderstandings with fickle girlfriends, one day besties, next day not, walking straight passed each other in the schoolyard.

Yet it was my journal back then that had been my very best friend, helping me find comfort in those lost and often lonely days. As a single child, I had found comfort in the unturned pages of my journal. And now almost 30 years on, it seemed I was finding my way back to my friend that once was, that beautiful pouring of my heart and how it aches, unravelling itself over blank pages.

With my thoughts expunged, I began doodling on the page, drawing an image of a naked woman standing high on a rock. Her long brown, sun kissed wavy hair reached all the way down her back, as she looked out to sea. I doodled some more, sketched a little, shaded too, until a perfectly formed drawing stared up at me from the page. I sat and gazed, wondering who this sketch of a woman now was, turning her head up toward me from the page.

"What are you waiting for Abigail?" I imagined her calling out to me, as if her hands were cupped to frame her mouth and echo her words from a distance.

I frowned and screwed up my nose to the sketch of a

woman in front of my eyes.

Sensing my confusion, she called out louder. "Embrace the artist within."

"Artist?"

She threw back her long mane, tossing it over her shoulder to dangle down her back, then looked straight out to sea, no longer staring at me. "Well I certainly didn't sketch this illustration of me," she chuckled, then leapt from the rock and dived deep through the water.

I imagined the image of a sketched naked woman, wild, untamed hair, wet and swimming in the ocean. Stroking effortlessly to the other side to swim to dry land, before heaving herself up onto a great big black rock.

"Let your art," she called out louder, "lead you to that place you have locked inside yourself and thrown away the key. "Let it take you to places deep within you are yet to explore, and...let out. Let your art touch parts of you that no man, no child, no other living soul can touch. Explore that part of you dear Abigail, that deep dark tunnel of the unknown. Let it lead you on unchartered waters. Let it lead you to your home, your heart."

I frantically flicked the pages of my notebook as if someone had hidden an entire story in it, comic strip style, without me noticing.

Exhaling, I looked back at the drawing once more, my original forming back on the page. The sketch of a naked woman, hair untamed, sitting silently on a rock looking out to sea.

I let my memory drift back to my school days, and recollected with fondness the art classes I took during and after school. A weekend workshop here. A semester at the local community college there. Remembered how much I loved art when I was growing up and all the way through my teens. Remembered how much I loved to lose time, sketching my heart onto the page. What made me stop I wondered? Then I wondered what made me never start. Wondered why when I left school, I left my art behind as if it held no meaning. I went headfirst into university, the intention of having the studies of Business, under my belt and the value I had somehow placed on majoring in Marketing and Finance.

Why did I do that when all I really wanted to do was paint? All I really wanted to do was lose time, travel the world, and set myself up in unknown places, quiet pockets of nature to sketch, draw and paint. How did I end up here? End up on a path so foreign to my heart but stable and reliable in the eyes of the laws of living. A practised life. A reliable life. A known life. But who could I rely on? My mother was dead. My best friend would soon join her. My marriage was falling apart, had fallen apart. I'd failed at being the mother I once dreamed I would be. Yet somewhere in all of this, I had lost me.

Dad used to plot at the dinner table I remember that now. Plot against my art. "Have something to fall back on," he would say. "The art you can always do...but the academic study you can and must, do now," he would demand." Once you have a family, a life of your own, you'll never have the time to go back to your studies but you can always find time for a little art."

I'd listened faithfully to my father. I have no idea why. I could so often see through the cracks of my parents' marriage long before either would have the courage to reveal them to me. The cracks that said they hadn't chosen wisely, chosen the wrong life partner in each other. But he was my father, and I relied on his word. What he said to me growing up meant something to me. But now I wondered with him so absent from my life, why I still let those words hold so tight.

An idea struck me. I grabbed my phone and texted Sal. "Thinking of you and...thinking of taking an art class. Thoughts?"

She texted straight back as if she had been sitting on her phone. "Stop thinking. Start living!"

I had to laugh. Sal always knew how to put me in my place.

Using my phone, I Googled local art classes in my area...then...after a frustrating number of detours, that directed me to art classes in some quaint town in the United States of America, I finally found something just 15 minutes from home. A five-session art class in Clovelly, every week on Tuesdays from 6:30pm - 8.30pm. And...it started next week. On no...Tuesday night is couples counselling...already thinking of putting me before us.

My phone beeped. It was Sal. "Make no mistake girlfriend. The time is now!"

Smiling and knowing that Sal often knew what was

better for me than I did, I dialled the number listed for the art class. Spoke to a woman named Monique who told me I had just taken one of the last two spots. Hadn't consulted Ed for his permission, approval or input and realised in that moment that somehow, I had been living parallel universes. I spent my childhood constantly seeking the approval of my father, permission to live from my heart. And now somehow, even at 42 years of age, I had been doing that all along with my husband.

Ed was due back this afternoon briefly, before re-packing and heading for the boys' kayaking weekend. I stiffened at the thought of revealing my new plans before he left. I could now hear the ogre in his voice when he called to speak to the kids. I knew it so well, for I recognised it in my own. When did parenthood become the trappings for guilt like a noose around your neck? A noose that made you feel guilty every time you tried to loosen the hold and step out from the scene that your life had become, just so you could inch out and claim a little freedom for yourself.

When he walked confidently into the kitchen, I noted Ed's eyes were still wary. Those deep blue eyes the colour of the ocean I had once fallen so desperately in love with. Those gorgeous eyes that had danced when he spoke to me during our long, philosophical conversations about life we once often had. Those deep dark confident, youthful eyes had become pale in comparison of late.

Now standing and looking at him looking at me, he was measured in his manner. Had I done this to him? I wondered painfully.

"Hi," I smiled, throwing him a lifeline to let him know it was safe to step into unchartered waters.

He kissed and hugged the kids and later stood in front of me, willing me to hold his gaze. He bent forward, kissed me lightly on the lips. It had been so long.

Then stood back to drink me in.

"How are you?" he smiled.

Faltering, still tasting the touch of his lips. "Er... ah... good...thanks."

"And you?" I asked using manners to steer me out of this unchartered path.

"You look good Ab," he said, looking me up and down. Oh no, he's doing it again. I've got to stop this before I get swept up in it all and forget my mission for myself.

He smiled, and gazed down at my mouth. Stop it with those sexy eyes would you.

"Yeah. You look real good."

"Do I?" I said flippantly, trying to sweep the compliments away. I just had to stay focussed on sorting myself out first, instead of getting lost in Ed. "You better get cracking if you want to be ready when Pete gets here," I said, looking up at the clock.

Checking himself and realising the time, he excused himself and hurried upstairs to pack.

I grabbed hold of the kitchen bench and shut my eyes tight. Please, please, please, let me have the strength to find my independence, before I find myself depending on a man again.

When Ed came back into the room, I found a hundred other things to do that avoided eye contact with him.

"I'm going Ab, he said stepping toward me then adding. "Um...I was thinking...after Greta on Tuesday... maybe we could grab a bite to eat. I'll ask my mother if she can stay longer."

Great! That's just dandy! Just when I want to go and re-birth myself and skip couples counselling for once, he wants to turn it into a romantic evening.

"Ab?" he said, repeating my name when I didn't answer.

"Oh yeah...um...about that," I said turning away like a coward to fill up the kettle with water.

"Sorry, what were you saying?" he wondered.

Oh...this is really more difficult than it needs to be. "Look...um...I'm going to need to reschedule Tuesday," I blurted out finally.

"Reschedule?" he asked, frowning. "But we rescheduled last session. I had to go away for work remember?"

"Yeah...um...look while you were away...I spent a little time thinking of something I could do just for me. And...well...I've booked myself into...a five-week art class. But it ...well...it kinda falls on the same night as our fortnightly sessions with Greta.

"Tuesday nights?" he questioned, surprise in his voice. "I thought we were getting somewhere Ab?"

"We are...I mean...ouch!" I banged my hand against the boiling kettle on the stove. "This isn't coming out right."

"So what...we're not going to counselling anymore?" He flared up.

"No. I didn't say we were stopping counselling Ed. I just said my art class was on the night we have scheduled with Greta.

"Don't you think counselling is a little more important than some art class you can do any time?"

What did you say! I fumed inwardly. That was it. Something inside me snapped. I couldn't be sure whether the girl inside me was shouting at her father now or the wife and overloaded mother was pounding at the husband. But whoever she was, she didn't hold back.

I ranted and raved about how I was sick and tired of consulting Ed on whatever I did and didn't want to do with my time, just because he earned the money for the family and I "sat at home" and raised the kids.

I yelled and screamed about his damn kayaking and how I had made so many allowances for him wanting to flit off here and there, simply because he earned the bread. "Not once, not once did you ever consult me," I roared when he dared to interject my wild violent verbal rage.

Well things were going to change around here starting with next Tuesday, I had decided. I may be, "sitting at home" raising three kids right now, but you can be damn sure that I'm not going to be sitting around for much longer. "I'm going to my art classes because I feel like it, and you can be sure to schedule that in your diary!" I fumed.

Pete was now knocking on the door, three kids who had made their way downstairs from the playroom, were now crying at the kiddie gate. Ed was cursing profusely and I was not remotely giving a thought for the language flying out of my mouth.

"Great," he yelled, finally getting in his say. He lunged down to snatch up his weekend bag and yelled at me over his shoulder. "Right back where we started." He pounded the floorboards toward Pete, now banging on the door.

"No," I said, my voice dropping down a scary decibel or three. My eyes turned greener than green, to become the full on Green-Eyed Mummy Monster once more. "Not back where we started. I have come a long way actually. We may not have moved any further along the road to recovery, but I am finally getting my shit together."

When Ed slammed the door behind him, I flinched and froze in my spot. The wails from my children were my undoing. I suddenly became overcome with an overwhelming amount of guilt.

I released the latch on the kiddie safety gate, got down on my knees and clung tight. Waited with the patience I didn't know I had for three little bodies to stop trembling. "Mummy's sorry."

Almost as if to myself but whispering the words in the air, I added, "I didn't mean for you to hear any of that. I wish I handled that better."

Later that evening with the kids all tucked up in bed, I decided now was the perfect time to break my incredibly unhealthy habit of guzzling wine on my own on the sofa, as if it were a religious ritual I had become devoted to. With Ed gone for the weekend and things ending the way they did before he left, I really wanted to try and have a positive, energetic and fun filled weekend with the kids. And, I wanted to get excited about art class starting next week.

As I sat by the quiet of the fire sober and solo, I thought back to the other night when Ed and I sat here together. It felt for every one step forward, we took five steps back. Thinking one quiet conversation by the fire sharing a bottle of wine could fix things between the two of us was naive.

My mind drifted further back into my memory bank all the way to my childhood. I remember my own mother shedding a tear in the quiet of her bedroom as if I was unaware. She never left my father. Stayed with him till the bitter end. And then she died. She settled for what she had. She didn't ask for more. At least I never saw her try.

My father never compromised his lifestyle for his family. Sure, he was home for dinner by 6:00pm most nights. But was he really there? He always wanted his own space, his own time in his den and of course there were all those affairs. I only know of them now, as the adult I am today. Where was his regard for the commitment he'd made to his wife? The commitment he'd made in having a daughter. The commitment he'd made in creating a family.

But now Dad was with Shirley and she had him

wrapped around her little finger. Maybe that's what he always needed? A woman who would dominate. Someone to put him in his place. Leave a very tight rope, vigilantly attached to him, ensuring he never strayed far from home.

But I'd be damned if I would live that life, the one my mother had subjected herself to. And yet, I could not be that other woman either. That dominant Shirley.

I wanted a man to love me for who I was, and for who I was yet to become. Maybe there's something to be said for divorce and finding your feet the second time round? Yet somehow I could see that I'd created all of this, whether consciously or not. I seemed to have re-created my past. But I'd be damned if I would take this into my future.

I had found strength of late in reflecting with honesty at who I did or did not want to be. I now knew the way through this messy marriage is not to fix what's broken, place band aids on hurts and pains with the utmost and delicate care. But instead, to move through all of this, was to rip open the wound and allow it to be blatantly obvious, in need of great care.

CHAPTER 19

I couldn't believe the day had finally arrived. Art class. Five whole weeks dedicated to me expressing myself. Me being creative. Me discovering another part of myself. Me having me-time.

As I stood in the u-shape art room with twelve other women, including our teacher Monique, excitement and nerves bubbled in my belly.

I was grateful that Ed arrived home so late on Sunday and left early on Monday. We hadn't said a single word to each other since our last argument. But now I was at art class, two indulgent hours, every Tuesday for five whole weeks, I willed myself not to think about my husband. Not to think about us, not to think about the kids, not to think about being a mum. Tonight I was a woman who was exploring her passion for art.

Monique appeared to be the stereotypical art teacher. Crazy, wild, curly hair, was a mop of random strands sticking out in every direction. Waves of colour ran through it in any old fashion. Highlights of blonde, red, auburn and gold. Who could really tell what her natural colour was? Who even cared? She certainly didn't. She was wonderful to look at. Plump in figure and short in stature. Her skin was a creamy pale white and her rose coloured cheeks tinted up when she grew animated in expression. I liked her instantly and felt sure that she was going to take very good care of my heart over the next five weeks.

I took in the scene. Five other women to my left and six to my right, all poised in anticipation in the u-shape set up in a large white room the size of a moderate sized dance studio. We were all different shapes and sizes, colours and races, yet we all had one thing in common. Besides being women, we all had that look of sheer awe at what might happen when we lost ourselves in the private space of art.

Monique had said that each session would have a theme and tonight's would be "Colour". She wouldn't reveal the next session just one week in advance. "Better to be surprised," she had said, her rosy cheeks tinting up at the time.

She lit a large red candle that had already burned bright, melted wax dripping down its sides. As the candle began to burn, its flame flickered, capturing the attention of twelve eager students in the room. Monique stood transfixed for a few moments connecting to the light. Then she closed her eyes and breathed in a sort of meditating fashion.

Twelve women's eyes transfixed on Monique. We held our breath too.

Monique eventually opened her eyes and the words started pouring out. She had the manner of a performer, as if she were speaking to a large auditorium packed with people. Her arms danced across the room as her voice spoke from her heart.

"This wounded heart and soul of mine, it would take some time to heal.

As I stripped away the layers, something vivid was concealed.

A dormant diamond locked inside, yet to be chiselled and cajoled.

A diamond with the greatest light, her truth it would be revealed.

It would start with painting the stroke of a brush.

Colour that would escape in a quiet rush.

Laying the foundations for artwork, to be framed and adored.

I have something to say in this world, I'll be damned if I'm ignored.

I will paint and hone my artistic skills,

A portrait, landscape or abstract I might fulfil.

Releasing my heart, thoughts and emotions thereafter

Would be the unveiling from my soul here and ever after.

The way of the wonder would come into its own.

It would chill me beyond my bone.

For my life is not defined by status or society.

But instead rests on the will to let go of propriety.

I will draw, I will paint, I will embrace the artist within.

I will let my emotions ooze out with a grin.

I will unveil the most almighty, for adoring and

critical eyes to see.

Yet what it will truly reveal, is the person that is me."

I wept. How did she know I needed those words? The tears dripped down my cheeks, falling helplessly onto the raw blank piece of art paper that lay in front of me ready to be filled with my emotions, my dreams, my heart, and my imagination.

All the fighting, the arguing, the anger, the struggle to get myself to this class, I was so grateful in this moment that I stuck with it and did not let the power of my family take hold of me.

I put the noose there. I put the oversized overcoat over my body that was three sizes too big for me. I had been wearing that noose, that overcoat for too long. It was time to lift the load...lift the almighty load of motherhood, and the draining scars on my heart and soul from a loveless marriage. From now on it was all about me and my desires. I needed to find my way through the dredge, find out what I was missing out on. Listening to Monique's words it became so clear to me. No escaping this anymore.

I thought marriage and motherhood would be enough, but I realise now it's not. If I'm to enjoy any of that, truly enjoy any of that, I must find what I enjoy most about myself first. This art class was the perfect place to start.

Monique began now in earnest. Tonight's session was titled, "Colour" she reminded us once more. She insisted it was time to leave perfection at the door, along with everything else we were trying to get right in our lives.

Tonight was all about expression and experimentation using colour, Monique had instructed with a melody in her voice.

Our brief was to simply place brush strokes on the paper before our eyes as only our heart desired. We were to complete three works by the end of the evening. Experimenting with different brushes, our hands, fingers, sponges, whatever utensils we wanted to use to form colour onto the paper. We would mix and splash. There were no rules. Oh, this is so liberating. Freeing myself of conformity and trying to be on 24/7. Trying to be the perfect wife and mother. What was I thinking?

In allowing myself to unravel now in amber, gold, yellow and the brightest of reds and wildest pinks, the palest blues and vital greens, my expression was on the page before me. My heart awakening with each new stroke. I was opening wider and wider and letting go of the burden that had become my motherload.

There was no turning back, I could see this now. This art class was just the start. I'd found my way out of the clouds to create this new path. It wasn't a path with Ed, Brady, Emily or Harry. It was a path just for me. A path to explore my womanhood.

I was on my way to opening up to a new enlightening Abby. I had no idea where she was headed but I wasn't focussed now on the how's or why's. As long as she was making something for herself, a woman she admired.

Later, when art class was coming to an end, I quickly grabbed my notebook from my handbag and on a fresh new page, drew a long pathway with stepping stones, three dimensional in form. I drew the first stone and entitled it, "Awakening the Artist Within."

When Monique finally wrapped up the class, I went straight up and hugged her. "Thank you!" I said, gushing with wet eyes and a full heart.

"You're welcome," she smiled. "Wait till you see what's planned for next week's session," she squeezed my hand, her pale blue eyes dancing lively now.

"Until next week ladies," she called to the door as we all shuffled out single file. We waved and said formal goodbyes to one another and motioned toward our respective cars.

When I arrived home, I sat in my car a little while longer, ignition turned off. I listened to the quietening within my belly, and a rumbling of sorts. I'd awoken something dormant in me, the diamond who'd be living it rough. There was no turning back. Not now. Not ever. I'd awakened the desire within.

CHAPTER 20

The next week went relatively smoothly, well...if you count Ed and I doing everything to avoid any possible dialogue with each other, other than to say

"pass the salt", it had gone well.

I'd managed to finally get us a new appointment with Greta, two Thursdays from now. Not sure if the silent treatment would stay this way for another two weeks but it would be interesting to see if we could survive. For me at least, I had art class to look forward to now, two whole hours to fill me up before facing the reality of my marriage.

Before I knew it, Tuesday evening had arrived again. I mused that I hadn't looked forward to a Tuesday evening when it was couples counselling in quite the same way as I do now. Tuesday now represented Artist Abby Day.

I hurried to the door as soon as Ed got home, kissing the kids briefly and calling back to let him know that his dinner was warming in the slow cooker. I had a youthful spring in my step, a lightness in my voice. I wasn't excited about what I was running away from, but what I was running to.

All twelve ladies greeted each other with polite, "Hi there's," and "How's it going?" But when we went to organically seat ourselves in the same place as last week, we paused. Noticing name cards were set up for this week's session in front of each artist station.

"Welcome ladies. Tonight's session is entitled perspective," Monique called out with a big wide grin and a tickle in her throat. "One can get a little complacent," she mused, "When one looks at things from the same angle."

She held her hands out wide to indicate the reason for switching our places from last week's session. "Art and expression is about seeing things from different angles. We will maintain the element of surprise during these sessions ladies, for art and matters of the heart. You see, for one to stay open and engage a wonderment about life, one must claim a freshness to their viewpoint, and to their stories yet untold."

Was this therapy or art? I couldn't decide. This Monique woman was gold. Where had she been all my life?

And then it struck me. Like a lightning bolt through my heart. It had been art that I had denied myself for so very long. Finding Monique was just a bonus.

I grew terribly angry with myself in that moment. Angry that at 42 years of age, I had dug my own quiet grave to mediocrity, complacency, and acceptance of the life I had quietly carved out for myself. No wonder Ed and I were miserable with each other. I'd been miserable with myself. How could I be happy with any man, any lover or life partner, when the one true partnership I had denied myself, was my partnership with desire.

This wildly expressive woman in Monique had

unleashed something inside me. She had dived deep and reached into my soul.

Monique commanded the centre of the room like she was taking to a grand stage. With her red candle from last week re-ignited, she closed her eyes briefly, opened them and then spoke as if she were delivering a sermon once more.

"I would find a way out from the darkened, blackened place,

I had lingered so very long.

I would glimpse at the light of this long and endless tunnel,

I had been crawling silently along.

I would feel hope, a deepening pleasure for me yet unseen.

I'd embrace this space, this quiet darkness and etch a little more.

I'd nurture and water it, for the richness and ripeness it needed to repair.

I'd sit in the stillness in this quiet hole, and find comfort in this despair.

What would it mean to hurl myself up?

Take one quiet step thereafter.

To break free from the cave I had shrouded myself in

And struggled outward that little bit further.

I would step and heave and grab the rope.

The lifeline left to dangle.

Hold with all my might and unravel from the space.

My soul and wounds so deep within this place.

It was a new perspective I was yet to climb.

A space high above the darkness.

Days filled with light and laughter.

An awakened spirit I would look after.

I thrashed about with all my might to climb from this deep dark cave.

I would claim it now, an unlived life, a future to seek thereafter.

What came next I do not know, for I shut my eyes so tight.

I hoped and prayed that with all my might, to glimpse into the light.

I felt a rushing, swishing move, rumbling from the ground,

So deep and with an almighty whoosh that I banished this cave unfound.

I was awakened by some unknown light; a light it did must save me.

I stretched and gently opened my eyes to sunlight that was the key.

I looked around in search of more, the greenest hills I would find.

I looked right down and saw it now, a daisy in the wild.

A fresh unpicked flower of yellows, whites and golds.

It was meant for me; I see that now.

To remind me of what I must hold.

My life was new, it was reborn.

A fresh perspective unleashed.

A new beginning, a life unearthed.

An unravelling released.

There would be no turning back.

To that deep dark cave.

For now; it had no purpose or need.

I'd seen the light; it was clear to me.

That enlightenment it would lead."

I wept.

It came as no surprise this time. Waves crashing down onto unpainted strips of bark that lay in front of me.

Silently, I wept.

"Perspective," Monique echoed with an eerie yet soothing tone in her voice. "Tonight's session is all about perspective. We can become complacent with our lives. But don't be hard on yourselves ladies, for we all do it. The routine of the everyday. The fastidious or lackadaisical way we go about things. Whether intense, fierce, simple or ordered, we become routine. In the mundane and order however, we restrict. The walls around us slowly become smaller. Neater, tighter, more conformed. But to open up to all that life has to offer," she said announcing this to us with wide open arms to the room, "to widen the scope further one must unhinge their perspective, one must liberate themselves from the cage."

Yep...I had definitely found myself in a therapy session masked as art class.

For the next fifteen minutes or so, Monique dimmed the lights and with her old-fashioned slide projector of negative prints, she clicked one image at a time and spoke. She showed images of places far away. Ireland, Italy, Iceland and India. "The 4 I's," she had said.

"What do you see?" She asked rhetorically to the twelve women in the room who were silently hanging on her every word.

"Mountains, cliff tops, rolling hills, water and ice. Nature in all its glory. Monuments and monasteries, churches and steeples and religious rituals, celebrated by all four countries. What do you see?" she continued to ask without waiting for an answer.

As each new slide clicked over, she invited us to dive deeper to find the answers within. "What do you feel? What is below the surface? Do you think it has been revealed?"

She had us searching in our imagination, steering us into unchartered waters. She was stirring something hidden deep within, rolling and roaring like a momentous thunder that needed to break out. After the last slide was shown, slowly Monique undimmed the lights. The red candle flickered at her art station that sat up front and centre.

She drew our attention to three pieces of material in front of us. A large piece of torn bark, a sheet of Perspex, and finally, a slab of washed limestone. "Now ladies," she said, her arms open wide like she was about to conduct an orchestra. "I would like you all to paint your own perspective onto the three materials you see in front of you. I won't be guiding you or giving you feedback or notes. You have everything you need. Just express yourself," she said, clapping her hands together with a loud bang and releasing them outward.

"I will play a melody mix of music in varying styles while you work. If you feel stuck or cluttered in thought, restricted or closed in, be sure to take a moment to close your eyes, and open your imagination. Reach deep inside your well of wisdom and let it out. Let out that expression, release your heart and pour your soul out onto the three forms in front of you. Be guided by the grace of you, the grace that is your light."

And so, we did. Deeply entranced and lost in time. My soul was unleashed, carefully creating a masterpiece of delight.

"Take a step back now ladies," Monique announced. "Stand up from your places and take a slow walk around the room."

As we weaved and darted, gently sashaying around each other, we were all blown away. It's true to say, we had each represented ourselves very uniquely. But all the same, we had expressed ourselves incredibly.

"And that's what we call perspective ladies," Monique announced. "Everyone has their unique viewpoint, a place in which they sit. A place to allow the stirrings that reside...an unleashing from within...a place for them now to fit. Your art is your true expression ladies, you must always remember that," she urged, her rosy cheeks glowing and a tenderness in her soft, gentle, blue eyes glistening with water.

Monique had a way of talking to our souls. We couldn't hide from ourselves in her class. She had a way of opening people up, to reveal themselves to themselves.

All twelve women said goodbye to Monique, some of us pausing to hug or kiss her gently on the cheek and thank her once more for the effect she was having on our lives, most personally.

Watching the other women leave the room one by one, I immediately felt a sense of kinship. A desire to get to know them further, for it felt we had already been truly intimate in this explicit heart space we now shared.

Later, as I sat in the parked car outside my house, I took some time for myself in the quiet comfort on my own. I reflected on the women in the class and realised that in my five years of motherhood, I hadn't made a lot of female friendships since leaving my full-time career behind me, except of course for Sal.

Most of my friends in the past were women at work. It seemed once I left my corporate days behind - between their over worked office hours schedule and my overworked, after hours, non-stop motherhood schedule - trying to find time to catch up ended up taking too much time. Time that none of us seemed to have in the first place, just to organise to get together.

I never did join that Mother's Group thing after I had Brady. Looking back, I think I had isolated myself from the world. Because the one person I craved most, the one I truly wanted guidance and support from, the only one who would really know what I was going through, was my mother. But with her gone, I didn't have the energy or inclination to seek out other mothers who might help fill that void. Other mothers who might help me feel nurtured and understood and guide me when I had absolutely no idea what the hell I was doing.

So much of the focus seems to be on supporting people through pregnancy and birth. But after you've done all that, you are very much on your own with the baby. There seems to be this massive abyss with what to do with the baby once you've got them home, and also what to do with yourself.

Sure, the whole Mother's Group thing is great, but really...it's the blind leading the blind. And then there's those comparison conversations one is continually subjected to in the park, or during a quick stop nappy change or a breastfeeding session in the parents' rooms at the local shopping centre. Comparing your children's measurements, sleep schedule, eating habits, breast milk or formula, natural or caesarean, drugs or no drugs...it's exhausting...and soul destroying.

What if we all just accepted that none of us really know what we're doing and every day of motherhood that we get something right, or even close to it, then that really is a great day!

What if mothers all around the world told the truth, openly declared when they were confused, frustrated, exhausted, overwhelmed, unhappy, and then some. What if we could find more compassion for each other, then maybe, just maybe, we might be able to find more compassion for ourselves.

But art class, it made things different. Sure, we were all women, but there was no conversation about whether we were or weren't mothers and how good we were or weren't at it. We were simply women finding our way through life, wondering whether art might provide a source of hope, inspiration and light.

I sat quietly a little longer in the comfort of my car. I'd taken to finding solace here of late. Ignition off, mind idling. My belly rose and fell as I stared out at the night sky stars. I looked up, as I often did, in search of my mother. Was she looking down on me, her spirit radiating from one bright star? I wondered if she knew just how much I missed her. Just how much I loved her.

I thought of Sal then. I wondered if I'd look for her in the stars one day too. Sal kept telling me to stop focussing on what was coming and enjoy what we have now, reminding me that none of us know when it's 'our time'. She told me I needed to stop focussing on the time we wouldn't have and start focussing on the time we did have.

Each morning, since art classes had begun a month ago, I had taken to getting myself up a little earlier than usual. With Ed sleeping on the sofa on a permanent basis, well, for now anyway, I had given to using my notebook to sketch something new each day.

Monique had encouraged us to stay with our craft, to practise that daily expression of ourselves. "Do you think a dancer doesn't stretch and move their body every day?" she had declared. "That a musician would go without playing or listening to a tune each day?" Then as artists, you should not deny yourself the opportunity to express your heart through art every single day."

I wasn't sure who I was doing this for more, Monique or me? Maybe it started off with my loyalty and dedication to Monique and wanting to do the right thing, but now I couldn't get up without propping myself up with my pillows and taking to my sketchpad like it was an extension of my heart.

I had found purpose and meaning and a reason to wake up and embrace the day. And it's funny you know...now that I was claiming just that little bit of time for me, I felt like I had so much more to give to my kids. I now had the energy and drive to immerse myself in making breakfast for the kids, feeding them food that made them feel good and happy. I found myself wanting to take them out during the day for our next big adventure, because I too was having my own deeply needed adventure. In taking more time for me, I could give more of myself to my children. Share that part of me, that deeply unexpressed part of me that had been unheard and unseen for so long.

I paused a moment and thought of Ed sleeping on the sofa downstairs. Would I be able to share that part of me with him? That untouched woman within that I don't think came out to be touched, caressed, longed and loved?

I wonder, if I had been the artist back then, instead of the unexpressed woman I had become, would I still be living in Australia or instead living in some foreign land? Would I have wound up living in the countryside instead of the city? A nice quaint little town where recipes for the best butterscotch sauce would be swapped over meeting other mothers in the street, instead of quick half smiles on the way to do our latte run?

But it was pointless wandering what might have been. Instead, I wanted to focus on what would become. A life where I would paint and dream. Not a week would be the same. An unearthed artist soul within would seek and look to find a woman cloaked in gold and jewels, a rare and cherished one to find.

CHAPTER 21

Time felt like it was flying lately. We were three weeks into art class, sitting in a different seat again; delight, excitement, nerves, hope and joy stirred around inside me.

Monique began her ritual of lighting a red candle and waiting for the words to come. Tonight's theme was, "Expression," she beamed. Her words for this were so simple but spoke volumes.

"Say it now, what you know is true,

This reality you have hidden deep.

For when the space connected you,

It was then your artist it did weep.

An artist is an unaccomplished soul,

Always in search of their next work.

Don't be complacent or cower in a hole,

Open up yourself, then let go, of that which irks.

Enrich your spirit, enlighten your heart,

Let your imagination run wild and free.

Don't let yourself get torn apart,

In the unveiling of what is meant to be.

Do not subscribe to that small hole,

The cell you once confined.

Instead unleash, unravel and release the soul,

And that almighty relieving of the mind.

Let her run wild and free,

An untamed shrew is she.

She has a message, a soul's purpose,

A heart, which rivals that of a furnace."

That woman gets me every single week.

With sermon ritual complete and the grand announcement of this week's theme, Monique turned off the lights completely. She fired up a clip on her computer that magnified onto the white wall in front of the room.

With my eyes still misty from Monique's class reading, I watched with the other women, an old black and white movie clip of Ginger Rogers dancing. She was moving, swaying, stretching, leaping, twisting, turning, bending. Fluid, graceful movements, where you could almost experience her inner most feelings. Expressed through the power of dance.

After the video clip ended, Monique slowly turned up the lights and began her routine questions. "What did you feel? What did you see?" And so on.

"Tonight, we will work simply in black and white," she declared. "Let's see you express yourself with just these two colours. One in oil, one in watercolour and the third in charcoal."

I now looked down at the materials in front of me that Monique had just announced and wondered how the blank white A2 scraps of paper might be filled by the end of the lesson.

"You must find your own expression on the page," she added, "With the two colours that are simply black and white. When you feel stuck, cluttered in your mind, restricted in your thoughts," she reminded us, as she always does, to close our eyes and open up to our imagination.

She reminded us to re-connect at times throughout the remainder of the lesson, to see the dance in front of our eyes, the fluid movements, the lines and flow of Ginger Rogers' grace and express that feeling on the page.

And so it began once more. Twelve ladies diving deep into our souls, to reach inside ourselves and tap into that untapped fragment, the movement that was yet to stir and release into solid form.

Later, toward the end of the workshop, we did what we always did and raised from our stools to quietly walk around the u-shape room and take in each other's works. No comparisons made. No judgements heard. Each unique and to its own. Twelve women proudly baring their souls to one another, without a care in the world, all our fears left at the door.

"Hey," Evelyn called out as she stood holding her car door open at the end of class. "Maybe we should all grab a drink after class next week? Or a bite to eat perhaps?"

As I clutched my own door, an excited independence within screamed to go out and have some fun. But then, as if from habit, I reeled it back in. "Ah...not sure."

"Oh sure you can," Felicity called out from her car now. "I'm in," she added, beaming at Evelyn.

"Come on girls. Let's do it," Evelyn encouraged, with mischief in her voice, as if we were about to play hooky from school or something. Well hooky from our family at least. A night out without purpose or occasion, such as a birthday or celebration milestone in sight. Simply a night out for the pure pleasure of it.

Knowing I just had to take that step. That step beyond art class to do more for myself just because, I cried out meekly, "Ok. I'm in."

Later, as I sat behind the steering wheel in the quiet comfort of my car, before stepping inside my house to the commitment of my family, I smiled. I had something new to look forward to now, a focus that involved pure pleasure.

CHAPTER 22

My insides twisted up in knots, tonight was the couples counselling session rescheduled three weeks earlier, because I put art before my heart. Or was it my heart that followed art? Whatever, these other matters of the heart needed to be addressed.

Three straight weeks of Ed sleeping on the sofa. Things had gotten more than a little uncomfortable between us, and I'm not just talking about how his body must be feeling waking up on that thing every day.

For me though, I'd grown excited with the extra space in bed. My bedroom had become my personal haven. I enjoyed my morning 'me-time' ritual of sketching on my notebook and sitting in the quiet of my mind. Stretching out and rolling over in my bed, only to discover I had more room than ever. I began to use my bedroom as my sanctuary, my special little space. Away from Ed. Away from the kids. A place just for me to play, sit, read, draw, sleep and just be. Ed may be uncomfortable downstairs sleeping on the sofa, but I've got to be honest, I feel pretty decadent in my own personal domain, all mine.

Even though Ed's mother had been roped into watching the kids while we went to see Greta, we decided we didn't want to alert her to where we were really going. What we were really doing. Pretended we were going out for a much-needed romantic date. Thought it best to keep up appearances and leave the house together rather than meet there with Ed running late. We travelled to couples counselling as a couple for a change.

Why did we have to be secretive though? Why couldn't we tell her the truth? Tell her our marriage was really crap. Tell her that we were doing whatever we could to hold it together. Why couldn't we tell her, so she could complement and praise us for giving it our all and daring to find the root cause, the key to us finding happiness again? Ed had scoffed at the idea. Told me in no uncertain terms not to let on. Instead of opening up ourselves and being vulnerable with his mother, we were meant to hold our heads in shame, riddled with guilt once more, as the failing wife, struggling mother, and inadequate matriarch I had become.

Ed and I sat in silence throughout the twenty minute car ride to Greta's. Not a word spoken, even on the long, cold walk through the crisp, winter's night air from outside the car park to her office.

"Hello Ed, Abigail. How are you both doing?" Greta asked reaching out to shake our hands in turn.

I'm wondering if she has to look so sensational all the time. I mean she's a psychologist...can't she see we're on the verge of breaking up! Messing with my fragile mind and my husband's loins was enough to send us both over the edge to crazy land at the sight of her.

Today she wore a tailored deep burgundy pencil skirt that hugged her buttocks and thighs. Reaching as long as her knees, with a split along the side to ease the tension when she sat. I'm not sure it eased any tension on Ed's groin. He shifted in his seat uncomfortably. Was that due to him feeling uncomfortable watching Greta in all her glory, or was it the anticipation of what she was about to make us say, make us feel? She wore a pale lemon shirt that sat crisp at the collar, one button too many undone, and a loose-fitting set of black pearls knotted just once, falling low into the gape of her cleavage. Only a woman with her exotic looks, luscious deep dark brown hair caressing over her skin and her year-round tan could pull the lemon off the way she did.

I felt defeated just looking at her. Somewhere between having three children I'd forgotten to look at myself in the mirror. Forgotten to take a little care with my hair. Forgotten to put some thought into what I wore that said more than 'comfort'.

I hadn't worn a feminine frock for a while, and certainly not a super sexy skirt like Greta's, since my days of leaving the corporate world. Well, there was that one crazy night in Byron Bay with Sal. I used to look smoking hot dressing for the day. Now I'm more focussed on how my three kids look when we leave the house. When did my life become about putting everyone else's needs before my own? When I became a mother no doubt.

I clenched my jaw. Determined not to rise to the challenge. Ok Greta, you want to see hot! I'll show you hot!

I glared at Greta with bitter envy. I knew that in her looking so fabulous each session, she was almost willing me to make an effort to do the same. I'd become so focussed on comfort and whatever was the quickest outfit to get on without three kids charging into my room while I dressed for the day. But even a lick of lipstick, a colourful scarf, a pair of dangly earrings would make a difference. Surely, there was something I could pull out from the closet to make me go from drab housewife to foxy woman in the making?

"So, you're comfortable with this new arrangement, sleeping on the sofa?" Greta now quizzed Ed.

"Well comfortable...is not a term I'd use for how my body feels every morning when I wake up. But...I've got to say," he paused, glancing in my direction briefly, "A little space from Abby has been good."

"Is that why you like going away for work? Away on your kayaking retreats?" Greta asked Ed, pen poised and resting on her clipboard.

I wonder what she'd write when we were gone? Perhaps she'd wonder why these two completely different people ever got hitched in the first place? She'd most certainly wonder why we still were. I wonder what she thought of us? Wondered what she thought from behind that mask of questions she hid behind each session.

"What do you think Greta?" I blurted out boldly before Ed had time to respond.

He jerked his head sideways and cocked his eyebrow at me.

"Pardon?" Greta asked me. Was that a mocking tone in her voice?

"Well, are you saying Ed is trying to do whatever he can to spend as little time with me as possible because that's what he'd rather do? Or are you just curious?"

"The curiosity should sit with you Abigail." Oh this woman is too sharp; it really unnerves me. "And you too Ed," she smiled at him now.

Much later, when Greta looked at her sleek and slim black watch that sat neatly on her right wrist, she issued out the 'homework' once more.

"Ask yourself these questions. For the next two weeks," Greta declared. "I want the two of you to question yourselves. Be honest in asking, what are you really running from? And what might you be running to? Are you escaping or are you immersing yourselves in your pleasures?"

Pausing to give us a little time to scribe her questions into our notebook, she flicked through the pages on her clipboard. "Journal them in your notebooks," she added. "Ask yourselves these questions at various intervals in the day. Do you take pleasure in what you are doing or do you sit in distaste?"

The next morning before showering, I stood facing the bathroom mirror in my winter woolly pyjamas. Looking very...well...unsexy. I wondered when I went from hot corporate chick to dowdy mother hen? I know Ed should love me no matter what I looked like but now, looking at my reflection in the mirror, I could see the un-appeal.

Later that evening, after the dinner and bath time routine, with Ed still at work and the kids playing quietly in their playroom, I stood in front of my chest of draws and began tossing clothes onto my bed.

"What are you doing Mummy?" Brady asked. Emily and Harry trailed close behind. "Can I help throw your clothes around the room too?" Brady asked, excitement in his deep blue eyes.

Emily piped in now, "Me too. I want to help make a mess," she squealed.

Not to be left out, Harry eased himself up onto my bed, with Emily giving his cute little bottom a nudge. He began tossing my clothes off the bed and onto the floor.

"No!" I screamed.

Three kids stopped dead in their tracks. Eyeballs on high alert.

"No. Mummy doesn't want to clean all of this up."

In the sixty short seconds of my kids entering my room, clothes were now strewn everywhere.

"Sorry Mummy," Brady offered. "We thought it was a game."

A smile slowly began to form around my lips. "Would you like it to be a game?" I asked, moving closer to Brady and crouching down to his height.

"Yes?" he answered with a question, caution in his eyes.

"OK, let's do it," I said, tickling Brady to the floor. Emily and Harry now jumped on my back, and soon fell hard on my head. "Ouch." We laughed and rumbled and tumbled all over the clothes strewn on the floor.

"What the hell's going on?"

I turned toward the bedroom door only to see Ed peering in, tie loose around his neck, suit jacket slung over his arm. The kids were frozen in fear.

"Finding my style Ed," I flicked back. "Seems I lost it a long time ago...along with my sense of humour." Grabbing a stray pair of navy blue jeggings on the floor and holding them up in pride, I added, "But it's here somewhere."

"Well it's your mess to clean up," he replied flatly.

Ignoring Ed, I now turned to the kids. "Ok little darlings, let's continue our search to find something that looks good on Mummy. Let's get me packed so I can go see Aunty Sal."

"What?" Ed said stepping fully into the room now.

"I told you. I'm seeing Sal this weekend."

"No, you didn't."

"Yes I did." I flared back.

"Well I've got stuff on." Oh this man always has stuff on!

I was determined to not let him get the better of me this time. "Ed, I even emailed you."

"Well too bad."

"Are you serious?" I glared.

"The kids don't stop being your responsibility just because you're focussed on finding yourself all of a sudden," he said, looking at the pile of clothes on the floor.

"Ed, she's not well."

"Is Aunty Sal sick?" Brady frowned.

Ed squirmed.

"Nothing for you to worry about darling," I said, reaching up to kiss the top of Brady's curls on his head.

"Look Ab, I know, but I've got a kayaking session lined up tomorrow. Then I've got a couple of clients out from the U.K. I've got to take them out tomorrow night."

I stared at him motionless, crouching on my knees on the floor. After a long pause, I turned away from Ed and focussed on my three children, patiently waiting to see how yet another disagreement between their parents ended. "Looks like we'll need a bigger suitcase," I smiled, reaching out to give all three kids a group hug.

"What...so you're taking the kids away for the whole weekend?"

"Fuck off Ed," I scathed, dismissing him as I brushed past, bumping him on the way out of the bedroom door.

We set off early the next day and left Ed alone with his morning ritual.

"We'll get breakfast on the road," I said to the kids when they groaned, still sleepy, tummies already rumbling. "It will be an adventure!" I declared.

After three toilet stops, two food stops, and one hunt for the missing teddy stop, we had finally arrived.

"My babies," Sal called out from the front door, arms opened wide.

I had to give it to her. A woman riddled with cancer, yet she still managed to scrub up better than I did. I released Harry and Emily from their seatbelts and carried Harry on my hip. Brady was now running frantically into the warm and welcoming arms of Aunty Sal.

"Careful with Aunty Sal," I called out, as all three kids were now pounding her with kisses and hugs with the excitement of oversized puppies. "She's not feeling well remember."

"They're fine," Sal soothed, while I grabbed our things from the car. "And, I'm going to feel a lot better after your weekend visit."

"I do declare," Sal said taking a second or two to look deep into the eyes of all three kids individually. "That... you've all grown taller since I last saw you."

"Really?" Brady said, puffing out his chest and stretching his neck taller.

"Oh...I missed you," I said, squeezing the life out of Sal as gently as I could. "You look wonderful."

"I feel wonderful," she replied, a soft sweet smile taking over her mouth.

"Really?" I asked surprised, hopeful. "Have things improved?"

"It would be a miracle if they did," she smiled, leading us into the cottage. She stopped in the centre of a sweet, old-fashioned kitchen that looked like it was stuck in the 1950's, only a little freshened up.

"A miracle in three life times," she added. "But, I just feel better being here," she declared, sweeping her arms out wide to show off her new place. "And happier," she added.

The kids all ran around squealing excited. "Where am

I sleeping Aunty Sal?" Brady demanded, pulling at her arm and leading her from the living room down through the hallway to discover where he might set up his stuff.

I stopped to take in the view. It just took my breath away. Floor to ceiling windows framed the open plan living space. The back of the cottage had been replaced with floor to ceiling bi-fold doors that opened out to the beach at our doorstep. Waves crashed on the shore below. The back of the cottage leading out to the sand had a long, deep deck attached to it, washed in lime. A weathered dark blue fence matched the trim around the house. I looked back into the cute kitchen, that I could imagine a grandmother baking scones in, and then over to the fire that roared in an old potbelly stove in the living room.

"This place is amazing!" I declared to Sal when she came back to join me.

"I love it here," Sal announced, shuffling on her feet toward me a little slower than usual.

We stood side by side, taking in the glorious ocean before us.

"Cuppa?" she asked, shuffling absently toward the kitchen without waiting for an answer.

"I'll do it," I said taking the kettle from Sal's hand.

"I'm fine," she said, ignoring my offer for help.

"Sal, let me help."

"It's good for me to keep doing things," she said without looking at me and began, in a slow rhythm, to take out old china teacups and a matching pot, milk jug and sugar bowl from the cupboard. "I want to enjoy all of this for as long as I can," she said, a little misty-eyed now. "Don't want to sit here all day with a blanket around me. However long I've got, I'm making the most of it Ab."

My heart constricted. I covered my eyes with my fingers, poked at the eyelids in the hope the tears would not fall. Knowing I would choke on my words, I walked back over to take in the view that spanned Seven Mile Beach. I wondered, as I looked out to the never-ending sea, how I would ever go on without Sal in my life.

The kids came racing back out to the living area, grabbing at my legs and talking over the top of one another, until I finally managed to work out that the consensus was a high demand for a walk along the beach.

"That's a great idea," Sal said, motioning to turn the kettle off. "Let's do the tea when we get back."

Reaching out to one of the hooks that hung near the back deck, Sal grabbed her scarf, gloves and beanie. "Rug up everyone. Spring hasn't quiet settled in yet."

We filed off to the beach one by one, walking down the private track to the sand, a set of stairs that ran along the side of the house. Once we hit the sand, the kids were off, running as fast as their legs could carry them. Harry fell flat on his face, then cried out for Emily to wait up.

"Don't go in the water," I yelled, running after them.

Once the enthusiasm of being on the beach had settled in, we found our rhythm. Slowly meandering along the shoreline, leggings, jeans and tracksuit pants all rolled up, collecting shells along the shore.

I turned back to Sal, who had slowed down to a snail's pace, trailing well behind us. "Are you ok?" I called out.

"I'm fine," she waved. "Go ahead."

Walking closer toward her, I called out again. "We'll stop and turn back."

"What and ruin all their fun," she glanced ahead at Brady, Emily and Harry who were now squatting in front of a sand crab, which was trying to claw its way out of a hole before the next wave came crashing down.

"We can come back later," I said gently, catching up to Sal along the shore.

"It's fine Ab. I just have to listen to my body. Stop when I need rest. Go when I'm good again."

Looking up ahead, further along the beach, Sal suggested the kids and I carry on. "Why don't you walk down to the mouth of the creek and have a look there. I'll stop here while you do. When you're done, we'll all head back for morning tea."

"I don't want to leave you," I said taking a step closer to Sal.

A fire burned in Sal's eyes. A history of twenty one years of friendship told me she was about to let me have it.

"Look, if you are going to fuss and sniff the whole time you're here, you may as well go back home now. I've got a nurse that fusses about every day, I don't need my best friend to do it too. I want to have fun," she pleaded with me. "I want to laugh and have a good time while you're here. I want to talk and sit up by the fire each night as long as my weary body will let me."

I looked at Sal and held her gaze, trying to extract the truth from her, staring deep into her pretty, caramel eyes, paler each time I saw her.

"Please Ab," she softened. "I want things to be as normal as possible. I love it here," she declared, looking around her along the shore. "Let's make the most of it." Dismissing me now, she took charge. "Go ahead with the kids. I'll stay here a while; then meet you back up at the house."

Later that evening, with the kids all settled in their respective guest beds, I relaxed on the sofa in the living room near Sal. I watched her slowly settle into the cosy grandfather chair next to the fire as she pulled the red and pink crocheted rug further around her tummy.

"They're beautiful, she said, staring at the fire. "Those gorgeous kids of yours."

I smiled and stared at the fire.

"They all comfortable?" she wondered, looking over at me as I tucked a blue and white woolly rug around my legs. "Got everything they need?"

"It's a wonder a mother manages to leave the house," I laughed. "Trying to remember to bring the favourite soft toy, the milk bottle, the water bottle, the soother, the special blankie, the night light, the torch...the list goes on!"

Sal laughed. "I've poured us a Baileys."

Lifting the glass, I raised it to Sal.

"Cheers," Sal said, raising her glass and clinking it with mine. "To friendship...and...memories made and treasured."

My eyes misted up for about the tenth time since I arrived that morning. Trying to lighten the moment I joked, "Well if you want me to stop sniffling, you'll have to stop saying such sentimental things."

"I'm allowed," she declared. "I'm dying!"

I winced, then sipped my Baileys and stared solemnly at the fire.

I thought back to when my mother was having her last weeks of treatment, when the cancer had fully taken hold of her body. There wasn't a single mention of the dreaded 'C' word. She wouldn't have it. Stoic till the end. "Hold your tears child," she had said. "Just give me smiles and those bright green eyes of yours to enjoy each day."

As much as it hurt like a sword daggered right through my heart every time Sal mentioned her impending death, I found it surprisingly refreshing to be allowed to be so open and honest about it all. To talk freely in knowing what we had ahead of us, somehow made us appreciate what we've right now, all the more.

"How's Ed?" Sal wondered, taking another sip of her Baileys.

I curled my legs up underneath me tighter and sighed. "I'm not sure," I said. "I really don't know where we're headed."

"What would you do...if it were you instead of me?"

Sal wondered. "How would you make your life count more?"

Taking a moment to gather my thoughts and sip more Baileys I pondered.

"If I were dying," I said, "If it were me instead of you, I'd end it with him. If I knew I had only a few months to live, I'd want to do just what made me happy. The kids, my art classes, hanging out with you, cooking in my kitchen, maybe taking in a movie or two each month. Walks along the beach no matter the weather or temperature. I'd grab a bite to eat with my art class friends and I'd paint every single damn day till the day I died. For as long as I could hold a paintbrush in my hand, I'd do that."

Sal looked at me silently and shook her head, then allowed a gigantic big smile to form.

"Well, well, well, look at you, I do declare you have come a long way to finding your way. Amazing what a little therapy and free expression through a few art classes does for one's soul."

My heart pounded. Had I really come this far in just a few weeks?

"Just imagine Ab, if everyone looked at their life that way?"

"What way?" I asked, turning my trancelike stare from the raging fire to look at Sal fully.

"If we all looked at life as if we were looking down the barrel of death."

"That's a bit morbid," I said, screwing up my nose

before taking another long sip of Baileys.

"No, you crazy woman," she laughed. "I mean, imagine if we made the most of the time we had. Only did things we wanted. Lived by our own rules. I mean, look at you Ab...I asked you how you'd spend your time if you knew you were dying and you didn't hesitate, not in the slightest. But on any other given day, you'd have answered with everyone else in mind first, before you thought of yourself."

"So where does Ed fit into all of this?" she asked tentatively.

"I'm not sure. I'm just not sure anymore. I'm not sure there's a place for him as my life partner or my lover. Sure, he'll always be the father of my kids...we'll always have that," I said, resting my hand under my chin in a fist and leaning on the arm of the sofa.

"Take your time with it Ab," Sal whispered.

CHAPTER 23

I hugged Sal tight on Tuesday after lunch when it was time to leave. We'd stayed an extra day, nothing to rush home for other than art class tonight.

Meredith, Ed's mum, was now looking after the kids. Ed said there was absolutely no way he could make it back home in time. I wondered how he could flip so suddenly from wanting to do everything in his power to connect again, to turning abruptly to run in the opposite direction.

Meredith had become moderately more available to help with the kids than usual. I wondered if she sensed I was on the verge of booting her son out the door if he didn't get his act together? Or whether it was because I had more reason to ask for help? Maybe it was because the kids were a little older, a little easier to manage, that she stepped in more? It was hard to tell.

I'd never grown very close to my mother-in-law. Shame though. I'd always hoped, knowing how hard it was to have my own mother out of the picture, she'd have wanted to step in and get more involved. But we'd always managed a superficial level of airs and graces and no-nonsense civility toward each other. All that aside, tonight I was so very grateful Meredith agreed to watch the kids so I didn't miss art class.

I switched off the engine and sat in the silence of my car, breathing in the stillness. It was the beginning of September, but the chill of winter still clung to the air like a frost yet to thaw. Dark by just 6:00pm. I smiled thinking of Monique and wondered what she might bestow upon us today. So far, we'd had colour, perspective and expression.

A tapping on my driver's side window startled me. Still strapped in my seat belt, my neck cranked. My cautious eyes turned sideways to see Tilly, one of my fellow art class colleagues, laughing and mouthing, "Sorry," as she waved her hand at me to come in.

I shook off the shock and laughed at myself to join her on the footpath.

"Sorry," she said out loud now. "Didn't mean to scare you."

"That's ok," I replied. "I seem to have found solace in the quiet of my car going from one appointment to the next lately. When the kids aren't there, I claim a few extra minutes for myself to be in the solitude of it all."

"I use the toilet," she remarked.

"Sorry?" I replied.

"My quiet time...I use the toilet," she declared matter-of-factly. "Lock it every time I go in. I mean there's nothing I can do to help a single one of them when I'm on the throne is there?" she laughed.

"And Steph", Tilly pointed to another art class colleague, with cropped brown hair that had streaks of auburn running through, framing her face in a short, messy bob. "She does it at the washing line. Asks the family if anyone wants to help hang out the clothes, knowing full well they don't...and won't," Tilly laughed. "So, Steph gets the extra time and space she needs by hanging around five minutes longer at the clothesline. Gets some breathing space from being in high demand from three teenage boys that seem to want their bottomless pit endlessly filled."

"I had no idea," I mused.

"Everyone does it," Tilly replied. "Otherwise we'd go crazy...if we're not already there!" she added, roaring with laughter, pushing open the art class door.

As we stepped into the magical world of Monique's art space and all that she created for us each week, she had us walking around as usual to find our name cards in a new location.

Standing at the front of the room now, a paintbrush tucked into her messy mane to hold it in place, or maybe it was a decorative accessory, there was no telling when it came to our much-loved, eccentric art teacher? A red candle burned bright, as Monique began to release her words of wisdom to the class and set the tone for the evening's session. She delivered rhythm like, an unravelling of sorts, to immerse us in the space to create art from our heart.

Tonight's theme was, 'Collaboration'.

"How can we rely on another to create our magnificent piece,

Without our spirit or gifts compromised in this crease?

Without our divine soul that is meant to be expressed,

Launching in a way onto the canvas that is meant to impress.

How do we reveal our self to another?

When we are still searching of a way to reveal it to our father.

How do we find solace and comfort in a collaborator?

Without it squashing our inner creator.

Yet it is said that two minds are greater than one.

Two souls are deeper than one.

Two hearts are fuller than one

So why not few artists to be greater than one?

It is our divine path as artists,

As women, and as individuals.

To find a way to express ourselves

Without compromise or becoming invisible."

I was now starting to believe that Monique had an insider's view into my life. Wondered how she could be so in tune with my state of mind, as if she were designing this workshop entirely for me. But then, when I looked around at the eleven other women joined in the circle with me, I noticed jaws dropping, heads nodding, tears forming. A surge of reassurance shot right through me, telling me I was not alone.

You see, I'd come to feel like this motherload of mine was unique just to me. That I was the failure, that I was the one who couldn't get my life right. But looking around the room, there were at least eleven other women in the world, in my local community in fact, with the same perspective on life as me. We were all struggling and striving in search of the perfect answer. Searching for enlightenment from the sanity of motherhood, and the commitment somewhere in all of that, commit to ourselves.

"Match up ladies," Monique clapped. "Get yourself into groups of three." As we organically sort of teamed up with the woman to our right and then our left, Monique continued. "The instructions for tonight's lesson are in the box in front of you. You have everything you need."

I teamed up with Tina and Heather.

Tina was a woman about five feet two inches, and a sweetheart in personality. Baby blue eyes and mousey dark blonde hair in a twisted knot on top of her head each week. She had two great big dimples that framed her infectious smile. She would no doubt bring enthusiasm, energy and childlike wonder to our project.

Heather was a lot more reserved than Tina. Older than both of us, possibly in her early 50s. She had black hair that was heavily accentuated with strands of grey. A neat cropped fringe sat just above her eyebrows. Her smile matched her grey eyes, friendly, a little reserved. My guess was Heather would bring planning, consideration and logical thinking to the project.

I would no doubt bring chaos, messiness and random wild thoughts to the project.

I reached in the box for the set of instructions. "Would you like to lead?" I asked Heather.

"No, you go ahead. We need someone with a little charge in her to ignite and get us going," she winked.

Shrugging my shoulders, I read out loud Monique's list of materials that were enclosed in the box, with twelve items and a brief that stated our piece had to, "say something," when people looked at it.

Now this is where I often come unstuck. So many thoughts rambling around in my head but never really knowing what it is that I want to say.

After ten long minutes stuck in our heads with nothing to show for ourselves, Heather spoke in a sort of old school teacher's manner. "This is not getting us anywhere. Why don't we do one of Monique's eyes closed exercises?"

"Let's do the ocean one," I suggested without thinking, while Tina cocked an eyebrow and said, "Huh?"

"You know, the one where she gets us to close our eyes and imagine ourselves sitting on a rock and looking out at the roaring ocean, to allow feelings and emotions to form. To bubble in our belly and then choosing the first word that makes its way up and out of our heart."

Tina and Heather smiled in agreement.

Closing our eyes now, I imagined myself by the water. Feelings of freedom, space, fear of the unknown, depth, darkness, plunged into my belly. It was time now to let that one word form that wanted to release from my heart.

"Truth," I said out loud without realising.

Tina and Heather opened their eyes and in response replied with their own word.

"Openness," Tina declared.

"Strength," Heather stated.

So, we had truth, openness and strength. That was the purpose and message we were to share for our art piece. We had to somehow find a way to say this visually while being in collaboration with each together.

"How do you want to say truth?" Heather asked.

"I want to say it with my heart," I found myself saying without thinking. "I want my heart to be big and bold and make a statement all on its own."

"Good," Heather replied.

"And for you Tina...openness...how would you like to show that?" Heather probed.

"I know," Tina declared, raising her hand enthusiastically in the air, "Why don't we use the box as our base material for the artwork. We can carve it into the shape of a heart with a Stanley Knife. Paint it in reds of varying shades to show depth, and then leave a space open at the top to feel that sense of openness. And then...strength," she continued, "That's where you come in Heather. Strength comes from it. Our art piece and its message will say that strength comes from having an open heart that speaks the truth."

"How should we show strength?" Heather wondered.

"Why don't we create a stairwell out of the remaining materials, joining them in an escalated fashion leading from inside the box at the centre of the heart? The varying materials will show that it's not just one way we grow strength in opening our heart, it's many ways and techniques. Trying different methods and using various resources to take one step at a time, in finding strength from within to open our heart."

Heather and I stared at Tina.

"You're amazing!" I declared.

"That's wonderful," Heather said, congratulating Tina on her ideas.

Turning to me now, Heather continued to speak. "Abigail, why don't you get started creating the heart from the box, keep an area open big enough to fit the materials, then paint it red, whatever shades you like."

Pointing to another section of the workstation, Heather added, "Tina and I will split up the materials and start the staircase and then join them together and glue them to the inside of your completed heart."

We began in earnest. Three virtual strangers, yet somehow in the space of wanting to collaborate, and accepting that talking about it wasn't enough, that the feeling we wanted was just as important...we found our voice.

As I cut away at the box and formed my heart, I wondered how long I had been living this way. Stuck in the thoughts going round and round in my head, yet never taking the time to sit with my feelings, and certainly not taking the time to voice them. Maybe that was a large reason for the demise of my marriage. I'd been shutting down my heart, rather than keeping it open.

Later in the class, when the final stages of our art piece were put together, I felt tears welling in my eyes and a lump forming in my throat. Tina buzzed around. Her cute little frame could have stood ten feet tall with pride. Even the demure Heather had wrinkles straining the corners of her eyes from the smile that wouldn't leave her mouth. Tina reached out and grabbed Heather and I in a spontaneous embrace. "Thank you," she giggled.

When Monique came around to inspect our work, we stood next to one another, trembling, like three schoolgirls waiting to receive our final assessment from our favourite teacher.

"Bravo," Monique declared, clapping her hands together. "I am so impressed with all of you. Three significant pieces of work, formed as one, created in well under two hours, and with two virtual strangers... bravo indeed. Now, if one might only apply that same collaboration in their lives...outside the solace and comfort of these four walls," Monique mused.

Turning to the whole group now, Monique commanded our attention with love and enthusiasm. "You are ready ladies to unleash yourselves, unravel your hearts, and find true expression in the experimentation of your art. You should go out and celebrate with one another. Have a drink to toast your success, after all, every artist must celebrate their first showing."

Twelve women looked at each other, green eyes meeting blue, brown eyes meeting hazel, only to meet blue once more.

As if sensing the excuses that would soon fall from on our lips, Monique held up her hand, palm facing outward. "It's only one drink ladies. Surely the load, the responsibilities at home, at work, with your family, can wait that little bit longer."

Waving her hand now at the door she said in a theatrical voice, "Be gone ladies, be proud. See you next week."

After making arrangements with the group to meet at the Beach House, a bar that sat almost on top of the sand at Bondi Beach, equipped with outdoor heaters, complimentary throw rugs and two large fireplaces burning inside, I jumped into my car to text Ed. Fear trapped inside my belly. Why was I so afraid to say what I desired?

Tina tooted and waved at me as her little yellow VW sped past. I knew it was now or never.

"You home yet?" I texted fast, as if this would somehow help my situation, then put on my seatbelt and got ready to roar the engine.

"Yep," came the reply.

"Not coming home straight away. Grabbing a drink with my art class," I texted back, then placed my phone in the console near the gear stick. I started the engine and followed the convoy of women in my white oversized 4WD Toyota, that said 'Family of Five'.

Ed texted straight back.

Looking down at my phone, I knew I shouldn't drive and dial but I was dying to know what he wrote.

"I've got an early start tomorrow," his text said.

Glimpsing at the words in bursts at various stop signs along the way, annoyance grew in my belly. Gee Ed. A simple, "Have fun," might have been nice.

Feeling bolder more these days since facing my fears of death with Sal, and facing my fears of insignificance in not being the artist that I think I was always meant to be, I wrote hurriedly at the next set of traffic lights. "I'll make sure I'm home before dawn," then stashed my phone into my handbag on the floor of the passenger side and laughed all the way to Beach Hut.

CHAPTER 24

It was the morning before our next couples counselling session. My week now went something like this...get through the weekend pretending to like Ed in front of the children. Weekday mornings were half to one hour drawing and sketching in bed before the kids woke up. After breakfast and getting three wriggly children changed for the day, it was trips to the park, beach or Kiddie Land when it rained. A treat day out to the zoo or museum, and sometimes for something very low key...a stop at the local cafe for hot chocolate and marshmallows.

I'd spend all Tuesday wishing away the hours in anticipation of art class in the evening, and every second Thursday dreading Greta and her brutal spelling out the reality of the failings of my marriage. I also spent quiet moments thinking about Sal and how much she meant to me, and wondering just what she might be going through.

After putting Emily and Harry down for their daytime sleep and setting up Brady in my bed with his own personal movie, headphones, cushions and popcorn, I smiled at him from the doorway before I went downstairs. His eyes were dancing, and his smile was as wide as the two ears on either side of his head. He shoved popcorn into his mouth, one oversized little boy's handful after another. The simple pleasures, I reflected. Kids have a way of uncomplicating life.

Then at the other side of life, I've got Sal facing the end. She's so clear too, really clear, of what she wants and she's doing it. What happens to all those years in between life starting and ending, when it all gets so messed up?

I sat on the steps that led to my backyard, carefully taking in the garden. In a matter of weeks spring would fully show itself in the blossoming flowers of, violets and pinks, deep reds and yellows. I would take comfort, then, in the pleasure of this garden that we started growing when we first bought the house just before we got married.

I took a deep breath, knowing that the simple pleasures of life no longer involved Ed and I. I'm not sure any amount of counselling could bring us back together. In fact, what the counselling had enabled me to do was come back to myself. I'd discovered just how I wanted to find solace not just in motherhood, but also in womanhood. I could see the burdens, one after the next, layer after layer, of walls that I built up.

In Ed and I growing apart, we were also growing up. He loves his life as the high-flying ad agency exec, wining and dining his clients. He takes pride in the work he produces, and gets a kick out of the hours he puts in to do it. He loves his kayaking and men's retreats. And, when he allows himself to let his guard down and not be in such a rush to fly out the door, he takes pleasure in sitting a while with the kids, or attempting to master his culinary skills in the kitchen, kick a ball with Brady or Harry, perhaps chase them around at the beach. When he's doing that, he actually looks happy.

But this marriage we are so desperately trying to have, trying to figure out, it's the least simplistic thing of all. It's the thing that's causing the great load, the greatest burden. I had recently come to this place in myself, through the work with Greta, Monique, and observing Sal's life being sucked away from her, of really wanting to live my life. Claim my own identity to be proud of the woman and mother I knew I was, and the woman who was still finding her way, to just maybe...if she's really lucky...make her living as an artist.

All those years of not knowing what vocation or life direction I should pursue. It wasn't the burden of motherload weighing me down, but instead that deep-rooted dishonesty that resided within. All that wasted energy and time blaming everyone else around me. Blaming my kids for taking up so much of my time, blaming Ed for not giving me much of his time, blaming my dad because he never wanted to spend any of his free time with me, blaming a mother-in-law, who didn't seem that interested in spending any time with my kids. I'd been sitting in constipation, too weighted to move, too incapacitated to find my freedom. But I saw it now, exactly who I was and all that I intended to become.

I reached for my phone and made a call to Greta's office, requesting her receptionist Annie change our appointment tomorrow evening from 6:30pm to 8:00pm. Annie told me that would be fine. Satisfied, I texted Ed's mother.

"Hi Meredith, I'm wondering if you could come by a little earlier at 5:30pm tomorrow and stay a little later? We would be home just after 9.00pm. Thankyou Abigail."

"Fine," came the reply after about 10 minutes or so. Brief as ever. I wouldn't pine or hope for a closer relationship any longer, or a few tender words, but instead accept that this was the way it was, and be thankful she could accommodate.

Ed was away in Melbourne pitching to a potential client. He was due back tomorrow afternoon. Picking up the phone again, I texted. "Can you get home by 5:00pm tomorrow?"

After twenty minutes or so his reply came through. "Fine."

I had to laugh. As curt in response as his mother.

The next evening, I took a little extra care getting ready. I decided on black pants that sucked everything in, my caramel leather boots with stiletto heels, a soft crème coloured blouse I had picked up on a shopping spree in Paris pre-motherhood. It fell loosely at the waist and the cowl frontage accentuated my full bust, at least that was one bonus of being a heavy curvy size 14, who was in denial she was really a 16. The sleeves were long and joined together at the cuffs with ivory pearl buttons that matched the row of buttons at the centre. I wore a sleek, white gold chain with a charm hanging from it, which I bought on a New York trip pre-motherhood. I twisted the charm in my fingers, sentiment tugging at my heart at the image of being back in my New York days, with all the charisma and confidence of a young carefree woman.

I placed white gold studs that dangled with a drop pearl in each earlobe. I marked my eyebrows with pencil, highlighted my eyes with soft brown shadow that made my green eyes look softer, smokier. I gave a lick of tint to my eyelashes and dotted my lips with pale pink gloss. I took a little care with my hair too, and tamed it somewhat with the hair dryer.

A knock at the door told me my mother-in-law had arrived.

"Oh! You look...ah...different tonight Abigail." Meredith commented, looking me up and down.

"Thank you," I smiled, holding the door open and closing it behind her as she set off down the hallway. I decided I'd take that as a compliment whether it was intended that way or not.

Ed arrived soon after his mother and after greeting the kids with more hugs than usual and kissing his mother on the cheek, he did a double take.

"Why are you wearing that?" he commented.

I laughed inwardly. I had finally begun to realise where Ed got his complimenting skills from.

"I felt like it Ed," I smiled, and then said goodnight to the kids and Meredith before heading to the door.

Once we were in the car and safely out of earshot from everyone, I revealed the change of plans. "Ed, I've moved Greta to 8:00pm so we can squeeze in dinner beforehand."

"What? You're not serious? You told me to race home for 5:00pm."

"Yes," I replied firmly.

"If I had known we were just leaving early for dinner, I could have swung by the office after I got off the plane."

"It will give us time to talk," I replied, trying not to let the tension that was building inside me reach my lips.

"What are you talking about?" he said impatiently, driving a little faster than I'd like. "That's what we do the whole time we're at Greta's. Why do we need to go through it all beforehand?"

"Because, there are things I need to say."

I sat fidgeting with the red and white chequered tablecloth that hung over the neat square table just for two. It was decorated with a single stem rose in a tiny glass vase, salt and pepper shakers and a carafe of water with two tumbler style glasses just next to it. A candle flame flickered in the centre of the table.

Taking a sweeping look at the other couples around us and the setting of our own table, I realised how romantic this place was. Dim lighting, small candlelit tables enough just for two spoke 'romantic couple' in volumes. It had been a few years since Ed and I had taken a date at our local Italian restaurant. Needless to say, they'd done it up since then.

The Italian waiter with a thick accent had taken our order with charm and enthusiasm, and left us with a basket of fresh sliced ciabatta bread and a dipping tray with olive oil and rock salt sprinkled in the centre.

"Well?" Ed questioned. "You've got me here, what it is?"

I sat silently looking at the man across the table. Staring at the man I had made a life with for the past fifteen years. In a single breath I was about to end any hopes we had of celebrating two decades together. I fidgeted, twisting the corner of the tablecloth around my fingers. This was harder than I thought it was going to be. I'd fantasized for so long about ending it, yet now I was doing it...well trying to do it...it wasn't coming easily. I knew once the words were out, I couldn't take them back.

"Ab, what's going on?" Ed said, irritation rising in his voice.

"Huh?" I replied.

"You wanted to talk. So talk!"

"Why do you want to be with me?" I asked absently.

"What?" he replied, screwing up his face.

"Why are you still with me?"

"What are you talking about?" He raised his voice, then noticed the short distance between our table and the couple to his right.

"Ed, I know we loved each other once, but I think too much has happened to ever get that back again."

He just stared. Said nothing.

"I know you're trying. Well, in your own way you're trying. And I know I'm trying. But the more work I do on myself, the more I realise how I want to be treated by a man."

"So, what are you saying?" Ed said glaring at me now, anger had well and truly reached his throat. His dark blue eyes grew blacker by the second.

"I'm saying...I really don't know why you're with me. You don't even seem to like me."

His turn to be silent.

We were interrupted briefly by our overfriendly Italian waiter, who looked, and sounded, like he had just arrived from the mother country last week. Thick Italian accent, early 20's, jet-black hair slicked back, big toothy grin.

"Ah, tis romantico no?" he gestured, his arms opening wide to the two of us once he had set down our pasta dishes and garden salad.

"Would Signora likea some parmegano?" he offered, while grinning and looking at me with the loveable affection that all young, Italian male waiters seemed to exude.

"Sure," I smiled.

He turned to Ed. "Anda for you Signor?" His Italian accent got thicker, his voice grew deeper as if he were about to break into song. "Parmegano?"

"No," Ed snapped.

I flicked an unfriendly glare at Ed. There was no need to be rude to this perfectly fabulous waiter when all he was doing was being his charming self. Ed used to be charming, I reminisced for a moment, remembering a time when he would have found a waiter like this entertaining.

"Will thata be alla?" the waiter said, already turning

his head to leave.

"Si. Grazie," I smiled.

"Prego," he bowed toward me. "Buon appetito," he added, as he smiled and left.

"I hate smarmy waiters," Ed spat.

"I liked him," I declared.

"You would," Ed snorted.

I sat silently looking at Ed and wondered how I could ever find the words. I didn't want to take a perfect opportunity to be romantic at a quaint little Italian restaurant only to have it ruined by the man facing me. I wanted him to want me. To make an effort and to damn well show me he gave a shit.

"I want a divorce," I blurted out without realising it.

Ed's reaction was brutal. No words, just a look that said he was ready to kill.

"So we're there are we? You've finally said it." Anger raged in his voice, but I could have sworn, looking into his eyes, that mist was slowly forming.

My heart ached. I didn't want to hurt him but, shaking off the guilt, I remembered what I came here to do. Strength stirred in my gut. Twisting the charm on my necklace for strength and to gather my thoughts.

I finally spoke. "Yes Ed, we're here. Someone has finally said it."

Silence.

He just kept staring across the table.

"No amount of counselling is bringing us back

together when we're already so far apart. I haven't been enjoying my life Ed. I've been trapped in the walls and layers and foundations of motherhood."

"What, so you're saying you shouldn't have had kids?" He flared at me.

I took a breath, connected with that inner strength I had found earlier.

"Ed, I love all three of our children, very much. But I have been struggling, I realise that now. Not struggling to look after them and do the day to day that is motherhood...running a house...running a family... but struggling to enjoy it. But I am now. Sure, there are some days I still struggle a little with the kids. Even a lot. That feeling, that overwhelming feeling that absolutely everything I am doing is shaping those three kids of ours. Wondering if I'm getting it right, hoping, that sometimes I do. But there are glimpses of successful mothering that I am witnessing in myself now, and not all of that has to do with what I do for them, but also what I do for me. You see, I finally realise, and I mean finally realise that the happier I am, the more I give to myself. And the more I do that, the more I am able to give to those three beautiful children of ours. I am finally getting so much of my life right for a change that the things that are so painfully not working out, are like someone is hitting me over the head with a wood paling, banging loud to get my attention, so I know exactly where the failures are."

"Ed, I want a divorce." Tears dribbled gently down my cheek.

It was hard to gauge Ed's mood or what he was

thinking. He pushed aside his half-eaten linguini marinara and glared.

"I want to say I'm sorry but I'm wondering why I have to be?" I sniffed. "Sorry it didn't work out. Sorry we didn't love each other enough to find our way out of the darkness. Sorry we didn't interest each other enough to want to be the first person at the end of the day we wanted to download with. Sorry that this new arrangement will unravel a family, change the living arrangements."

Silence.

Ed just stared at me.

"Ed, say something," I pleaded, using my red paper napkin as a tissue to dry my eyes and blow my nose.

I looked over at our Italian waiter briefly, who shuffled his feet from side to side, an indication he wanted to clear our plates, but hesitant to take a step closer toward the scene unravelling before his eyes. I gave him a small smile as if letting him know it was now or never.

He darted quickly toward us. "I takea these plates, awaya?" he asked. "Finito?"

"Si. Thanks," I spoke softly, choking on tears.

Ed moved his hands away from the plate so the waiter could remove his dish but spoke no words.

Once the waiter had left, I looked back at Ed. "Say something, please."

"What's left to say? Looks like you've been thinking about this for quite some time. So what do you want me to do, thank you for finally getting that off your chest? What you've been so desperately wanting to say for so long?"

There was no denying rage was running through Ed's veins.

"Ed, I didn't plan this. Didn't plot," I said leaning forward, wanting to reach out and grab his hand and look into his eyes to show him just how much I hurt too.

But I didn't reach out. The natural loving part of me that wanted to help him through this, ease his pain, ease his own load at the failures of our marriage. I felt sick inside. Uneasy, knowing the hurt I was causing him. I couldn't help the man I once loved overcome his own grief in learning to live without our marriage. Help the partner I had made a life with start a new beginning that didn't have me in the main frame.

Our waiter hovered again, looking to me for guidance. For permission to intrude on this very intimate setting, so far from romantic it became tragically funny.

I gave him a smile, a look of reassurance. "The bill please. Grazie."

He gave me a nod, replying. "Si bella," And then glanced sideways at Ed. And... ehhh...bello."

I peeked into my handbag to check the time on my phone. "We're going to be late if we don't leave now."

"What's the point?" Ed sulked.

He looked like he'd aged ten years since the start of dinner, yet his actions, his thoughts, were child-like.

"Because Ed, every ending deserves the best chance at a new beginning. And I don't honestly believe that you or I have the foresight or experience to help make that so. With Greta's help, we have a chance."

CHAPTER 25

Ed and I were now facing Greta with gravely solemn expressions.

"You look lovely today Abigail."

"Thank you Greta. I realised in letting go of my corporate image and falling into motherhood, I had yet to find an image of everyday womanhood. How I wanted to dress for me, in a way that made me feel good about myself when I stared back at the mirror."

"Good for you," Greta smiled.

"Now, let's hear what new developments have taken shape over the past two weeks." She peaked an eyebrow and turned more toward Ed.

He sat in silence, as did I.

"What's going on?" Greta asked. "Ed, Abigail, what's happened since we saw each other last?"

I exhaled. I knew it was going to be up to me to do the big reveal.

"Greta," I said gently. "Ed and I have come to a point." Ed flared his eyes at me, rage pouring out of them. Shifting in my seat, I continued. "I should say, I've come to a point...a place of realisation...and well...I've just explained this to Ed during dinner before we came."

"Go on," Greta encouraged, looking to me, then

turned a measured look at Ed.

"I can't do this anymore Greta."

"Do what Abigail?"

Oh, did I really have to spell it out? But I had to remember she was a psych, trained in extracting information out of people.

Looking firmly into Greta's eyes and placing my hands under my thighs, sitting on them as if to find strength, I blurted it all out.

Blurted out that I wanted a divorce. That I wanted to move on with my life. How I had started to appreciate the time I had left now that my best friend was dying. Had started appreciating the kids more, seeing my time with them as precious, rather than a burden. I'd uninhibited myself in taking art classes. Yet in all this finding myself, what I also found out is that I didn't want to share my life with Ed anymore. Could see the long dark path we would continue to take each other on. But now what I really wanted was to give us the opportunity to finally find a bit of lightness in our lives.

Greta sat and listened, made notes. I often wondered if she ever read back over them or if she was just making a show that she was paying attention.

For a few moments we were all silent.

Taking in the finality of my words, I exhaled loudly without realising how much I needed to get that out. To have Ed really listen to me, to everything I had been going through.

Greta laid the foundations of the sessions from the

very beginning. When one speaks, the other listens. Our therapist asks the questions. Ed and I do the answers. We do not criticise the other or comment about them in response to what the other has said. Instead, our response is to come from how the other's words make us feel. So, knowing the rules, we both sat in silence waiting for Greta's next move, like an astute chess player.

"How do you feel, now that you've let that all out Abigail?" She asked, glancing at Ed when she spoke.

"Relieved," I blurted out.

"Go on," she encouraged.

"Relieved...er...guilty...exhausted...enlightened   too actually...and really scared...but mostly...relieved Greta, because it's been burdening me for so long."

After a short pause she turned to Ed. "And how do you feel Ed?"

"Empty," he replied with a flatness in his voice. Void of expression.

"What else Ed?"

"Nothing. I feel nothing," he said, turning to face the window.

Greta was silent before probing a little deeper. "And if you could go beyond the emptiness, the nothingness, what would you feel?"

"Pissed off!" he flared.

"Good Ed. What else?"

"Angry. Cheated on. Lied to. Used. Taken advantage of. Threatened. Mislead. Made a fool of. What more do you want me to say?" he said, standing up from the chair and sweeping his hand through his dark brown, wavy hair in frustration.

"Are you feeling hurt Ed?" she asked.

"Hurt?" Ed yelled back at Greta, taking a step toward her in rage then turning his rage now on me.

"That bitch," he pointed at me. "Married me, had kids with me, said she'd make a life with me and now she wants to throw all of that away. Well she can forget it if she wants me to tell her how sad and sorry I feel about all of this. I'm angry, seriously pissed off that while she's been off finding herself, I'd been hoping she'd find her way back to me."

I clutched at the sides of my black tailored pants, pulling at them for strength.

"So, what would a life without Abigail mean for you Ed?" Greta wondered.

"I'd be gutted," he said, surprising both himself and me in the same breath.

His eyes clouded over with tears as he looked down at me. "I love you Abby. I thought we signed up, 'for better or worse'?"

He turned to Greta and let go. "I don't know how to do this any other way than I am."

I sucked in my stomach, held tight to the fabric of my pants and hoped the tears would not come.

"Abigail," Greta turned her attention to me. "How does that make you feel, listening to everything Ed has just said?"

"Sad," I replied. "Sad that it has to come to me leaving, for him to want me to stay."

"Do you want Abby to stay because she's leaving Ed?"

His eyes closed briefly. Opening them again, he stared directly into my own. Yet his words were for Greta.

"I want her because I've always wanted her. Loved her through it all. Loved her more each time with the birth of each of our children. Wondered how I could love her any more than I already did. I love the way she cooks and makes our home so cosy. I'll never make poached eggs the way she does. The way she creates something from nothing. I'm always in awe. I loved travelling with her all over the world before we had kids, meeting up at sneaky locations in the middle of a work trip. But it's now with three kids in our lives, that I love travel just as much even if it's a trip to the beach as a family of five. One child on my shoulders, one on her hip, and the third taking turns to look up into our eyes, waiting to be swung a little higher than the last. I'm in awe of how much she has achieved in motherhood. But I'm gutted Greta, and deeply pissed off...as much with myself as I am with my wife...for leaving it so long to get a life. She suffered for so long, never said a word. Sure, she may have cloaked it in cynicism. A snide comment about being late here, a peaky comment about not making the bed there, a snigger about not throwing my clothes in the laundry right after I took them off. Sure, she spoke of her dissatisfaction in me, but never did she reveal her dissatisfaction in herself."

He floored me. I couldn't speak. Don't you dare ask me to respond now Greta! I haven't a word. Not a single word in response to this revelation. He never let on.

Greta allowed silence to fill the air.

Eventually she said, "Ed, are you ready to take a seat again?" Motioning her hand toward his chair.

Taking a seat next to mine with a heaviness in his manner, Ed sat in silence as I did. Greta stared back at the two of us. We stared back in return. Ed and I dared not look at each other.

"It hurts, doesn't it?" she said, taking turns to look at each of us. "It hurts when you feel betrayed by the one you love. And it hurts when you realise you have contributed to that. It hurts when you realise you've been taking someone else's happiness for granted and relying on them to pick up the emotional load that you were too slack to pick up yourself. Relationships take work guys. And I mean real work. And then when you add a commitment like marriage and children on top of that...that's a load in itself. We go through a lot as human beings, so fragile and sensitive to the goings on in the world. But the saddest thing about our vulnerability is that we take it out on the ones we love most...our partner...and quite often our children...not to mention on ourselves."

Greta took a breath and a moment to pause. "Now, you two have to decide whether you want to do the work or not. I'm not talking one or two sessions with me, I'm talking about the work you want to do all on your own. The work you want to put into your relationship with all three of your children, not just as a collective, but the unique relationship you have separately with each one of them. The work you want to put into being co-parents, there's that relationship, then there's the relationship between the two of you as partners, life partners, the commitment you made in marrying one another. Then there's the relationship of sex and intimacy, your relationship as lovers and of course your relationship as friends. Not to mention your relationship as sharing a space together, a home, like a housemate, and all that goes into running a household. Then there's the relationship of money, finances, paying the bills. And of course...there's the relationship with yourself, the most important relationship of all."

I looked down at my hands, now resting in my lap, and contemplated everything Greta was saying. I heaved a heavy sigh.

"What is it Abigail? What's going through your mind right now?"

Still looking at my hands, I said, "It's a lot."

"A lot?" Greta wondered.

"A lot to take in and a lot to take on."

"You're right. The problem with marriage and with starting a family is that no one tells us what to do. We don't go to marriage classes to learn how to be married. There's a saturated market on pre-natal classes, but how often do you see classes on what to do with the baby when you get it home? What to do with yourself when you get home. What to do with your partner when you get home? Parenthood is one of the most vulnerable places you can exist."

Taking a breath and leaning forward, compassion filling her eyes, Greta spoke. We listened. "This is what I want to say to you two now. You know I don't often give my opinion. But I'm going to give it now."

Ed and I shifted in our seats.

"I think if you don't give this a real go, you'll regret it. All relationships take work. Even if you move on to new partners, you need to know that will take work too. Neither of you have given this marriage a real chance at success. Neither of you have had role models in your own parents to model what a loving partnership and life mate can truly be."

Turning to me, she spoke gently. "Abigail, it seems like your father spent far too much time having affairs and indulging himself on the high-flying life he had grown accustomed to, to notice how much his little girl wanted to be acknowledged and adored. Because of that, you became stoic, learned to shut out your feelings for fear your desires would not be met. It's affected the way you are with Ed."

"And with you Ed," Greta said turning to him now, "You lack real intimacy with your mother. She's cold toward you, doesn't spend long enough to get close. Too concerned with her social set and what's going on in her friendship circle to make a real connection with you. Even both your brothers have made their lives very separate from the family. You are all incredibly independent, never calling on one another for support. This distant, emotionless relationship with your mother, has deeply affected your ability to get close to your wife."

Turning fully to both of us now, and stretching her back a little upright, Greta continued. "You see, both of you, you were on the back foot when you started this commitment called marriage with one another." A strength rose in her voice now, willing us to listen hard. "But you are so much wiser now, in knowing what it truly means to be married. To make a commitment to someone you love."

Exhaling and putting her clipboard behind her on the desk, Greta spoke with a full heart and a head loaded with wisdom. "I don't think any couple could not have had a real, deep, and enduring love for each other by the things that came out of Ed's mouth earlier. And Ed," Greta turned to him fully now. "Abigail had no idea just how much she was struggling. That's why she could never tell you, because she didn't even know it herself. But she's telling you now."

Holding her palms open and gesturing her hands toward us, Greta continued. "One of the real problems is you both stopped talking to each other. Stopped speaking up, and I don't mean yelling at the other person or rude comments here and there. You stopped communicating and remembering you were a team. I think this marriage deserves a chance. I think you both deserve another opportunity to make things right. And here's what I want you to do to get started."

Greta reached back for her clipboard. She was going back into homework mode. I knew the routine.

"I want you to look at the household as a shared

responsibility. Ed, you'll need to look at what you can do to contribute more, and I don't mean financially. You're already doing a great job of that. You'll also need to look at the way you spend your time with the kids. Start giving each other the opportunity to have one-on-one time with all three of your children. I know you don't have a lot of time, but it doesn't take much to have real connections with kids. They are openhearted sponges who love to soak up any bit of personal attention and love they can get, especially from their parents."

"Abigail, this art of yours, it really sounds like you've found something there. I think you need some time to think how you might do more with that in the form of potential paid work. I understand you are with the kids 24/7 and there's little free time to explore this art, so how about this for an idea? Look at putting your kids in care either one, ideally two, days a week. If you want to have someone come to the house instead, fine. But you need to have your own space to create. By the way the passion comes through your voice when you speak of your art classes, I'd say you have a real untapped talent there. Something you should certainly pursue. I'm sure for the time being with Ed's salary, you can find a regular sitter or day care. Before you know it Abigail, your art will bring in enough to cover the fees. And, one last thing...I want the two of you to take dance classes."

"What?" Ed said speaking my own mind.

"You heard me. Dance classes. Take a course. A full term, six to eight weeks or so. Partner dancing. Where you have to touch, look into each other's eyes, connect. Not speak with words but with the language of body rhythms, emotions and trust. The two of you need to learn to trust each other again, and to find a way to communicate and rely on each other. I think you'll find the dance classes will help."

She reached to her business card holder that sat on her desk and flicked through the cards. "Here it is," Greta enthused, pulling out a business card for couples dance lessons on it.

She looked at the clock on her desk. "We're almost done here tonight. I feel like we've finally made some real progress. I want all of that underway before our next session. And...I want a progress report."

Turning to me with a hint of tenderness in her voice, Greta wondered. "Abigail, would you hold off your decision to take action on the divorce proceedings until the dance classes are over...just six to eight weeks?"

Hesitating, I finally nodded.

Turning to Ed now Greta continued. "Ed, you have to make these real changes over the next few weeks to see if this is a marriage that either of you want to stay in. Understood?"

Ed shrugged his shoulders. "Yep. Sure."

On the way home neither of us spoke. A heaviness filled the air in the car. We were processing.

CHAPTER 26

The next morning, I woke feeling as if my head would explode. I wasn't sure if a massive head cold had miraculously entered my over worked brain overnight, or, if it was the beating that my mind took while I tossed and turned, trying to process everything Greta had said.

Tears formed in my eyes from the pounding on my head that did not let up. I wanted to curl back up into bed and hide under the covers all day. I didn't want to play mummy today. No drawing this morning. Didn't have the energy, or heart for it. A rawness crawled around in my gut. I just felt so incredibly alone in all of this. Really, really alone.

I could hear the kids already up, rattling around in their room. No doubt Harry would have a nice full, not to mention stinky, nappy for me to change. What a way for a woman to wake up!

I stumbled out of bed and threw on my slippers, drawing the dressing gown string tighter as if it would help hold me together today. I opened the kids' room to find all three jumping up and down on their beds, laughing and throwing pillows and soft toys around. I'm constantly amazed how much damn energy kids wake up with...every...single... day.

Wincing, I touched the palm of my hands to my

eyes in the hope it would help the throbbing dissipate. Releasing my hands now, I waited for the miracle that didn't happen. The pain was still very much present, and growing at a rapid rate.

"Back in a sec kids," I said, running to the bathroom. Reaching up to the medicine box on the top shelf of the bathroom cabinet, I grabbed the bottle of ibuprofen and swallowed two tablets, washing it down with water from the tap like a puppy dog. Hoping, praying, the pills would take effect sooner rather than later.

I shuffled back into the kids' room, trying not to dry reach when I picked up little Harry for a cuddle. Yep he had a good one trapped in that nappy of his. After swiftly changing Harry, more for my benefit than his, I moved the kids downstairs.

"Mummy's got a pounding headache this morning. It's breakfast in front of the tele."

"Yay!" Brady and Emily shouted in unison.

Harry jumped up and down now to mimic his two older siblings.

All three kids shouted out loud, jumped up and down and danced around, throwing their hands up in the air. I winced at the noise. Ohhhh please kick in ibuprofen... like now.

With all three kids plonked at the coffee table, sitting on their knees, glued to the box shovelling cereal into their mouths, I used this window of time to have a cup of tea and a slice of vegemite toast, minus the butter. Once I was seated, I noticed a note resting under the fruit bowl that sat in the middle of the island bench. As I opened it, I noticed it was a letter from Ed.

"Dear Abby.

I love you. I'm game if you are."

Tears stung my eyes. Turning to check on the kids I returned to the letter.

"I'm sorry I let things get to this place. I'm sorry I let you down. I'm sorry I didn't buy you flowers on your birthday when I knew how much they made you smile. I'm sorry I forgot to say I love you at least once every twenty four hours. I'm sorry I didn't kiss you every night, every day. I'm sorry I forgot to be the man you married in every imaginable way. I'm sorry I hurt you. Sorry I took you for granted. So very sorry I stepped away.

I can't imagine any other woman in my life. Abby, you will always be my one true love. Making those three kids of ours was no accident. I loved every bit of you when I did. I loved you before, during and after, and I will love you forever more.

I forgot when you became a mother that you were once a talented, creative woman too. I'll do whatever I can to make this work and support you in your artistic pursuits.

I'm not giving up, not in the slightest. I'll be damned if I do. You chose me to make a life with and I'd like a chance to show you that I can be that man. A man you can depend and rely on. A man to hold your hand. I want to show you I can be a husband to love. Can be your children's father that you can depend on. I want to be a man you can share yourself with too.

I want to show you I can be all those things and so much more.

I gave no other woman my name Montgomery but I now want to give you a reason to keep it. To be proud to carry and share my name and be proud of the man at your side.

I thought my job was to provide for the family, but I can see now how much I have denied you. I want you to find your wings and have your freedom as well. I want you to make a life of your own. Not separate from me but one you can share with me too.

I am contacting dance classes today and will let you know later what they say. Greta's right. We've got to find a way to connect, communicate and trust one another that allows us to meet in the middle.

Get set up with a part-time helper for the kids. Get on to that straightaway Ab. You need some space for yourself. Daycare can come later but for now, let's get someone in. What about the neighbour, the lady who retired recently that helped the night Sal went to hospital? I know it was all a bit crazy that night, but I'm sure she'd love a bit of extra cash and the company. Why don't you approach her about doing two afternoons or mornings a week to get started? But I'll leave it to you to do what you feel best, whatever you want.

I want to make this work Ab. We've got six to eight weeks of dance classes to see what we've got.

I love you. Always will.

Ed. x"

I rubbed my eyes. Grateful the headache pills had finally kicked in.

I couldn't face the kids just yet. Needed to regroup. "Mummy's going to have a quick shower."

No response. Three muted small children glued to Mr Spot on the television. I had to laugh. I hated using television to distract my kids and give me some peace of mind, but now I'm wondering why I have denied myself that for so long too.

An hour later, one fresh dressed mummy and three smartly dressed children stood patiently waiting at our neighbour's front door.

"Let's knock again Mummy," Brady declared, eager for an excuse to pound harder on the frosted glass panel.

"Wait darling," I said, reaching to grab his hand before it struck.

An older woman who I knew as Eva opened the door to three enthusiastic little faces.

"Hello there," she smiled.

"Hi," I replied. "Sorry to intrude, but I was err...ahh."

"Yes dear?" she enquired.

"I...um...wanted to say thank you...for well...helping with the kids in that emergency a little while back, when my friend had to be taken to hospital."

"Of course dear," she said. "Is your friend ok now?"

"Ahhh...mmm...she's fine. But...what I was also here for was...well."

"Yes dear?"

"Well...you see...I'd like to get a regular part-time sitter for the kids. A couple of mornings a week and well...you were so good with them in that emergency... and well...I understand you're retired now and wondered if you would be interested?" I finally managed to get it all out.

"Well that is something to consider," she smiled. "Would you like to come in and have some morning tea so we can talk about it?"

Without waiting for me to reply, Brady pushed his way through the door, followed by a super eager Emily. Harry wiggled his way off my hip, wanting to be released from my grip to ensure he didn't miss out on the action.

Eva laughed. "Seems it's settled then. Why don't you come in dear...Abigail, isn't it?" she questioned stepping aside so I could make my way down the warm beige carpeted corridor.

"Yes," I smiled, "It is."

Eva wore her hair in a fuss free, cropped short style that framed her angular face. Fresh blue eyes that sparkled when she smiled and smooth, lightly tanned skin that looked like it stayed that way all year round. I understood her to be originally from the Netherlands but apparently she had been in Australia for some time, so the man at the fruit shop on the corner mentioned to me once. Even though she had retired recently, she hardly looked a day over 50. Her grey hair was the only hint of her age. The rest of her looked incredibly vibrant and well...youthful. She had a lean body that looked great in her dark denim jeans, tennis shoes, polo shirt and cardigan.

She placed a box of toys in front of the kids that included books, blocks, barbies and bears. "I call it the 'B Box'," she laughed. "When my grandchildren come to stay." Oh no, grandchildren. She'll be busy enough with them without wanting to overload herself with mine.

"I love to have something on hand for them to play with. The kids can add anything they want that starts with the letter B to the 'B Box'. I change the alphabet from time to time. I've got all the letters," she said, pointing to a stack of big square red boxes with big blue letters brightly painted on the front, representing the alphabet.

"But I don't see them nearly as much as I'd like. They live in Adelaide."

"Oh. Really?" I brightened now.

"So, tell me, what did you have in mind?" She was seated on the chair opposite me, sipping her tea. I looked briefly to the kids who were now fully engrossed in 'B Box' land.

"Well," I said shifting a little in my chair. "I need to take a little time for myself."

"I'll bet you do," she declared, gazing her eyes over the kids.

"I've been taking art classes and...well...it seems I might be able to make something of it...pursue it professionally perhaps."

"That's wonderful," she smiled biting into her

homemade lemon teacake.

"And well...I was thinking that if I had a little extra help...I could take the time to see if I really have something."

"I'd love to!" she declared.

I laughed. "But I haven't told you what it involves and worked out a suitable payment."

"I'm thinking you want a few hours to yourself, perhaps a day or two each week. And...if it works out... that might grow into a night out once in a while? And," she said winking at me, "If it's cash, that'll help ease the pension pittance I get from the Government."

I grinned. I knew Eva was perfect.

"So I was thinking...maybe a Tuesday and a Thursday? Say 9:30am till 1:30pm? Say...$25 cash per hour? Would that work ok?" I wondered, taking a sip of English Breakfast tea.

"Oh, what an old lady could do with a little extra cash!" she chuffed. "I'd love to," she beamed with enthusiasm. "Besides, I'd love the company."

Eva looked over to check on the kids, a natural maternal habit it seemed, then wondered. "But what about your mother? And...your husband's mother?"

I softened, thinking of my mum. "Mine died a long time ago. She never got to meet the kids I'm afraid. And Ed...that's my husband, his...well mother...let's just say she prefers tennis, high tea and ladies lunch day to running around after three energetic children."

Looking over at the kids and then back at Eva, I

added, "I think she'd love to be let off the hook actually.

"Well, it's settled then," Eva said wiping her mouth with her napkin. "Would you like me to start next Tuesday?"

"I'd love it," I beamed.

I wanted to reach out and hug her.

"Oh, one more question," she asked. "Would you prefer the kids to come here to my place or me come to you?"

"Gosh...well...that would be wonderful if the kids could come here. Then I'd have the house all to myself and could get messy with my art." My mind began to daydream at the wonder of all that precious time to myself at home, without a single member of my family there. Bliss.

"My place it is then," Eva confirmed. "Bring the children at 9:30am on Tuesday. Now," she added with a hint of humour in her voice, are you going to tell me their names or should I play a guessing game? We didn't quite get around to that the night your friend was taken to the hospital." She got up from her chair and sat crossed legged on the floor to play with the kids.

"Oh. My. God! Where are my manners?"

CHAPTER 27

Ed texted around 5:00pm. "Can't get home till 9:00pm. Big pitch then client drinks but I REALLY want to see you. Talk before you go to bed. I've got good news re dancing. Ed x."

Smiling, I thought of my own good news about Eva. I actually felt excited about being able to share something with Ed for a change when he got home.

It was around 9:30pm when he eventually got in. I was sitting by the fire, feet curled up underneath me, flicking through a hard cover art book I had picked up at the National Art Gallery in Canberra. I hadn't looked at it in at least ten years.

"Sorry, took a little longer," he said. "Thanks for waiting up."

I smiled.

"Can I get you something?" He asked, "Before I join you...cuppa, glass of wine, Baileys?"

Baileys made me think of Sal. She was getting worse but she wouldn't let on. I'd strangled it out of her nurse last week when I called while Sal was taking a nap. I needed to get back down there and soon. Tears welled in my eyes.

"You ok?" Ed asked, stepping a little closer.

I choked back tears but I knew it was important for me, important for us, not to shut him out. "Just thinking that the last time I had Baileys was with Sal."

"Oh," he replied softly. "How's she going?" he asked stepping even closer.

"Not great," I managed to get out.

"I might take a couple of days again. Head off with the kids in the morning. Come back Monday evening."

"Go on your own," he said walking over to the drinks cabinet. "I'll look after the kids. I'll take Monday off work."

"What?"

"The pitch went well. They owe me, big time. I'll let my assistant know in the morning."

"Here," he said, passing me a large glass of Baileys on ice with fresh lime slices through it. "To Sal," he said clinking his glass to mine.

"To Sal," I said, tears misty in my eyes.

"Can I join you?" he asked tentatively.

"Sure," I replied.

He stretched out on the sofa, keeping a healthy distance between us.

"I phoned up about the dance classes today. They've got a beginner's class on every Wednesday at 7:00pm. Goes for about an hour. They said we can join any time. I've signed us up for the next eight weeks."

I looked at him in surprise.

Smiling he continued. "We start next Wednesday."

"What about work?" I asked sipping my Baileys.

"I'll work around work. This is more important. You are more important. We are more important."

He reached for my hand and squeezed it in a way that made me nervous. I could feel he was trying, really trying. But how long would it last?

"Any luck with the sitter?" he asked, releasing my hand.

I smiled. Relief and hope filled my insides. "Eva is all set. Recently retired. Loads of energy and super keen. Two mornings a week. Tuesday and Thursday. And, she's going to have the kids at her house so I can have our place free to paint, to do my art."

"That's great news Ab," he said squeezing the back of my neck and massaging a little.

Nervously, I shifted in my seat.

"Ab, I want you more than ever," he whispered, massaging my neck deeper. "I've missed you. Missed touching you." Oh no. He's moving closer. "Missed kissing you...touching you...making love to you."

I gulped Baileys and shifted uncomfortably.

"Ed, I'm um...I'm not ready. I need some time. Please understand I just need time to...well...see if this is what I want anymore."

"Sure," he said, dropping his hand suddenly from my neck.

"Don't be angry with me Ed."

"I'm not angry. I know, I know...we need time," he

said, absently running his fingers through his messy brown hair. "I just miss you that's all."

"I know. Just give me a little more time."

Rising from the sofa, Ed headed for the shower, suggesting I take off early in the morning to make three full days of it with Sal. He assured me the kids would be fine. Better than fine. Told me to get to bed and get some rest before the long drive.

Before leaving the room, he reached down and held my gaze. I could see love roaming around his gorgeous blue eyes. Eyes that I had never grown tired of looking at.

He stopped just short of my mouth.

I held my breath.

And then...he kissed me. Lightly swept his lips over mine. So tender and so sweet. He didn't tell me he loved me, but the kiss told me he did.

CHAPTER 28

Sal stood in the doorway, a great big smile on her face. But her body spoke volumes. She'd dropped a lot of weight since I saw her last month. A lot can happen in four weeks when you have cancer eating away at your insides.

"Come here you," she said, holding out her arms, wincing a little at the effort.

I hugged her and felt bones beneath the layers of clothes hanging on her body. I planted a firm smile on my mouth in defence, but she knew me too well.

"I know...I know," she said leading me into the house. "I've dropped a massive amount of weight. But there's not a thing I can do about it. One way to lose a few pounds though," she laughed.

"Not funny," I replied.

"Better than moaning about it," she smiled. "Cuppa?" she asked, walking into the kitchen.

"I can get it," I said, stepping in to take the kettle from her hand.

"Ah...let me do it. Trust me, if I need help you'll know."

Turning on the kettle with a slow, methodical order to her movements, much like that of a frail old lady, she let me glimpse into how life was for her now. "I start out ok but find I need a rest by the afternoon, to see me through the evening."

Looking out to the spectacular view that was Sal's new backyard, Seven Mile Beach in all its glory, she suggested we take our tea out onto the deck and soak up the warm sunshine.

Tasting one of the mini blueberry sugar-free muffins Catherine the nurse had made earlier that morning, I asked where she was.

"Sent her out for supplies," Sal replied, as she took a little time to get comfortable in one of the two wicker chairs on the deck, complete with footrest. I gazed out at the blue ocean for miles and miles. Breathed in fresh air that told me summer was on its way.

"It's beautiful down here Sal," I reflected, taking up the other chair on the deck and sipping my tea.

"I love it here," Sal replied. "Couldn't think of a nicer place to die."

Bitter sweet filled my mouth.

"So, Ed gave you a leave pass did he?" she asked peaking her eyebrow.

"Oh Sal, I don't even know where to begin."

"Well you better get started with it then," she encouraged. "You've got three whole days to fill me in, and, for us to solve all the world's problems," she laughed.

Barely pausing for breath, I downloaded for almost two hours before Catherine returned, armed with an oversized box of fresh produce. Leeks and celery, loads of green leafy vegetables, carrots and crisp pink lady apples sticking out over the top of the box.

"So what do you think?" I asked Sal, as she eased herself slowly from sitting position to stretching out further to lay down.

"I'd say that either way, you'll both be good dancers at the end of it."

We both burst out laughing.

Taking a sober moment now, Sal held my gaze, took a breath and spoke.

"I'd say it's about time you got a little extra help with the kids. About time he took care of them on his own. About time you did something with your life that you actually enjoy doing. You've always had a flair for the arts, for creativity Ab. You're just so damn talented you got scooped up by the first employer who'd take you straight after uni. And regrettably, you never looked back. Never gave a thought to whether the jobs you were taking one after the other, were something you enjoyed doing, and not just paying the rent. I'd say we should break open the bubbles tonight girlfriend and celebrate!"

Motioning to sit up, Sal suggested we take a walk on the beach. "Catherine will have lunch all set up by the time we get back. I'll rest after that," she assured me.

Later, with Sal resting and dinner being taken care of by Catherine, who seemed to prefer quietly, diligently doing her duties on her own, I decided a little art therapy might help fill the gap.

"Kids ok?" I texted Ed before getting stuck into the art paper with charcoal that sat on the floor of the deck overlooking the beach.

"We're fine. Be with Sal. Ed x."

I wanted to do something for Sal, sketch something for her to enjoy when I went home on Monday. A gift to show her how much she meant to me. Crouching on my knees, I frowned at the paper on the lime washed deck, growing frustrated the ideas weren't coming, under the pressure of trying to master perfection.

Then, remembering what Monique always said when we were stumped or blocked, to close our eyes and open to our imagination.

I diligently closed my eyes, took a deep breath, and opened up to my dreaming mind. I breathed in the smell of the ocean, allowed the sound of the waves to crescendo in my ears. Opened to the sounds of birds and laughter in the distance.

With my eyes still closed, I began remembering a time when Sal and I went to New York. We really did have the time of our lives. I was dating Ed at the time, but it was still early days, so Sal had said a little flirting wouldn't hurt. "Besides, it would keep him on his toes if he discovered he had a little competition," she had insisted.

I remembered this one bar Sal and I went to, laughing all the way down the stairs. An upmarket jazz bar uptown, with the finest of men to devour with our eyes, not to mention our mouths.

We let them buy us drinks, and talked early into the next day. Two 28-year-old outgoing Aussie women with enchanting accents and everything to look forward to in life.

My mind drifted back to Sal in the other room, taking a much-needed rest, now that cancer was slowly sucking the life from her body. With my eyes remaining closed, I forced myself to return to that scene in the bar. "Cocktails & Dreams," we had declared that New York trip, playing homage to the infamous Tom Cruise movie. That's what I'd paint for her, I decided.

Opening my eyes, I began sketching on the page, creating the framework for a bar. Two girls in tightly fitted dresses, one red, Sal of course, and the other pale blue. Sky-high stilettos, long luscious red curls on Sal and dark blonde sleeked blow-dried hair for my own. I drew men lined up on either side of us, a single file leaning in. A sexy dark haired waiter in the background with a cocktail shaker in his hand, muscles bulging from his arms. The men were gazing inward, to the direction of Sal and I, having the time of our life in the middle of it all. "Cocktails and Dreams", I scrawled above the bar in the sketch and smiled when I took in the scene. Pleasures of memories made with my best girlfriend would forever be etched in my heart.

"How much longer do you think Sal will be resting?" I later asked Catherine, about an hour of sketching under my belt. Looking at the clock on the microwave, she replied, "Another half hour or so I'd say."

I informed her I would quickly run into town and be

back before Sal woke up.

I stowed the drawing in the cupboard in the spare room where I was sleeping and ran out the door. I wanted to grab some paints from the art and craft store in town and put the paint on the sketch later. Have it all dry by Monday when I left.

The next morning, Sal and I started it with a walk along the beach before breakfast, dipping our toes, then all the way up to our knees in the water. It was ice cold, but I loved that it shook me to the core. Woke me up and told me I was alive. I felt like I finally had things to look forward to. It's like I'd been in a holding pattern for the past few years. A mere observer of my life, so deeply entrenched in the harshness of it all. It's been a lot, I reflected, as I took a breath to stop and look out at the ocean.

"You ok?" Sal asked, linking her arm in with mine.

"Yeah," I sighed.

"Out with it," she urged.

I remained staring out to sea before I eventually began to speak. "It's been a lot. I didn't realise how much I was struggling, or maybe I did. I thought I'd make a fantastic mother."

"You are," she squeezed my arm.

I stayed fixed on the horizon of the ocean. "Not the kind of mother I imagined I'd be. Pictured me being more patient, more tolerant, and a whole lot more fun. Imagined I wouldn't have wasted a single moment being miserable. Expected to love it more than I did."

Streaming my fingers absently through my hair now, I continued. "Oh, look, I love it, I really do, but I love time for me and doing my own things too. I pictured myself devoted like my mother was with me. One hundred percent focussed on the kids. But I find myself craving free time in the toilet just to get away from them. I've been ridden with guilt about it for years."

"Let's put things into perspective here," Sal said firmly. "Your mum had you and only you. A good kid through to the core. You were more of a companion to your mum from what I can gather. A shopping pal, out on day trips together. Kept her company when your dad was off travelling around the world on work trips and racking up mileage in the torrid affairs department. You were there for your mother as much as she was there for you. But Ab, you've got three kids, not one. And two of them boys. Boys who love to burn up energy all day long. You've been an amazing mother to those three kids and you've really tried your best to make Ed happy. But being a wife and mother, you've given up a part of yourself, a big part of yourself."

"I'm not saying there's anything wrong with that. But you're bound to miss her from time to time. That deep longing we get when we miss an old boyfriend or a friend who we're not in touch with anymore. Abby, you miss that part of yourself. That unique and wondrous soul. That woman who is pure woman, regardless of what her family setup looks like."

Sal squeezed my arm. "I want you to do something for me when I'm gone."

I let out a sudden moan. "Oh Sal, I" said squeezing back.

"Ab, I know I don't have long."

I looked into Sal's eyes. The sparkle had been slowly fading. No amount of makeup could hide the dark circles under her eyes or hollowness in her cheeks.

"I mean it. I won't be here to remind you of this and I don't want to leave without knowing you'll be ok."

I choked back the sob locked in my throat.

"Abby please, my darling friend, stop giving yourself a hard time. Stop trying to measure up to everyone else's expectations. Stop trying to be perfect. I don't know if you realise this, but that little girl inside is still looking for her dad's approval. But no amount of perfect parenting, perfect wifely duties, perfect homemaking, will make your dad acknowledge you the way you have always hoped he would."

"Sure he loves you Ab, in his own way. But you've spent so long trying to impress someone in the hope it would make him come home, come to you, come to your mother. But Abby, he's where he wants to be, doing what he wants to be doing. Let it go. Let all of that go and just know that you are enough. Know that everything you are doing is enough, more than enough."

I wiped my eyes with the heel of my hand, trying to hold back sobs. I reached out for Sal and hugged her, painfully aware of the bones. "I'm going to miss you so much Sally Douglas."

"I know. Just promise you'll do what I said."

"I will Sal...I will," I sobbed into her ear.

Later with Sal having her afternoon rest, I set to work on the remainder of the painting. Every brushstroke felt like a gift. A layer of love I wanted to share. I wanted Sal to feel with each fresh stroke of colour I brushed onto the painting, just how much she meant to me. She said she didn't have long, but I wanted her to have the painting all the same. I wanted to show her just how far I'd come and how so much of that was due to her friendship.

On Monday, I decided I'd leave after lunch when Sal had her rest. With my bags in the car, I had one thing left to do. I was nervous.

I'd dashed out earlier that morning to grab a large picture frame from a discount store in town. I whizzed back and placed my painting inside it. I had wrapped it in soft tissue paper layered in pink and white and tied it in a bright red bow.

I walked out to Sal who was lying outside on the wicker chair, feet up, wrapped in a chocolate brown and cream chequered throw rug.

With her eyes closed, I whispered. "You asleep?"

"Just resting my eyes," she smiled. She tilted her head up and covered her hand with her face to protect it from the sun's glare.

"I'm going to get going but I have something for you before I leave."

As she slowly motioned to sit up, I almost thought I could hear her bones creak when she moved.

"Here Sal, let me help."

I gently sat her up and puffed up the cushions behind her back. She smiled, but her eyes were tired, weary, almost lifeless.

My heart panged. Every time I said goodbye I wondered if it would be the last time.

"What you got there?" Sal asked, mustering up energy from an unknown resource.

"A present," I whispered.

"Well, let me have it," she said reaching out her hand. "Beautifully wrapped," she beamed, carefully peeling away the layers of tissue paper. Sal held the gift, now unwrapped in her fragile hands, taking a minute or two to take it all in. "What a beautiful painting Ab. This is gorgeous."

Sal glanced in more detail. "Wow. It looks just like you and me in New York," she laughed. "Where did you find it? It's exquisite. But you shouldn't be buying me presents." She looked closer at the detail. The tall New York City skyline at the top of the frame, two women sitting at a bar in the centre. "Cocktails and Dreams," she whispered in a floating reminiscing style voice. "Ab, this is amazing. It's like it was made just for us. Where did you get it?" she asked turning to me on the wicker chair next to her own.

I smiled. Said nothing.

"Ab?" She quizzed me, turning her head to one side and peaking her brows.

"Look closer," I urged.

"Closer?" she quizzed.

Turning back to the painting once more, her blue eyes opened wide in surprise.

"Abigail Montgomery. Oh. My. God. Abigail Montgomery. This is you. Is this you? Did you do this? Is this your signature?" She said holding the painting away from her and then closer to check the signature.

Smiling, I slowly nodded my head.

"When? Oh. My. God. I'm so proud of you. I love it," she said, hugging the painting close to her chest.

"It's my first official piece of framed and signed artwork. I started it on Saturday when you were resting. Completed it yesterday when you rested some more. Let it dry overnight and voila," I declared, raising my hands toward the painting in Sal's arms.

"Ab this is really good," Sal beamed with pride.

"You think so?" I wondered, softly.

"Abigail Montgomery, you're an amazing artist. Don't you ever forget that."

"Really?" I questioned.

"Ab," Sal said, tearing her eyes away from the painting, blue eyes staring into green. "I can see all the love, the care, the emotion. The memories of what we had in New York. It's brilliant!" She declared, kissing the framed image of two women having the time of their lives in their youth.

After hugging Sal and struggling to let go, I finally said goodbye. The car radio played softly in the background on the long road home. My mind drifted in and out. Thinking of Sal, of New York, of Ed, of the kids. I drifted back now to my childhood with my mum and my dad, overseas travels in my 20's, my home now in Bondi, and my art.

"My art," I whispered the words out loud.

I'd created a place to pour all my emotion, all my thoughts, feelings, dreams and memories into a frame. An image that was unique to me and now I'd just shared it with Sal. I mean truly shared it. I smiled and pushed a little harder on the accelerator, to meet the 110km speed zone. I was ready to get home. Ready to get on with my life.

CHAPTER 29

Tuesday morning gave me a brand-new reason to get out of bed. With the kids due to spend all morning at Eva's, I got to spend almost four hours sketching, painting, and immersing myself in my imagination.

I don't know who was more excited when I dropped them off, Eva or the kids. She had everything prepared. Super precision and order. Had a schedule all worked out that had the kids squealing with delight.

Eva had set up three different breadboards on a coffee table in the centre of her kitchen. First, they would make scones and place their initials on top. Then they'd make shapes with Play-Doh she had prepared earlier while the scones baked in the oven. Later, they'd stop for morning tea in her fenced off backyard, eating their warm scones along with fruit skewers. Then they'd come back inside to read stories and listen to an audio book. "One each visit," she had smiled. Then they could have free time with the 'B Box' for an hour before Mummy came back to collect them at 1:30pm.

"No cleaning the house dear," she had said, holding up her finger and waving it about when I left. "This time is just for you and your art," she had instructed. "The washing will always need doing."

When I walked down the road to grab my morning

latte for the first time during a weekday sans kids, my heart panged. Not because I missed them, but because I realised how much I'd been missing, how much the kids had been missing, how much we all had been missing, in not having a grandmother part of our everyday lives. Sure, Ed's mum was around, but she loved her independence too much to spend all day baking scones.

I should have done this years ago, I realised now. Got a grandmother figure in to help out and become a part of family life. But Eva was working before, so maybe, just maybe, I'd been waiting for her all along.

I held my breath, hoping it would all work out. Then stopped myself worrying about it, remembering what Sal had said. "Don't waste time hoping something will turn out. Just enjoy it for all it is right now." And right now, it was perfect. Better than perfect.

It was the last class of the art term and I already knew I didn't want it to end. As usual, Monique had prepared something unique, something new. She always kept us on our toes. "Expect the unexpected," she would say.

"As an artist you must stay open, it's key to keeping your creativity alive, and your eye sharp," she had mused.

Tonight she turned off the lights. It was completely dark when we entered the room, all except for one bright red candle that flickered at the front. She stood in the doorway, greeting us one at a time before leading us in by the hand to our stations.

With all twelve women now seated, silent and still, Monique took her place up front and centre, commanding our attention once more. Red candle burning brightly, eyes fluttering closed, she held her hand to her heart and breathed. We were in complete darkness, just one bright candle providing the light and Monique's voice leading the way.

When she opened her eyes, words poured out, from the only place she knew how...her heart and soul entwined as one.

"It is often in darkness,

That we wonder alone,

What it is we are yet to find.

This search in body, spirit and mind.

The space within we want to crawl and climb,

To reach out, call out, look out and wonder.

If we could have anything, our true heart's desire,

What would it be that makes us so much stronger?

Would I desire, a career, or two,

Perhaps a lover in my bed?

What about the pitter patter of children?

A place to rest my head?

Would I desire a life unlived?

Untraveled and unearthed?

Would I desire a place to settle?

To comfort and re-birth?

Would I journey alone or have a partner walk with me?

To hold my hand along the way?

Would I go out, stay in, dress up or down?

What secrets would I find from within?

If I could step out from the darkness and into the light,
A place, a life lived so bright.
What would I see before me?
That I truly would delight.
Would I hug myself with sheer wonder?
For all that I created.
Or would I turn off the light?
For fear or growing hatred.
If I could have anything I would truly love,
A world that is my creating,
What would I discover and make uniquely mine?
A life that has been waiting.
I would create my castle, my great domain,
A place to sit and ponder.
A place to be, eat, loved and adored.
A place to be shared and grow fonder.
If I could have anything, what would it be?
A place that is so mighty.
When I sit alone in the dark each night,
A place to grow old into my nineties.
But if I close my eyes and embody the dark,
Knowing it has a place in its purpose.
For without it, I would not search for the light.
I would not hope and wonder without growing nervous.

I would not dig deep to my insides,

And reach to the place where my soul sleeps.

I would not wake it up and shake it about,

And encourage it to take a giant great leap.

For without the dark,

There can be no light

No wondering where might be.

No striving for your best,

Not desperate to see

Just what could possibly be."

When Monique completed her sermon and held her hands out a little longer, as if on the grand stage, I held my hand on my belly, willing it to stay settled. I carefully exhaled and allowed Monique's incredibly deep and gifted words to affect me once more. I soaked in every letter, every syllable, every word, and every intricate line. She had bypassed my heart and spoken directly to my soul.

Monique walked around the u-shape room with her candle in her hand as the hot, red wax dripped onto the glass stand that held it in place.

She carefully lit individual candles from her own that sat in front of each art station. Only now did I notice they had been there all along. The whole room lit up now, twelve candles plus Monique's, created the only lighting in the space.

"Tonight we will work by candlelight," she declared. "When you think you cannot see, when you are struggling to find the shape on the page, close your eyes, look from the darkness and turn to the light. You have one hour to use the sheet of paper in front of you."

Standing up front and centre once more, she announced that tonight's topic was Life Creating.

"If you could have anything in your life, what would you desire? What scene would you create?" She invited us to explore. "What would you do? Where would you go? What would you dream of?" She wanted us to draw our life as we truly desired it.

"Now," she added, "I know you cannot clearly see the page. But sometimes in life it's exactly the same. We must first begin to look, before we can truly know what is already before our eyes."

I sat and wondered a while, fear kicking in, afraid of what I'd draw on the page. Afraid of what I would see, afraid of what I wouldn't.

As if sensing what was going on inside my brain, Monique said out loud, "Get out of your head and into your heart. Close your eyes, reach down to the depths of your soul for it is there that you will find your truth. Your happiness, prosperity, love and joy. Your triumph at creating a life you love. A life full of all the colours of the rainbow and every shade in between."

I looked at the flickering flame before my eyes and began to sort of meditate on the light. I allowed my mind to drift in and out, float off to somewhere unknown.

I closed my eyes, allowed them to rest, focussed on the natural rhythms of my breathing and searched deeper within. I allowed the image to form in my mind and take shape and movement now.

An idea struck, a feeling inside, and I wanted to get it all down and allow it to organically form. Opening my eyes, I began on the page, charcoal leading the way. I sketched and smudged, stroked and drew, closing my eyes from time to time to reconnect with the image that framed my heart.

After well over an hour, I finally came up for air, placing the final touches on the life sketch before me.

I had imagined my kids running along the beach, Ed and I chasing them through the waves that crashed on the shore. High on the hill at the end of the rocks I'd sketched out a house. A cute little log cabin, smoke wafting from the chimney, wild flowers overhanging the gate. We were on holiday it seemed, but comfortable in the space. Perhaps it was where we would retreat? Yes, that's what it was, a place down the coast, a place we could lose time. I drew angels high in the sky, two of them smiling and looking down. The faces of my mother and Sal smiling through the clouds. I stared back at the picture, holding its gaze. I could see it clear as anything now. Yet with only a candle to guide me there, it seemed perfectly formed somehow.

I began to notice that familiar fear kicking in. Fear of the unknown and the known. What if it didn't work out with Ed? Then from somewhere within I heard a voice... what if it did?

The next morning while lying in bed, taking my 'sketch time' just for me. I reminisced on the evening last night and the way it had ended with my treasured art class friends over a glass of wine. We had taken Monique out for a drink, well three actually. We didn't want to say goodbye. All twelve women had pleaded and begged, urged her not to let us go. By the end of three drinks, we had managed to get her to commit to another five weeks. Another new beginning to look forward to.

Now, as I lay on my bed feeling content and hopeful inside, I realised it was now Wednesday, which meant something new for Ed and I too.

With Eva relegated to babysitting the kids tonight, I felt like I could truly let go, switch off and really enjoy the night. Ed's mum had helped over the last few months, but it dawned on me that I was always on guard, waiting for a call, something to go wrong or being asked to hurry up and return. But with Eva, I just knew she wanted to be there, you could tell. I could completely exhale and be free.

I'd worn a dress with heels. Gee it had been a while. A dusty pink 50's style that swung in swirls when I spun. It tapered in at the waist and was held in place with a dusky green belt. Green heels and emerald earrings that dangled completed the outfit. I'd taken a little more time and care with my hair and, makeup and having dropped a few pounds recently, I was really content, happy, to gaze at the woman in the mirror.

Ed had taken a breath, a gasp of air, when he saw me come out of the bathroom. He had reached for my cheek, kissed it tenderly then whispered in my ear to tell me how beautiful I looked.

Now, standing at the bottom of the stairs to the dance studio two flights up, we looked upward and then sideways to each other, hope filling the lungs in our chest and resting deeply in our heart.

He reached for my hand, caressed my palm, then squeezed it and whispered. "Ready?"

Looking over to him now, a smile filled my mouth that reached all the way up to my eyes. I allowed my heart to fill with love, to overflow all the way through my body. I allow myself to open up to a future where anything was possible. I squeezed his hand with all my might, and whispered the words, "I am."

He squeezed my hand in return, then pulled my fingers up to touch his mouth. He stroked his lips gently against my hand, and smiled.

Giving my hand one final tight squeeze, we kept our fingers interlinked and turned to look up toward the dance studio, to the long flight of stairs that was ahead of us. I had no fear now in climbing them, but instead a desire to take a leap of faith in knowing that it was simply about taking one step at a time.

THE END